Hawthorne & Heathcliff

By R.K. Ryals

To my parents whose lives and deaths inspired me. You taught me that it takes more than the desire to do something to succeed. It takes a willingness to walk the road you chose. All with a sturdy pair of shoes. For that, I will always be grateful.

Mirror

*I am silver and exact. I have no
preconceptions.
Whatever I see I swallow immediately
Just as it is, unmisted by love or dislike.
I am not cruel, only truthful,
The eye of a little god, four-cornered.
Most of the time I meditate on the
opposite wall.
It is pink, with speckles. I have looked
at it so long
I think it is part of my heart. But it
flickers.
Faces and darkness separate us over
and over.*

*Now I am a lake. A woman bends over
me,
Searching my reaches for what she
really is.
Then she turns to those liars, the
candles or the moon.
I see her back, and reflect it faithfully.
She rewards me with tears and an
agitation of hands.*

*I am important to her. She comes and
goes.
Each morning it is her face that
replaces the darkness.
In me she has drowned a young girl,
and in me an old woman
Rises toward her day after day, like a
terrible fish.*

~Sylvia Plath~

Prologue

In my life, there were three words more powerful than *I love you*. In my life, there were three words that carried me, three words that made everything I'd done, everything I'd gone through worth it. In my life, love was never *I love you.* Love was *for my sake*.

I knew the moment I saw the water falling from the sky that my life was changed forever. We walk through moments in our lives, each one marked by something. For me, it was rain. Anytime anything bad ever happened, there was a downpour, as if the clouds, the sky, and the world somehow knew that I was getting screwed. It was as if the old adage *when it rains it pours* was written for me. And when it rained, I prayed and cried and shouted. It often made me wonder which was worse: the rain or the prayers.

"I've got news," my Uncle Gregor said, swallowing audibly.

My uncle was the definition of unkempt. No matter the occasion, he always appeared to be falling apart, as if he were afraid looking like he was put together would ruin the world. There'd never been a moment in my life when he hadn't worn a button-down white shirt only half tucked, his hair a brown spiked mess, and his black tie pulled loose. His pants were always a tad too short, which made no sense because he'd never been very tall.

That day, he'd been even more unkempt than usual. I remembered it because his eyes had been bloodshot, his mouth twisted, and his shirt stained. Even half-tucked, his top was never dirty. That day, it was.

My feet were frozen to worn, carpeted stairs, my hand clutching a wooden banister. My uncle was an odd man who spent his life pretending he was a scientist while living in a ramshackle plantation somewhere between Mississippi and Louisiana. The name of the town never mattered much. It was the plantation that mattered. It was as unkempt as he was, and yet it was alive.

That was the day I'd turned six years old.

That was the day I was wearing a pink sequined dress with a frilly tutu skirt, and shiny black shoes strapped just the way they were supposed to be strapped.

That was the day I wore my mother's coral lipstick, and a plastic, silver tiara sitting lopsided on my perfect coiffure.

That was the day I wore the pearls.

That was the day I grew up.

Outside, it was raining.

It was raining because that was the day my parents left me.

"Are they coming back?" I'd asked my uncle.

He'd tugged on his tie, and I'd known simply from the gesture that they never were. Oh, my parents weren't dead. I wasn't that lucky. What an odd and cold way to feel, I know, but with dead parents, maybe there would have been good memories, this hope that with their last breaths, they would have cared … just a little. Alive, they'd simply never cherished me. Alive, they'd given up. Alive, they'd abandoned me.

Outside, the rain poured.

That was the day I quit trying, not at life, just at myself.

That was the day I'd pulled the pearls from my neck and watched as the beads rolled from the carpeted stairs to the hardwood floor below, the *clunk, clunk, clunk* a loud reminder that I had a heart.

That was the day I'd pulled the tiara from my perfect coiffure, and then screamed, my fingers digging at the hairstyle, tugging my hair so hard my scalp burned.

That was the day I learned why my uncle stayed unkempt. Because if someone was already messed up, then maybe being put together wouldn't hurt so much.

That was the day my uncle looked up at my reddened cheeks and smeared coral lipstick, his fingers pulling at that awful tie, and he said, "You've got this, Hawthorne. Together, we've got this. We may not do it right, but you've got to try. For my sake."

Hawthorne wasn't my name, but that day, it became my name. I often wondered why my uncle called me that, but that day it didn't matter. The only words I heard were *for my sake*.

My uncle's home wasn't much of a home, and he was a very *not* typical father, but he climbed those stairs that day and tried unsuccessfully to straighten out my hair, his eyes reddening. That climb and his trying fingers were enough to make him a dad. He cried, and I cried with him on those stairs.

"For my sake," he'd said.

The sobs were drowned out by the rain.

If you want to know the truth, this is a love story, but it isn't the kind of love story you think it is. Because this story isn't easy, it's hard. This love story is full of fear. Life is downright scary, and if you survive it, no matter how easy you have it, then you're brave. You don't live life, you tackle it, jump on top of it, and pound the shit out of the earth all while it rains around you.

Life happens while it's raining.

Life happens when you're falling.

Life happens when you exhale.

Life just … happens.

For my sake.

11 years later ...

Chapter 1

The first time I ever met him, he was sitting in the back of my last period English class. He was the kind of guy that girls looked twice at but didn't approach, because no matter how attractive he was, there wasn't much you could do with a guy who didn't talk.

Maybe that's why I noticed him. It wasn't just because I sat next to him, it was because I wasn't much for talking either. Our mutual respect for silence was the reason we were relegated to the back. The only difference between us was our appearance. He was handsome enough to be remembered. He was handsome enough to have poems written about him, the kind that called him solemn and stoic, the kind of brooding soul I'd always imagined Heathcliff from *Wuthering Heights* to have. I was just the strange, unkempt girl with the weird uncle and no parents. I was a bunch of sad stories.

Truth was, life had taught me that words were better spoken when they meant something. Which meant I spent more time talking to my uncle and to myself than I did to those my age. It's funny, really, how much one moment in your life can separate you from the people you're supposed to relate to. I'd lost that. I'd lost the need to talk about clothes, dating, and sex. I wanted to talk about the things everyone else wanted to forget; life and death and symbolism.

It was true. I was weird.

I'd only had three loves in my life: my uncle, books, and an overwhelming desire to become a philosophical chef with a Classics degree, because who doesn't want to eat great food and spend hours lost in history?

It was true. I was weird.

And yet, in many ways, he was, too. So it began, this odd dance of sidelong glances and uncomfortable shifting, as if neither one of us wanted to admit the other was there across the aisle from the other, not talking. For half a year, I spent my last period pretending the guy didn't exist, that the girls didn't whisper about him, that the other guys didn't throw him strange, murderous glares.

He didn't care.

In passing, I'd heard one of the girls refer to him as Max Vincent, but I'd quit thinking of him as a regular name. In my mind, he was Heathcliff. He was a quiet, young man too large for his desk, his legs always stretched out in front or to the side of his seat to accommodate for his height. Occasionally, his beat-up tennis shoes rested next to mine in the aisle, and I'd stare at them—my foot and his—as if they were more than shoes and feet, as if they represented something larger than that.

Two shoes, my size seven and his much larger undisclosed number.

Hawthorne and Heathcliff.

Two names that didn't belong to us. Two shoes that did.

I obviously needed a better hobby than baking and philosophy. Last period English class was a sad reminder of that. Six months of sidelong glances and comparing tennis shoes, and sadly it was a Friday afternoon and Sylvia Plath who did me in. There's a mystery to silence that, once broken, can't be returned.

Poetry was Mrs. Callahan's favorite form of senior torture. Poetry is an acquired taste. It's a deep look at life in an odd, sometimes broken way. It turned life into a puzzle, and puzzles weren't something my class was interested in solving. Their lives were already bursting with perplexities, and they were too occupied with trying to figure each other out, trying to figure their hormones out. High school was like a zoo packed with predators trying their best to scent out the weak.

Poetry handed them the weak.

The moment Mary Callahan read *Mirror* by Sylvia Plath, I was riveted. Call it fate, but the poem spoke to me. That was the point of poetry, I guess, but this poem wasn't about romance or nature or death, it was—

Suddenly, my musings were interrupted by Rebecca Martin.

"I love my mirror," she teased, her throaty voice enough to enchant a room.

A masculine snort answered her. "I bet you sleep with it, too," Hunter Green said, his brows wagging. "You know … bow—"

"That's enough," Mrs. Callahan called, her short but lithe figure leaning casually against her desk. "We'll start there. Do you think the poem is about someone's love for their reflection?"

"No," Jessica Reeves replied, "it personifies the mirror."

Mrs. Callahan tapped a pencil against the top of her desk. "Sure, it brings the mirror to life, but what—"

"It's ridiculous," Rebecca remarked. "Who cares about a mirror?"

The teacher's brows rose. "And yet you admitted to loving yours?"

Rebecca shrugged, her highlighted brown hair falling over her shoulder.

Brian Henry whistled. "Well, if it had *that* to look at every day ..."

Rebecca threw him a wink.

Mrs. Callahan smiled. "I wasn't quite looking to make that point, Mr. Henry, but now that you've touched on it, why do *you* think the mirror is so important in this poem?" She glanced at Rebecca. "Why do you think the woman keeps it? Why does she keep coming back to it over and over again, even when she's trying to mask what she sees in it? She obviously doesn't always like what it shows her? So why—"

"It's honest."

The room went silent, and for a moment, I was as surprised as the rest of the class. I was surprised because the words were mine.

Mrs. Callahan pushed away from her desk, her eyes squinting at the back of the room. I wanted to hide, but there was nowhere to go. I'd never meant to speak. Speaking got you noticed, and I was the master of disguise. Speaking replaced mystery with sad stories.

"Miss, um …" The teacher bent to glance down at the grade book on her desk, but was interrupted by Hunter Green's quick cough.

"Hawthorne," he coughed again, "the girl whose mirror should tell her she needs a brush."

Rumbling laughter filtered through the room. The laughter didn't bother me. His words didn't either. It only bothered me that I'd spoken, that I'd broken this strange pact my tennis shoe had made with Heathcliff's bigger tennis shoe.

Mrs. Callahan crossed her arms. "What's honest, Ms. Hawthorne?" she asked.

Hawthorne wasn't my first name, and it wasn't my last. It just *was*, but I didn't correct her.

"The mirror," I answered. "The mirror is honest. I-it's what makes a poem about a mirror *more* than a poem about a mirror."

There was no laughter now, just scattered coughs and hissed *freaks* echoing throughout the room. Mrs. Callahan didn't reprimand anyone. I think she figured, like I did, that it was pointless. You can't change people's minds about someone. You can only change how you feel about the title. I was above the words. I'd learned that life was deeper than teasing laughter and whispered names. It was so much deeper.

"And what makes it more?" Mrs. Callahan asked.

It was too late to pretend I was suddenly mute.

My eyes met hers. "Mirrors don't lie. You may not like what they show you, and you may try to change what you see, but they never lie. The woman keeps coming back, because no matter how much she dislikes what she sees, she craves the honesty. The mirror gives her the truth, and it can't walk away from her."

"Pathetic," Hunter coughed.

The large shoe in the aisle moved, sliding with careful precision away from my desk. The movement shouldn't have hurt as much as it did, but there was something about the way the shoe left me. It was as if, by speaking, I'd told it good-bye.

"Is it the mirror that's pathetic or the honesty?" a deep voice asked.

My gaze flew to the desk next to me, to the way Heathcliff's legs were suddenly alert, his feet flat against the floor. *He'd* spoken.

There was no doubt Hunter Green was insulting me, the "pathetic" comment directed at my person and not the poem, but Heathcliff changed that. He re-directed it. I'd broken our silent pact, and he'd accepted it.

Hunter laughed. "I'm thinking you need to fu—"

"That's enough," Mrs. Callahan said firmly, her gaze passing between Hunter's desk and Heathcliff's. I couldn't bring myself to look past his shoes. "I think," the teacher continued, "that you may have something there, Ms. Hawthorne. And since I'm curious to see what each of you take away from this poem, I want you to go home, look in the mirror, and write a paper or a poem about what you see. You're going to have the rest of the year to work on this. Perceptions often change over time, so I want this assignment to change with you."

It was with those words that my life transformed. Mirrors are often terrible things. They don't just make you look at yourself, they make you look at your life.

The bell rang, the sound of shuffling feet, zipping backpacks, and chatter drowning out the tension in the room. Girls cast glances at Heathcliff's desk, their demure smiles and faint murmurs full of lustful secrets. I couldn't make myself look at him. I knew what he looked like—tall, broad, and muscular with flippant brown hair framing hazel eyes—but I didn't want to see his face. I'd developed a strange relationship with his shoe and his silence, and I knew that looking at him would change that somehow.

Picking up an old black messenger bag covered in handwritten quotes, I slung it over my shoulder and walked from the room, my feet carrying me into a brisk January afternoon. It wasn't quite cold enough to see my breath misting on the wind, but it was cold enough to make me tremble. Dry leaves and pine needles crackled beneath my shoes as I marched across the school lawn toward a dirt road leading through the woods beyond, my hands stuffed into my blue jean pockets. Behind me, his shoes followed.

It should have been strange, I suppose, that he crept after me—his feet following my feet, his silence as comforting outside as it was in the classroom—but it wasn't. Hunter Green had a history of anger issues, and Heathcliff had goaded him. For me no less.

The crackle of leaves, the feel of the frigid air on my face, and the faint sounds of cars driving away echoed around us. Rays of light filtered through the bare tree limbs above us, leaving glowing dust-filled streaks across the air like magic fingerprints. Birds called to each other, but we didn't speak.

Heathcliff kept his distance, as if staying far enough behind would keep that strange, silent world we'd lived in alive. Even as cold as I was, my back was suddenly full of life, his presence causing my skin to tingle. Every swallow, every breath, every step was too loud. My feet were clumsy, my brain working hard to concentrate on each footfall. I was seeing the woods, *my* woods, in a whole new light.

My uncle's house was a few miles away from the school, the acreage he owned separated from the woods by a rusted barbed wire fence. I'd been walking the distance for years now, but I'd never been so disappointed to see the fence.

With less grace than usual, I threw my bag over the barbed wire before climbing over the barrier, the rust coming off on my sweaty palms. His shoes followed me, his larger feet landing on the other side easily. He should have turned back by now, but he hadn't. He remained behind me, our feet shuffling through knee-length, brown grass toward a long drive shrouded by crepe myrtle trees and overhanging gray clouds, the sun dimming with the threat of rain. The looming house beyond looked more haunted than majestic, and maybe it was. Not by ghosts but by memories.

We traversed the lane, the soil beneath our feet clinging to our shoes, the dwelling now a monster in front of us, not because it looked dangerous but because it was the end of our trek.

The door to the house swung open, and my uncle's unkempt figure came stumbling into view; his reading glasses perched sideways on his nose, his hair tousled, and his loose white shirt hanging over a pair of too short, wrinkled khakis.

"That you, Hawthorne?" he called, his absent-minded gaze on a stack of papers in his hand. "I've got something I've got to show you …" His gaze slid up, his loafers stopping short when his eyes met the figure loitering behind me. With a quick sweeping glance between us, he straightened, his brows arching. "I didn't realize you had company."

Shifting the papers to one hand, he swiped his palm down the side of his leg, his gaze sliding over my face as he moved past me to meet Heathcliff. "Welcome, son. You belong to the Vincent bunch, I bet. No mistaking that height and build. Would you like to come in?"

There was an uncomfortable pause, a lengthy silence, before he replied, "No, sir. Just wanted to make sure your niece made it home okay." He grew quiet, and then, "I noticed you've got a lot of untended work on the property. You wouldn't be needing any help out here would you?"

Even with my back to them, my pulse sped up. The papers in Uncle Gregor's hand rustled. "You noticed the mess then," he laughed. "I'm not much for home repairs, I'm afraid. The house could use new paint, and with the temperatures still down, we always need wood, but I couldn't pay you, son."

"I don't need the pay, sir. Just the work."

Another long pause before my uncle answered, "Well, then. I wouldn't want to turn down free labor. You're welcome whenever you have the time."

There was shuffling, the sound of hands meeting and then shoes hitting the lane as Heathcliff left us.

Uncle Gregor stepped back, his lined but kind face suddenly gazing down into mine, his glasses making his eyes appear bigger than they normally were. "That was strange, Hawthorne," he mumbled. "Tell me I didn't just invite a criminal to fiddle around our house."

I stared, my cheeks heating. Uncle Gregor could read me like a book. "You know you didn't," I answered.

For a moment, he watched my face, his throat clearing. "Okay, then. Want to see what I found?" He grinned, and I knew he'd been tinkering in his lab. It wasn't a typical lab, just a room full of used equipment, most of it useless, and shelves of overused books.

My grin met his. "Bigfoot doesn't exist, Uncle."

"There's no proof of that," his smile grew, "but this is better. I found new slime."

Following him, I swallowed back a laugh. "I didn't know there was old slime."

He was still holding the papers in his hands, and my gaze fell to them, the words *medical* and *urgent* jumping out at me.

My feet froze, my smile slipping. "You don't want to show me slime, do you, Uncle?"

He paused, too, his fingers gripping the papers. "You don't know that," he whispered.

"But I do," I whispered back. "You don't ever show me your experiments unless it has something to do with food and recipes."

His shoulders slumped. "I've got news."

Outside, it began to rain, the hard sound loud on the roof.

It was like being a little girl again, only this time it wasn't my parents leaving. This was worse. My gaze slid once more to the papers. "There's something wrong with you, isn't there?"

He glanced back at me. "Hawthorne—"

There were no pearls to pull from my neck or a fancy hairdo to mess up. There were only tears, slow and hot down my cheeks. "How long?" I asked.

I knew in my heart he was leaving me. Uncle Gregor never talked to me about sickness. He wouldn't be talking to me now if it wasn't serious.

The rain on the roof was louder, harder. "They're not sure," he answered.

My gaze traveled to his, to his bright, reddening eyes. This was different from my parents. Unlike them, this wasn't his choice.

My cheek suddenly met his soft chest, my feet moving faster than my brain, my tears sinking into Uncle Gregor's shirt. His hand cupped the back of my head. "We've got this, Hawthorne," he said. "I promise to make it until you graduate if you promise to stay strong. For my sake."

The tears came harder. "I want to stay with you," I sobbed. "School doesn't matter."

The papers fell to the floor, his hands coming up to grip my shoulders. "It matters. It really matters. You can do anything. *Be* anything! I'm going to take care of you, Hawthorne. The house is yours—"

"Stop!" I cried, my nose running, my eyes dripping as I tried pulling away. "Just stop!"

Uncle Gregor refused to release me. "It's been in this family for generations and has long since been paid off. I have enough put back for your—"

I wrenched myself away, my red eyes and swollen face staring up into his. "I don't care." I meant to yell it, but it came out as a jarbled murmur.

For a long time we stared at each other, tears falling; his lined face and my young one. Uncle Gregor and his Hawthorne. He was my love story, the man who'd made sure I'd eaten and dressed and loved after my parents left. He was the only person I felt comfortable talking to. This house was home, the four walls a place I could breathe. He wasn't just my uncle anymore.

"For my sake," he said suddenly, and my chest throbbed.

"For your sake," I replied.

I was back in his arms again, my cheek against his safe shirt, the world beyond his embrace suddenly too big and too scary.

Outside, it rained.

Chapter 2

The following Saturday morning brought no rain, only sunshine and glittering frost-covered bark. Light spilled into my room, the beams playing over a sun-bleached brown carpet before climbing up chocolate striped wallpaper. In a weird way, the room should have felt like a prison, the stripes bars holding me in. Instead, they were inviting, the window seat built in front of my large second story window complementing it, the seat covered in faded cocoa-colored cushions. Brown was such a simple color, unexciting and plain, but it felt stable and reliable. I treasured reliability.

Sleep hadn't come easy the night before, and I'd spent a good amount of time in the shower, the cascading water like my own personal rain cloud, before falling into bed with wet strawberry-blonde hair I knew would frizz by morning. For hours, I'd stared at the ceiling, the faintly glowing moon and creeping shadows replaced by the sun's inching fingers.

For my sake.

My eyes misted, my heart so heavy in my chest that it felt like it would fall through me and the bed to the floor below. Life shouldn't be about good-byes, but I felt like mine was. I was a revolving door. There was no way to enter my existence without exiting. In and out. Like breathing. Only it was the kind of breathing that hurt.

For my sake.

Those three words wouldn't let me quit, but they couldn't stop me from grieving either.

Throwing my legs over the side of my bed, I stepped toward a golden framed mirror I kept propped up on top of my dresser, the small rectangular-looking glass angled so that it faced the window. My fingers wrapped around the frame, and I lifted it, my face wavering as I fell back onto my bed, the mirror held above me. Mrs. Callahan's assignment suddenly seemed more important than it should, as if the dead poet who'd written the poem had known I'd be holding this mirror the same way she'd probably grasped hers.

"It's honest," I whispered.

Gray eyes stared back me, the unremarkable orbs framed by wild, curly hair that saw fingers more than it saw an actual brush. Pale skin flushed by tears highlighted high cheekbones and full, downcast lips. She wasn't an ugly girl, the girl in the mirror, but she was too old for her age. She was tears and heartbreak and fear. She was full of dreams and a million lost opportunities.

"Who are you?" I asked her.

A loud *whack, whack* answered me, and I sat up, the mirror falling forgotten to the bed, my bare toes digging into the carpet below. Slowly, I made my way across the room to the window, my palm resting against the wall, my knee sinking into the brown cushions as I glanced out into the yard. My eyes fell on curling mist in the field beyond before sliding through the crepe myrtles to a small shed visible from my room. It was a dilapidated structure, the door's hinges rusted so that it wouldn't completely close. Two small windows flanking the entrance were busted, the jagged glass sparkling in the sun. It was home to outdated yard equipment, pests, and vermin.

Next to the shack was a cutting log, an ax, and Heathcliff, his old sneakers replaced by sturdy well-worn boots. His head was down, his plain gray work shirt unbuttoned at the wrists and rolled up to his elbows despite the chill. He was splitting wood, the *whack, whack* loud in the still morning. Across from him, his sleep-rimmed eyes full of curiosity, was my uncle. He was holding a thick black mug full of dark coffee, his assessing gaze on Heathcliff. They were speaking, albeit not much, each of their lips moving occasionally as Heathcliff worked and my uncle watched.

Hugging my knee-length, blue plaid sleep shirt, I sat hard on the cushions, my eyes on Heathcliff's obviously repaired boots. Shoes, I was beginning to learn, could say a lot about a person. For one, Heathcliff rarely bought new ones, despite the fact that his family owned a fairly lucrative gas station slash hardware store in town. I deduced three things from his not so new footwear: he didn't like change, once he had something he kept it, and he took care of his things. He was also patient. How I knew this, I had no idea, but I was sure of it all the same.

His head suddenly lifted, and I looked away, my gaze flying to my lap. Scooting to the edge of the window seat, I stood and edged behind the wall, my feet carrying me to my closet. There wasn't a large array of things inside, just rows of durable jeans, sweatshirts, and loose button-down shirts I'd stolen from my uncle. It was one of those shirts—a light blue one—that I tugged on now with a pair of jeans and black work boots, my body tingling with anticipation. I didn't understand why Heathcliff was here, why he'd taken it upon himself to enter my safe world, a plantation where only my uncle and I ruled.

My well-worn boots found the hallway beyond the room, moving carefully down the carpeted stairs, my feet both giddy and wary. It was as if my shoes knew that once I opened that door, they'd be stepping into something new, a different reality from the one we'd always known.

The door creaked, my fingers gripping the knob so hard my knuckles whitened. My uncle's head swung toward me at the sound, his brows arching as I slunk into the yard. My gaze slid to Heathcliff's boots and the growing pile of split wood beside him. There were three fireplaces in the house, and we used them often in winter to keep the residence warm in place of central heat.

Uncle Gregor cleared his throat. "I've got a new experiment I want to try," he mumbled, his warm gaze meeting mine as he passed me.

Even in Gregor's sudden absence, I didn't speak. I simply walked to the newly chopped wood and filled my arms, carrying first one load into the house before returning for another. I'd made a third trip and was stacking what was left in a pile against the shed when he spoke.

"Who walked away from you?" he asked.

I froze, my back to him, my eyes on the shed. A small brown spider was climbing up the side of the paint stripped building, scurrying so quickly I was sure the arachnid was as afraid to hear me speak as I was to answer.

"In class," Heathcliff began. He paused before inhaling, the exhaled words that followed coming rushed and low. "In class, you said mirrors couldn't walk away."

I straightened, my back stiff when I murmured, "My parents."

There was a moment of silence. My parents weren't a secret. The whole town knew my parents' story, but it was nice of him to ask, nice of him to want to know more.

My hands returned to the work. Stacking wood wasn't a science, but I was suddenly obsessed with the need to make it perfect, to make sure the split logs lined up a certain way.

There was a single *whack* behind me as the ax was returned to the chopping block and left there.

"You don't talk much," he said.

Six months of silence, of resting shoes and swift glances, and now ...

"Why are you here?" I asked.

Boots moved behind me, stomping over dew-covered grass before resting next to mine. "Maybe I like quiet people," he replied. I felt his eyes fall to my untamed hair. "You sort of intrigue me."

My stomach clenched, my insides filling with crawling insects, and I was suddenly at a loss for words. Or maybe, I didn't say anything because there wasn't anything that could be said. There was nothing *worth* saying.

"And that's why," Heathcliff murmured, "your silence now. It's as if you don't feel the need to fill space with noise. But the one time you did speak, it meant something." He leaned close. "What's going on inside your head?"

My breathing grew harsh, my pulse quickening. "Are you one of those *I find wounded animals to heal* kind of people. I can promise you, I'm not wounded."

My words surprised me, and for a moment, I think it did him, too.

"Maybe not," he said finally, "but you do need a friend."

My gaze shot to his chest, my eyes wide. "I don't!"

He leaned against the shed, the muscles in his arms pushing against his rolled up sleeves. "Why won't you look at me?"

I swallowed. "I know what you look like."

"And yet you won't look at me. Why?"

My lips curled, the smile as much a surprise as my words. "Because I don't commit to faces."

Heathcliff chuckled. "You only commit to shoes?"

My smile slipped. "Faces leave," I mumbled. "Shoes walk away. You learn a lot about people by what they wear on their feet. I'd rather see what's going to leave than what I'd miss if it left."

There was a long silence, and my gaze found his shoes. I was waiting for him to leave, for his boots to stride past me and my odd words. But they didn't.

"And if the shoes don't walk away?" he asked.

My heart jumped. "Then the face matters … once it's earned."

His boots remained. There was rustling as his torso shifted, another long pause, and then, "I think there's some paint at my father's store that would look good on this house. For now, I can start with the yard. It needs a lot of work before spring comes."

His words registered, but they didn't matter as much as his frozen boots.

Chapter 3

There was something wrong with Heathcliff. Maybe it was his persistence, his dogged determination to fix whatever little problem he could find on our property, but he found a reason to stay all of Saturday and most of Sunday. An ax, a hammer, garden gloves, and rotted pieces of wood all lay haphazardly around the lawn, and when he wasn't working, he was talking. Somehow his boots found me. The first time was in the house, in a corner of my uncle's bizarre library. He was fixing a leak in the ceiling, and I was attempting, unsuccessfully, to write Mrs. Callahan's paper.

"You made any progress with it?" he asked.

He was standing on a ladder, and I stared at his jeans. "Not much," I admitted.

He hammered away at something, the sound driving out the need to converse, before remarking, "I haven't written a word. You have any idea what you're going to write about?"

My gaze went to the notebook in my hands, at the glaringly empty pages.

More hammering, and Heathcliff climbed off of the ladder, the tool in one hand, the other slapping the side of his leg. "I'm betting most of the papers will be exaggerated descriptions of appearances." He stooped and attempted to meet my gaze, but I avoided him. "What do you see when you look in a mirror?" he asked.

My fingers pressed against the paper's blue lines. They were like veins, those lines. Straight, perfect veins waiting for the words that would breathe oxygen into them. "I … devotion."

Speaking to Heathcliff was constantly surprising me, as if by talking I was learning new things about myself. Maybe I'd been too quiet in the past, too shut away, and the things I was saying now were things Uncle Gregor and I had never thought to discuss.

Heathcliff's fingers suddenly brushed mine before moving away just as quickly. "Do you know what I see when I see you?" My lips parted, but he didn't give me a chance to reply. "Strength," he said, "loneliness, and confidence. That sounds contradictory, I know, but you *are* a contradiction."

He stood then, but I surprised myself by reaching out to grasp his wrist. We both froze. "You …" I inhaled. "When I see you, I see a disregard for things. Not for important things, but for things you should probably be interested in." I should have released him then, but I didn't.

He didn't pull away. "And what am I supposed to be interested in?"

My gaze traced a streak of dirt down the side of his jeans, the soil sinking into the fabric. "Parties … girls."

My fingers released him, but he didn't move. "Oh, I'm interested in girls. It just happens to be one girl."

After the statement he could have walked away, but he didn't. In the end, it was me that left. Standing, I wedged my way past him, my head down, my wild halo of hair hiding my burning face as I moved from the room.

In the hall, I paused, my back going against the wall next to the open door, my heart beating too quickly. Heathcliff moved inside of the library. The ladder snapped shut, his boots pounding over the scarred hardwood floor. There was no carpet in the house's first story, and the wood made his boots yell, the *thud, thud* louder than it would be outside or upstairs. My lips curled.

Something fell lightly against the wall behind me, but I didn't startle because I knew it was Heathcliff, his back resting against the wall that I rested against, the only thing separating us an open door and wall panel.

This time, I was the first to speak. "Why me?"

Heathcliff chuckled. "Why not?"

"You like to fix things?" I asked, changing the subject.

"It's better than breaking them."

I swallowed a laugh. "I like to cook."

It was such a corny thing to say, but I wasn't a pretentious person. I was too blunt to be flirtatious, and the lack of wit just made my words sound silly.

"I like to eat," Heathcliff said after a minute.

This time, I didn't even try to hide my amusement. "Maybe you'd like to stay for supper then?"

As soon as I asked, I wanted to take it back. The question took more from me than he probably realized.

There was a momentary silence. "I'd like that."

"Okay, then." Stepping away from the wall, I didn't glance back as I walked away. If he stayed, he stayed. If he left, he left. It was enough I'd been able to invite him.

My smile followed me through the day and into the kitchen, the room suddenly a hazard it never was before. I second guessed everything, the recipes in my slate blue index card holder, the ingredients, and the time it took to cook. Uncle Gregor came in a few times, his mouth twisting with hidden enjoyment.

"Are you nervous about cooking?" Gregor asked.

I threw him a look. We'd not discussed his illness since Friday afternoon, as if we'd made a silent pact to pretend it didn't exist. He was tired, his eyes lined with weariness, but he played it off well, and my heart hurt with the deception. He didn't need me reminding him that he was sick. I'd seen the papers, and I knew what they meant.

"My fingers feel too big suddenly," I admitted.

His calloused hand picked up a Granny Smith apple. "Apple dumplings for dessert? You can't go wrong there."

My gaze found his face. "What am I doing?"

Smiling, he answered, "Flirting, I hope. I like him."

A lump formed in my throat, and I swallowed past it. "We don't know him."

Uncle Gregor leaned close. "Then we get to know him. He comes from good people, Hawthorne. The Vincents are hard workers, kind, and stubborn as hell. I'd swear his grandmother was the hand of God. I felt her rod on my back quite a few times as a child." He chuckled. "She's a mean spirited witch with a heart of gold hidden under all that crass."

I frowned. "I guess I just don't get it. Of all the girls at school—"

"None of them are you. It's that mysterious beauty." He winked. "But it's also just you. Men don't always want simple. Some of them want complicated."

"I'm not—"

Uncle Gregor winked again. "You are all kinds of complicated and that's okay. There's nothing wrong with emotional scars. Sometimes those are deeper than physical ones."

I stared at my hands, at the scattered ingredients I'd begun collecting on the black marble bar. "I had you," I whispered. "You were all I needed."

Uncle Gregor's hand covered mine on the counter. "But that doesn't erase the pain. It doesn't erase the questions and the doubt being abandoned at six years old would cause." I started to pull away, but he wouldn't let go. "It's okay to have wanted more. It doesn't make you selfish. It doesn't mean you loved me any less. It makes you human, Hawthorne. Human is good. It means you still have the capacity to care. Give the Vincent boy a chance."

My hand grew still. "Heathcliff," I muttered. "In my mind I call him Heathcliff."

Uncle Gregor laughed. "That's my daughter."

Those words made us both freeze, his hand on my hand. If my palm hadn't been trapped, it would have trembled. Gregor wasn't my biological father, but in many ways he'd become that.

For a long time, there was silence, the only sound distant hammering outside as Heathcliff worked.

Suddenly, I whispered, "Dad."

The word didn't feel strange on my tongue. It felt right. It felt certain.

Uncle Gregor's hand tightened on mine and then lifted, his palm patting me awkwardly before his throat cleared. "Make your meat loaf. There ain't a man alive who could leave that."

He left then, and my gaze followed him, my lips whispering, "Dad."

My heart had never felt so full and so broken at the same time. The feeling remained with me while I worked, and I poured love into the meal, the kind of love you have for someone that hurts so much that not having loved them would be worse than never having them in the first place. What a strange kind of love that is. I had that with my Uncle Gregor. There were so many people who didn't have that with anyone, and I counted myself lucky. Yet my uncle was right, too. It was okay to still hurt, to be afraid to trust more than just him with my heart.

I was setting the table in the small dining room to the side of the kitchen when Heathcliff came in, his boots resting awkwardly near the door. The dining area was more of a nook. A small wooden table rested in a corner alcove surrounded by windows on three sides, its view a part of the yard badly in need of weeding. We had a formal dining room, but it was covered in dust and never used.

"It smells good," Heathcliff murmured.

My uncle's voice answered his. "It always does with Hawthorne. She's been playing with food since I first let her use a stove. Even before that, she'd spend hours flipping through food magazines."

My cheeks burned as they entered the small space. My uncle took the seat at the head of the table nearest the windows, as it was his custom to do so, and I took the seat next to him. Heathcliff sat across from me.

I stared at my plate, at the food so carefully laid out on it. I'd taken Gregor's suggestion and made meat loaf, roasted potatoes, and butter beans slow cooked with bacon. Apple dumplings sat in a chipped china bowl in the center of the table. It wasn't a fancy meal, but it was well made.

Heathcliff took Uncle Gregor's lead, waiting until he'd taken a bite before following suit. After a moment, he sighed, and I fought not to grin at his mumbled, "Wow."

"So," Heathcliff said aloud, "is this what you want to do after school? Cook?"

I pushed at the food on my plate, my gaze sliding to his hand as it lifted and lowered. "Sort of," I answered. "I'm also really into history."

Silence fell, and I felt Heathcliff's boot sliding toward mine under the table.

"What about you, son?" my uncle asked. "What kind of plans do you have after graduation?"

Heathcliff coughed, his foot tapping before resting. "Well … I like to piece things together. Especially machinery. So, I'm thinking something in engineering. Maybe welding."

"No plans to go into the family business?" Gregor asked.

"Not really. It's always an option for me, a fallback plan, but I've got a brother who'd do better with that than me, sir."

"True," Uncle Gregor chuckled. "It isn't very good business for one to work on someone's house for free."

I could feel Heathcliff's gaze on me, and I squirmed. "Not necessarily for free, sir. Sometimes keepin' busy and doing things can be as much for pleasure as for money."

"Right then," Gregor murmured. "You know I don't think I caught your first name, son. You're a Vincent, so are you the eldest or the youngest of the boys?"

Heathcliff set his silverware down, the fork clattering against his plate. "It's Max. I'm the youngest."

Gregor gestured at me, a piece of meatloaf speared to the end of his utensil. "Did you know my niece calls you Heathcliff?"

My head shot up, my startled gaze flying to my uncle's face.

"Heathcliff?" Max asked.

I refused to glance in his direction, my gaze remaining on Gregor. His eyes twinkled, his cheeks rosier than I'd seen them in days, and I knew this conversation was filling him with life. It made being angry at him hard.

"Heathcliff?" our guest repeated.

I cleared my throat, my hands falling to a cheap paper towel I'd draped over my legs. "It's silly."

"It's romantic," Gregor argued.

Heathcliff's boot slid even closer to mine. "The Heathcliff from *Wuthering Heights*?"

"You read?" my uncle asked.

"It was for school junior year." Heathcliff's throat cleared, the weight of his gaze heavy as it found me again. "Wasn't Heathcliff cruel and sadistic?"

My eyes slid to his chest. His work shirt was no longer clean, the fabric marred by dust, rust, and oil. "It's not his character that reminds me of you," I mumbled. "It's his ability to defy being understood. No reader comes away from that book feeling the same way about him. It's always different."

"And so I'm a brooding, romantic yet sadistic hero?" he asked.

"No," my eyes found his chin and stopped, "you're misunderstood."

Silence reigned, and Heathcliff's shoe met mine under the table. Boot against boot.

"There's apple dumplings," Gregor pointed out, his words breaking through the tension. It was such a relief, I almost laughed.

Eating replaced silence, the rest of the meal moving quickly before Heathcliff stood. He thanked me for the food, thanked Gregor for the hospitality, and then promised he'd return. After the declaration he left, his boots charging out into the clear and darkening Saturday evening. Burgeoning stars winked in the crisp sky, and I watched as his shoes disappeared down the lane.

I'd been sure he wouldn't return.

I was wrong.

His hammer woke me the next morning, the sound filling the day and the afternoon, replaced occasionally by the *whack* of an ax or rustling as he pulled up wilted, brown weeds. I kept busy as he worked, my heart wanting to see him, but my mind wanting me to avoid all contact. It seemed wrong to be so conflicted, but isn't that what romance was? Conflict?

He found me at the end of the day, his shoes stopping just beyond the wooden swing where I sat on the back porch, a food magazine next to me, and an empty notebook in my hand.

"Is Hawthorne really your name?" he asked.

Laying the notebook aside, I pulled my legs up onto the swing and hugged them. I wasn't very tall, 5'1 exactly, and I rested my chin on my knees. "It's not my real name, no."

Heathcliff pushed aside my things and sat, his body causing the swing to shift. "And your real name?"

When I didn't answer, he used his boots to propel the swing slowly backward and then forward again, the swaying motion creating a strange sense of comfort, as if we were moving in and out of reality.

"Is it like my face?" he asked. "Do I have to earn your name, too?"

My arms tightened on my legs. "It's Clare."

He scooted closer to me, his warmth chasing away the encroaching chill as night fought day. "Clare," he repeated. "I like it."

"I prefer Hawthorne."

My hand fell to the swing between us, and one of his hands fell next to mine. Not quite touching but close enough the electricity the proximity created caused my entire body to tingle.

"Because your uncle calls you that?" Heathcliff asked.

His fingers brushed mine, and I swallowed hard, my body squirming with the discomfort. It wasn't an awful discomfort. It was needy somehow, even desperate.

"It's the name that defines me, the one that matters," I whispered.

His palm was covering my hand now, his fingers slowly stroking my fingers. "Clare ... Hawthorne ... they both suit you."

Heat erupted from his hand to mine, and the wonderful discomfort grew. Fingers against fingers. Stroke after stroke. The darkening sky was suddenly aflame with color, with bright purple and pinks, the sporadic star breaking through streaks of violet and fuschia. In my head, I heard music.

"Why do you believe I'm misunderstood?" he asked suddenly.

I glanced at our entwined hands. "Because you've let yourself become as much a mystery as I have, your silence lighting people's curiosity. So many girls want you, and so many guys hate you because they want to be wanted the same way you are. They assume things. And then you come here ..."

My words trailed off, but he jumped on them. "To the wild girl's house," he finished.

"I'm not wild," I pointed out crossly.

"Your hair is," he returned.

My lips twitched. "It's a curse."

"It's sexy as hell."

His words startled me. "That's a new way of putting it."

"It's the truth," he replied. He scooted closer, his hand tightening on mine. "Tell me, *girl with the wild hair*, what would you do if *this* Heathcliff wanted to know things about you?"

My chest rose and fell, my heart thudding. "Depends on what you want to know."

He leaned so close, his mouth brushed my ear. "Everything."

I gasped, the sound lost to the creaking swing chains. "You can't come back!"

Startled, he leaned away. "Give me a good reason why."

"Because this isn't a good time."

"Is there ever a good time for anything?"

I tugged my hand away from his. "My uncle—"

"Is dying," Heathcliff said abruptly.

I froze, my throat constricting. "H-how do you know that?"

"Because he's been going to the same treatment center as my grandmother," he answered. "They've been talking ..."

My head filled with noise, my heart a puddle in my chest. My uncle, my *father*, was dying. He was dying, and I couldn't take the pain.

"Hawthorne," Heathcliff whispered, "you need a friend."

I stared at the night's first stars, as if their twilight-dimmed glow would reveal something to me, give me answers to the universe I didn't understand. My world had been so small up until now, so small and yet so painfully safe, too.

"Did you only come here because you think I need a shoulder to cry on?" I breathed.

Heathcliff sat back against the swing, the accompanying creak loud. "I only found out about your uncle last night from Mams, my grandmother. I came here because I'm interested. I'm staying because I'm interested. I'm offering you comfort because I *care*, because it wouldn't hurt to have a friend of my own who's going through it, too."

My gaze traveled to his profile, not quite reaching his face but coming close. "What's she ..." Swallowing, I left the question unasked, but he knew.

"Cirrhosis," he answered, and then he laughed, as if the amusement would chase away the grief. "Too much of her homemade tonic, the doctor says."

Maybe I should have laughed the same way he had, but I didn't. Instead, I reached once more for his hand, my fingers entwining with his, and I said the scariest words I'd ever uttered. "I could use a friend."

There'd been no conversation after that, only creaking swing chains and wild splashes of color amongst leafless trees as the sun set. Shoes and fingers skirted each other.

The sky was clear. There was no rain.

Chapter 4

It's odd how life works, how when we tell our story, its told in large, dramatic pieces. There are no small moments because there doesn't seem enough time for the small moments. We don't use our last breaths telling people about the food we ate or the clothes we wore, we talk about what it was like to love, to lose, and to succeed. We talk about the highs and sometimes we talk about the lows. We don't talk about the between moments.

I fell in love during the between.

The Monday after Heathcliff's weekend visit, our feet met in last period English class. As soon as his backpack hit the floor, his body sagging into his chair, his tennis shoe slid across the aisle, his foot resting against mine. No one had to step over them. That was the beauty of sitting at the back of the class.

I stared at his shoe, a small laugh escaping when I realized there were words written on it, my gaze darting to his desk to find an orange washable marker dangling from his fingers before returning to his foot. There on the side of his shoe was *Got meatloaf?*

There was a light *clunk* on the worn, tile floor, and a blue marker rolled against my desk. Leaning down, I snatched it, my fingers gripping it so hard my knuckles whitened. This was it. Heathcliff had not only found a new way to talk to me, he'd found a way to talk to my fear, my fear of walking away.

There'd been a test after his shoe's question, another short discussion about poetry and a new required reading book, and finally free time. I'd started working on the mirror assignment then, but first I dropped a sheet of paper, the marker in my hand as I knelt to retrieve it.

My shoe bumped against his shoe as I sat upright, a clumsy, blue *cookies instead?* written on the side.

It was then I found the words to start Mrs. Callahan's assignment. Every now and then, words just happen. For me, these words were like a recipe, an odd order that may not make sense at first, but completely works together when it's finished.

Hawthorne Macy

I'm a cook. I like making food because I can take a variety of components and make something old, comfortable, new, or unique out of it. My life is like a recipe. In my mirror, I see the ingredients, my uncle and me. I'm not sure how we work, but we do. Each time I've glanced into the glass growing up, I've seen him behind me. At first, I was a little girl with terrible hair, my bewildered uncle standing at my back, his flabbergasted eyes on my tangled head. I think that's how we came to be, Gregor and me. He was left with a terrible muddle of a girl, and he had to figure out how to put her back together.

The bell rang, and I startled, my notebook snapping shut. The classroom emptied, busy feet rushing for the door. Only one pair of shoes other than mine remained.

His shadow loomed over me. "You said something about cookies?"

Standing, I stuffed my things into my messenger bag, my face averted. "Today?

You don't have anything else you have to do?"

Heathcliff rocked back on his heels, his hands finding his blue jean pockets. "One delivery. You wouldn't want to go with me, would you?"

I hesitated. I wasn't sure what Heathcliff saw in me, why he felt this need to keep trying so hard. He was taking me out of my comfort zone, and while it bothered me, it also felt oddly exhilarating.

I was quiet too long, and he leaned close. "Come on, ride with me. I've got my truck today, and I'll take you home afterward."

With a quick, unsure glance at the door, I found myself murmuring, "Okay."

His shoes rocked forward, his step light as he led me from the room and out of the school, his feet pounding over brown grass and pavement. An old two door Toyota truck sat in the parking lot, the red paint having seen better days.

Heathcliff pulled the squeaking passenger door open, and then patted the roof. "1985, four wheel drive, 22RE motor, and over 200,000 miles on her. She's not young, but she's strong."

My gaze fell to the cracked and faded black leather bench seat within, and I ducked under his arm, my messenger bag hitting the leaf and dust strewn floorboard.

Heathcliff rounded the truck, his fist tapping the hood before he swung open the driver's side door and climbed in. Reaching for the floor, he grabbed a work jacket, shook it off outside, and offered it to me.

"I've got to do a little work on the heat and air," he admitted. "I kind of like riding with the windows down though. Even in winter."

My fingers dug into the rough blue jean coat, my arms sliding into the insulated sleeves. It smelled faintly of oil and pine needles.

He started the truck, his arm falling over the back of the seat as he pulled out of the parking lot. "You seemed distracted at the end of class. Finally started writing on the paper?"

A couple of turns, and the road began disappearing under the truck, the yellow lines moving faster and faster. The wind rushed in through the open windows, roaring through my ears and chilling me. It smelled like bark, exhaust, and ice, even though it wasn't snowing and rarely did in our hometown.

When I didn't answer, Heathcliff's voice rose above the wind. "I know why you won't look at me."

My head shot up, my gaze on his windshield. There was a crack in the glass, one line that curved upward over the windshield wiper before sinking back into the hood.

"You're scared I'll see the pain." His fingers brushed the jacket I wore, his hand dangling near my shoulder. "You're not hiding anything, Hawthorne."

My lips parted, my fingers gripping the open window, the metal cold against my palm. "Why are you trying so hard to get close to me?"

The truck slowed, the wind becoming less desperate, its fingers no longer ripping at my hair.

"You're genuine," he said. "I could use genuine."

We passed a large *Vincent Hardware & Quik-Stop* sign, and Heathcliff pulled the truck into the parking lot. Vincent's was one of those one stop kind of places. There were three wooden buildings, all attached in some way, all square and mostly unadorned. The largest was the hardware store, a separate dirt parking lot behind it. The middle building, attached to the first by a breezeway, was a small café, and the smallest was a convenience store with four gas pumps. The smell of wood, gas, and greasy hamburgers infiltrated my nostrils.

Heathcliff's door creaked. "I've just got to grab a few things."

Leaving the truck idling, he jogged into the hardware store. There were a wide variety of vehicles parked in the lot, most of them newer and older model pickups. A group of rough, oil-stained men stood outside chatting. Kids from school crowded into the café, yells rising over strains of country music.

Curious gazes met me through the window, and my eyes fell to my lap.

The truck's tailgate came down, voices rising as wood hit the bed. The truck shook.

"This needs to go to the Parkers. If there's no one around, Kenny said you could just stack it in the old barn," a deep male voice ordered.

The tailgate slammed shut, and Heathcliff's door re-opened.

A large figure paused just outside my window, rough, work-chapped hands curling over the edge. "Got company, I see," a man greeted.

I glanced up, my gaze meeting a kind, lined face that reminded me of my uncle's. This man was rougher around the edges, broad and tall, a denim work top buttoned over a white T-shirt. His hair was black, a bit of silver touching his sideburns. A name tag was stitched to his shirt, the name *Dusty* sewed across it.

"Yeah ..." Heathcliff hesitated, and I wondered if it was because of me or because I'd met the man's eyes. The thing was, I wasn't afraid of looking at people. I was afraid of looking at the ones I might care for. "This is—"

"Clare Macy," the man muttered. "We don't see much of you and your uncle in town." He studied me. "It's amazing really. You look just like your moth—"

"It's Hawthorne now, sir," I said quickly.

The man's startled gaze met mine, something akin to pity crossing his features. "Hawthorne," he repeated. Stepping back, he reached into the truck and offered me his hand. "Dustin Vincent. I'm Max's daddy. Tell your uncle I'd love to see him more."

Accepting his offered hand, I mumbled, "Yes, sir. I will. Thank you."

Throwing his son a quick glance, he backed away.

Heathcliff eased the truck out of the lot. "I'll be home a little after dark, Dad!" he called.

Gravel crunched, the tires spinning out onto the road, the wind rushing once more into the cab. It helped chase away conversation, but I felt Heathcliff's gaze when he glanced at me. He shifted gears, the afternoon sun glinting across our faces. Outside, fields rolled by, bare and brown but full of idle life, the soil antsy for spring.

We turned onto a dirt strip, dust flying up along the Toyota's thin, red paint.

"You like speed?" Heathcliff asked.

My head had fallen back, the wind's cold fingers a welcome relief on my too busy scalp and chaotic thoughts. But while the air felt good, it didn't mean I liked going fast.

I shook my head, and Heathcliff hit the brakes. "Do you even know how to drive, Hawthorne?"

My hands clutched the leather bench seat, my fingers pushing through the cracked material to the yellow stuffing beneath.

Heathcliff parked. "You're what … seventeen? Eighteen at the oldest?"

"Seventeen," I volunteered.

He glanced out the window at the pasture next to the road, the ground flat and the grass low. "Want to learn?" he asked.

My stomach lurched. "I'm not sure that's a good idea."

He laughed. "Of course it is." Flinging open the door, he climbed out and rounded the truck before entering the passenger side, his hand falling to my hip, urging me gently to scoot across the bench.

Moving carefully behind the steering wheel, I sat stiffly, my back tense.

Heathcliff slid as close to me as he could get without impeding me. "You know," he said, "I like driving. It clears my head. The windows down, the wind in my face. The air kind of speaks to you when you do that. It drags away the cobwebs and leaves behind an odd kind of resilience."

I grimaced. "More like the smell of road kill on the back roads."

He chuckled. "I was thinking more along the lines of honeysuckle in summer. I thought girls found that kind of stuff romantic."

My brows arched. "The road kill or the honeysuckle?"

Heathcliff's hand found mine on the bench, his fingers lifting my fingers. Placing my palm against the shifter, he snorted with amusement. "You've got a lot of sass for a quiet girl." He should have released me then, but he didn't. "Let's drive. I'm going to shift with you at first until you get used to the sensation. Once you figure out how to use the clutch and get the feel of the gears, it's pretty easy from there."

He went through the steps, walked me through the operation and the feel of the different components, his words carrying me and the pickup into the pasture.

It was one of those days—the sun shining and short brown grass swaying around the old truck—that I couldn't remember exactly how we ended up racing through the field, our laughter rising through the cab and out the open windows. In truth, I was a terrible driver, and we lurched more like a boat in the middle of a storm rather than sailing smoothly.

"Slow it down a little," Heathcliff laughed. "You're doing fine."

Turning sharp, I literally grinded to a stop. "I'm going to kill your truck," I gasped, my ribs sore from the laughter. "Don't you have a delivery?"

His hand tightened around mine on the shifter. "It was worth the stop." Releasing me, he pushed open the door and trudged through flattened grass to switch places with me. "It was good to see you smile." Once behind the wheel, he faced me. "Admit it, driving clears the cobwebs."

My low chuckle filled the cab. "If you like being seasick and all."

"Look at me," he pleaded suddenly. "Look at me when you smile like that." My grin slipped, and his fingers found my chin. He didn't force my face in his direction but I felt the frustration. "You looked at my father."

"I don't know your father."

He was staring at me, but I gazed past his shoulders at the pasture.

"You don't want to know him, is that it?" Heathcliff asked finally.

My eyes fell shut, the breeze from outside brushing my cheeks. "I do want to know him. I'm just not looking to *keep* him."

Heathcliff's breath fanned my face, and my eyes tightened. "You want to keep me?" he asked, chuckling. "You do realize that sounds kind of strange."

I was suddenly imagining a glass figurine version of Heathcliff sitting on my dresser, and my lips twitched.

And then, the smile was gone, stolen by his lips, the sudden pressure causing me to stiffen. It was quick, the kiss. A simple warm press of skin against skin before he was gone, his mouth replaced by wind and the smell of pine and woodsmoke.

He cleared his throat. "Better get this timber to the Parker's."

Turning my head, my eyes flew open, my breathing rushed. The urge to touch my mouth was strong.

Grass slapped the truck, the engine revving.

Pulling the pickup back onto the dirt road beyond, Heathcliff asked, "Was that your first kiss?"

My gaze remained on the landscape beyond the window, on the passing trees and scattered houses. The wind beat against my face, but it wasn't clearing away the cobwebs in my head. I didn't want them gone. His kiss *was* my first, the feel of it strange but nice, as if by kissing me he'd exposed something. Like a stubborn jar of pickles, the lid finally wrenched open.

He drove, and I watched him from the corner of my eye, my heart pounding. There was no music in the truck, only wind, but the air was suddenly our dirt road song, the rattle of wood in the back of a short bed pickup the chorus. Everything about me felt funny, like I'd eaten way too many lemons, my stomach on fire from the acid.

His head turned, and my gaze flew forward.

"It *was* your first, wasn't it?" he asked.

There was a smile in his voice, and I placed my hand on the dashboard to steady myself as he drove over rough spots in the road.

"Just drive," I said.

I didn't have to look to know he was grinning.

Chapter 5

It hadn't taken long to deliver the wood. With Kenny Parker's help unloading the timber, Heathcliff had finished twice as fast, shaken Kenny's hand, and then driven away.

Kenny's curious gaze followed our disappearing pickup. His wife joined him, her graying hair pulled away from her face. From the side mirror, I watched his arm circle her waist, their heads close. It'd be all over town by nightfall that the Vincent boy was seen with a Macy.

My heart sank. There's this thing about small towns. Rumors festered here, growing until they became open wounds that never seemed to heal. My parents were gone, but I'd heard the whispers growing up. I was living in the shadow of my parents' sins. It didn't matter that I hadn't been the one to leave, I was marked.

"She'll run off and break Gregor's old heart," I'd heard people say. Because, in their minds, the running was in my blood, the antsy need to see the world and never

return in my veins. That's what people did here. They either stayed or they never left.

The pickup turned down the tree-covered lane that led to my uncle's plantation, its ramshackle appearance not quite so disheveled after Heathcliff's work.

"I'm bringing the paint I promised this weekend," Heathcliff said, his hands spinning the steering wheel as he eased into an empty spot next to the shed.

We climbed free of the truck, the ill at ease, after kiss moment gone. It had been so fleeting that it seemed an imaginary moment now rather than a distinct memory.

"Tell me you really have those cookies," Heathcliff added.

Slinging my messenger bag over my shoulder, I stepped toward the house. "Are you looking for an invite in?"

He trailed after me. "I'm looking for a reason to stay."

My feet froze, and his shoes paused next to mine, the marker questions still scrolled on the side. I stared down at them. "I have chocolate chip cookies and pralines, and ... um, would you want to work on Callahan's assignment with me?"

"Perfect," he responded. Leaving me, he headed for the door.

I followed. "Are you sure there's nothing you'd rather be doing instead?"

"Trying to get rid of me so quickly?" Stopping at the door, he pulled it open and stepped aside.

"No." I walked past him into the dark foyer. "I'm just finding it hard to believe you want to do homework."

"I have an idea." He snapped his fingers. "Grab the cookies and show me your room."

Heathcliff had the uncanny ability of making everything he said sound like it was perfectly reasonable. Cookies and my bedroom *wasn't* remotely close to that, but I found myself marching into the kitchen anyway to grab the covered plate on the counter. My feet were traitors, their love affair with Heathcliff's shoes making them blind. It was my only excuse.

"I'm upstairs," I mumbled, the thud of my shoes quieted by the carpeted stairwell.

Heathcliff's muffled steps followed.

Musty flooring and moth-eaten curtains assaulted my nose and eyes, the hallway

suddenly new to me, seen and smelled the
same way I imagined Heathcliff saw and
smelled it.

"We aren't really into decorating here,"
I muttered.

I nodded at a door, and Heathcliff
breezed past me, his hands removing the
plate of cookies from my palms as we
entered the room. My bedroom. My
sanctuary.

There was silence, and then, "Wow,
Hawthorne. No posters or tubes of lipstick
anywhere?"

My cheeks heated as my gaze scanned
the room. It was barren other than my
dresser, my bed, the window seat, and a
shelf of books. The only decoration was the
gilded mirror propped on the dresser, its
current reflection a tall young man and an
uneasy young woman with windblown hair
and a bulky work jacket.

Removing my messenger bag and the
coat, I held the jacket up before tossing it on
the end of my bed. "I forgot to leave it in the
truck."

Heathcliff set the plate of cookies down
on the dresser and moved past me to the

bookshelf. "Don't worry about it." His fingers ran along the books' worn spines. "No TV or anything here?"

The books were in alphabetical order by title rather than author, and his hand wavered over the W's, over my tattered copy of *Wuthering Heights*.

"My uncle was never one for television, and I guess he didn't think I needed it."

My gaze fell to my feet as he glanced at me. "That's where it comes from," he said thoughtfully. "This genuine air of yours. It hasn't been corroded by things."

I snorted. "You don't read much do you? There are tons of sordid, not so innocent stuff in books."

Heathcliff stepped toward me. "Like what?"

Clearing my throat, I backed away, my hand falling to my bag, to the notebook that lay within. "We're supposed to be doing homework."

"Oh!" Heathcliff exclaimed. "That reminds me! My idea!" Leaning close, he took my bag from me, his hands digging through the contents for the composition book and pens within. "Let's make this more interesting. I'm going to write your paper and you're going to write mine."

"What?" I gasped. "No!"

"It'll be your words, Hawthorne. I'm just going to write them down while you speak and vice versa." His hand found my hand, and he tugged me toward the bed. "Sit," he ordered. My tailbone hit the mattress, the mirror from my dresser suddenly appearing in front of me. "Look in this, and tell me what you want me to write."

Handing the mirror off, he sat behind me on the dark comforter, and for the first time I stared at his face. It wasn't a direct look. It was his reflection, but it was his face nonetheless. He had a strong countenance, a hard jaw and straight nose. His hazel eyes teetered on bright green, the color in stark contrast to his dark brown hair.

His eyes met mine in the mirror, and he froze.

"It's just a reflection," I defended, the words slipping free before I could grab them back.

One of Heathcliff's hands rested on the bed, the other poised above my notebook, the cover open to reveal the page I'd written in school. His gaze fell to the words, scanning them before his eyes rose again.

"An honest reflection," he murmured. "Isn't that what you said in class? The mirror is honest."

My gaze studied him before sliding to my face, to my gray eyes and reddened cheeks.

"Let's write, Hawthorne," Heathcliff prompted. "What do you see?"

"My mother," I whispered. My mouth choked on the words, desperate to draw them back in, but it was too late. Thoughts I'd never shared with anyone but Gregor fell against my lips and there was no holding them back. I guess when you dam something up long enough, it's bound to explode.

"I see my mother," I repeated. "I see her eyes and her face, but I don't see the storm. When I was a child, her eyes always looked like the sky right before the tornado sirens go off, like funnel clouds of wildness. I used to envy her those eyes. They flashed like lightning. Now, when I see the same color in mine, I'm angry."

Heathcliff wrote in the notebook, but mostly he stared at my reflection, an odd expression on his face. "Angry?" he asked.

I swallowed hard. "Because she took that away from me. She took away my right to be wild or irresponsible. I couldn't do that to my uncle, and if I did, if I decided to be rebellious despite that, I'd prove them all right."

"Them?"

"The town," I replied, my gaze on my eyes. "They'd look at me and say, 'she's just like them', and that's the one thing I never want to be."

Heathcliff sat up behind me, the notebook forgotten. "Why do you care? Why not be wild and free. You can be both. Being free spirited doesn't mean you're going to leave."

My gaze found his in the glass, the storm I was fighting so hard to control swirling in my eyes. "Doesn't it?" He started to reach for me, but I gripped the mirror. "And what do you see? What do you see when you look at yourself?"

His gaze swept from my reflection to his own. "One of the Vincent boys," he answered. "Tied forever to hardware and gasoline."

Surprised, I asked, "And you don't want that?"

"No," he shook his head, "I mean, yes. I'm proud of it. There was only a hastily constructed shack in the wilderness when my ancestors came here. I've been bred on stories about how my family built everything they have out of timber, tools, and sweat. I just want to do something different."

Realization dawned, and I stared. "You want to leave."

He glanced at my reflection. "Don't you? I see it in you, Hawthorne. You're like a weed in the middle of a field of flowers waiting to be pulled loose."

My gaze fell. "I'm not my parents."

His hand slid across the comforter, his fingers tugging on the hem of my shirt. "No, you are *you*. They're not allowed to steal that."

Maybe, once, I wouldn't have allowed them to take those choices away from me, but now …

"He's dying," I breathed. "The paperwork he brought home," I hiccupped, "they said terminal cancer. Stage four."

There was sorrow in Heathcliff's eyes, but there was also something beyond that. "And when he's gone? Have you thought about that?"

My eyes closed. "I don't want to think about it."

Heathcliff's fingers found my face, turning it. "Look at me," he whispered. "Really look at me." My eyes squeezed tight, and he sighed.

Tugging my chin away from his grip, I murmured, "Two days of work, driving a stick shift, and a quick kiss doesn't earn you that."

I expected him to get angry, to call me crazy and leave, but he didn't. His body sank into the mattress, his hand falling to mine on the comforter.

"I'm not going anywhere, Clare," he said.

"Hawthorne," I corrected.

"*Clare*," he insisted. "It's too late for me to leave. I'm invested now."

I laughed, my eyes opening, my gaze on our hands. "You make me sound like a bank account."

Releasing my hand, he reached over me to grab the mirror, and I glanced into the glass, his gaze finding mine in this alternate reality, in the world of looking glasses. "Maybe it is kind of like that," he remarked. "I'm investing in you, Clare."

I cringed when he said my name, but I didn't look away. "Why?"

"Because that's what I do," he stated, and shrugged. "Ask my family. I invest in things, and I keep at it until I wear it down." He smiled. "My brother found an injured dog once on the side of the road. Everyone, even the vet in town, said he wouldn't survive. They decided to put him down. But I stole him."

My eyes grew round. "You took him from the vet?"

He nodded at our reflections.

"And did he?" I asked.

"What?"

"Die?"

Heathcliff's grin widened. "I nursed him for weeks. Brought him food and water, bathed him, accepted medicine from the same vet I stole him from. My parents didn't get angry. I think they thought it would teach me something about life and death. That maybe if I saw him pass, I'd learn what it meant to let go."

"And?" I prompted.

Heathcliff leaned forward behind me, his mouth near my ear. "His name is Rat, and he's ten-years-old now. Lives with Mams. You can meet him. He's not as active as he was when I was eight, but he's a good dog. Loyal."

Staring, I mumbled, "And they call me the odd one."

His lips brushed my neck. "I just don't like giving up on people."

How my shoe found this boy's shoe is beyond me. I'd always run away from people, from possible relationships. I'd made it my entire school career avoiding relationships of any kind, romantic or otherwise. Until his shoe met mine in English class.

"I'm not a good investment," I whispered.

"I beg to differ," he argued. "I think you may be my best yet." He leaned away, and I released a pent up breath. "Now, come on, we have an assignment to do."

In the end, Heathcliff left that night, a sheet of paper dangling from his fingers. I held the other. We'd placed them side by side before he departed, his gaze sliding to my profile while I avoided his. The assignment wasn't officially over until the end of term. But we had a start.

Hawthorne Macy

I'm a cook. I like making food because I can take a variety of components and make something old, comfortable, new, or unique out of it. My life is like a recipe. In my mirror, I see the ingredients, my uncle and me. I'm not sure how we work, but we do. Each time I've glanced into the glass growing up, I've seen him behind me. At first, I was a little girl with terrible hair, my bewildered uncle standing at my back, his flabbergasted eyes on my tangled head. I think that's how we came to be, Gregor and me.

He was left with a terrible muddle of a girl, and he had to figure out how to put her back together.

Other times, I look into the mirror, and I don't see my uncle or even me. I see my mother, her stormy, tornado-infused eyes taunting me, telling me that I can't be daring or free. Her eyes tell me I have to fight too hard not to be like her or my father. Her eyes tell me to be afraid.

Finally, I look into the mirror, and I see myself. There are yearnings there I'm not sure I'm ready to explore. There's grief I'm afraid to face. There's courage, but there's also regret.

My uncle is living on borrowed time. He did more than fix me, even with my doubts, even with the things about myself I'm not sure of. He loved me, and I loved him back. He took my heart, and he kept it safe. He guarded it. I think, if I'm being honest, I'm afraid that when he's gone, I'm going to break what he worked so hard to keep strong.

Max Vincent

I'm a Vincent. When I look into the mirror,

I see a name. I see wood, nails, gasoline, and sweat. Then, I see fire. Figuratively speaking, I want to use the gasoline and the wood to burn down what I know is expected of me. I want to see more, be more, and do more. I don't want to spend my life staring into a mirror pretending I don't want to be somewhere else, be someone else.

I want to be who I am. I want my name, but I want more. I'm not ashamed of that. In truth, I don't really know what I want to do or who I want to be. I just want the freedom to find out.

Closing the door behind Heathcliff, I turned, my back settling against it. There was a light on in the kitchen, and I knew my uncle was sitting, as he often did in the late afternoon, at the kitchen table, a newspaper in front of him, a cup of strong coffee in his hand.

My feet found him.

I sometimes wondered if my body worked as a whole, or if my heart ruled it rather than my mind. My feet often took me places I'd never thought of going until I got there.

"He kissed me," I blurted.

Uncle Gregor's head shot up, his coffee midway to his lips, his gaze sweeping my face before going to the hall beyond.

"He's gone," I supplied, and repeated, "He kissed me."

"You said that." Setting his coffee down, he peered at me over the brim of his reading glasses. "You know to be smart, don't you, Hawthorne?"

My feet took me to the table, my stance uneasy. "I'm not quite sure what to think about all of it."

Shifting uncomfortably, Gregor gestured at the chair next to his, and I sat. "Well," he cleared his throat, "I don't really know how to begin …"

His face reddened, and I took pity on him. "I'm seventeen, Uncle. I know about sex. I just don't know about Heathcliff."

Uncle Gregor released a relieved breath. "Follow your heart. It won't fail you. Not yours."

My fingers played with the edge of his newspaper. "You have too much faith in me."

He smiled. "Maybe, but I know you, Hawthorne, and I'm willing to bet I'm not wrong about your heart."

His chicory-enhanced coffee tickled my nose as I leaned over, my gaze scanning his face. "Do you think I'm like my parents?"

Startled, Gregor stared. "Your parents?" My lips parted, but he didn't give me a chance to respond. "Your parents weren't runners. I know what the people say in this town. I know the rumors. Being from a small community makes us all afraid of losing people. It's a comfortable but often boring life. Young people come and go. It doesn't mean they're running. Your parents didn't run, they quit. There's a difference."

A tear fought a battle with my eye and lost, the moisture rolling down my cheek. "Why did you keep me? Why didn't you go after them?"

The paper rattled as Uncle Gregor shoved it aside, his gentle hand finding mine. "They were terribly young, Hawthorne. I lived away, working for a pharmaceutical company when my parents passed. I was twenty-eight. My brother was only sixteen, and I became responsible for him. A year later your mother told him she was pregnant. They were *so* very young. Very restless people with few responsibilities. They had you, but it wasn't enough. Oh, they gave it a good show for the first six years, but it wasn't to be. They wanted that chance to be young, I suppose."

"They were irresponsible," I spat.

His kind gaze captured mine. "Maybe."

My shoulders slumped. "They've had their chance to be young by now, but they haven't returned."

Gregor's hand tightened on mine. "That's real fear they're facing now. You grew up while they did, and I don't think they know how to come home to a stranger."

There were no words for the emotions that churned in my gut, the uncertainty, the anger, and the confusion. In many ways, I'd learned to cope with my past by loving my uncle and his home too much. I'd planted my soul here, and then I'd met Heathcliff's shoes. The young man wearing them was making me search deeper within myself than

I wanted to. He was making me care about him, care about something other than this house and the sweet Southern air beyond the windows.

"Let yourself bloom, Hawthorne," my uncle whispered. "Open yourself up."

Taking a deep, chest-expanding breath, I breathed, "And if I'm making a mistake? If I'm making the wrong choice?"

Uncle Gregor patted my hand. "Choices aren't always mistakes, but they are always defining."

"I wish I had your confidence."

"If you did, you wouldn't be young."

Tugging my hand away from his, I stood and stepped away from the table, my back to him. "Do you believe in love?"

His chair scraped the floor. "I do, but ask me *why* I do."

Turning to face him, I mumbled, "Why?"

"Because I believe in you. Because no matter how many times your heart is broken in life, your love will always be worth it."

His words warmed my heart, but they also filled me with fear. "You think my heart will be broken?"

"I think your heart will learn. The heart can't be broken if you don't let it break. Let it, Hawthorne. People are so afraid of being broken that they don't allow themselves to learn from the pain. The heart can't be taught if you don't give it something to learn."

My chest felt funny, heavy and uncomfortable. "He plans to leave one day."

Uncle Gregor stood and stepped toward me, his gaze full of warmth. "Then let him, but give him a reason to wish he'd stayed. You won't understand this now, and I don't expect you to, but know this: sometimes love isn't forever. Sometimes it's just moments in your life that teach you. If it's the forever after kind of love, it'll find you again. If it isn't, don't let a broken heart break you. Let it make you love harder. Love is a mistake worth making."

There was passion in his voice, strong and sure, and I found myself smiling. "You know, you're kind of wise, Uncle."

He snorted. "No, I'm old. Now what's for supper?"

I laughed, my gaze scanning his face, my eyes tracing the lines around his lips.

Gregor was only forty-six years old. No matter how old that seemed to me right now, it was still too young to die.

Swallowing past the sudden lump in my throat, I gasped, my question broken when I asked, "Are you afraid?"

"Afraid?"

A tear slid down my cheek. "Of dying?"

"Oh, Hawthorne." Closing the distance between us, he pulled me into his embrace and tucked my head under his chin. He smelled of chicory and menthol. "I'm not dying. Not really."

My sobs shook me, my nose and eyes leaking into his linen shirt, staining it. "I don't know if I can make it without you."

Gently, Gregor pulled me away from him, his eyes capturing mine. "You can do anything, Hawthorne. I won't be leaving. Not really. People don't die, we pass into memory. I'll live through you, through your heart and your mind. That's the wonderful thing about life. Our bodies die, but memory allows us to live in those we love."

My sobs shook me. "I'm so scared. I want to pretend I'm not, but I can't. I'm so sorry. I'm so very sorry."

Uncle Gregor gripped me. "Shhh …" he soothed, "I'd be more worried if you weren't."

We were doing a lot of hugging lately, my uncle and me, as if we needed every possible moment we had to say good-bye.

"You know," I gasped, my voice shaking, "you're supposed to be all against my having a relationship with someone. The whole protective *I've got a gun* bit."

Uncle Gregor chuckled, the vibration a welcome comfort against my ear. "Is that so? I'm afraid I'm going to fail you there. The last time I held a gun, I managed to shoot up my grandma's prized roses rather than the target."

It was the first time I'd heard this story, and I smiled. "That's not so bad."

"It is when the target was on the other side of a creek opposite the house."

"Oh," I laughed, "that's pretty bad."

"It was considered safer that I didn't have anything with a trigger after that."

My chuckle mingled with his.

"Tell me your stories, Uncle. All of them," I urged.

He grew still. "Some of them involve your parents, Hawthorne."

There was silence, and then, "You said people don't die, they pass into memory. I want you there in mine, the hard moments and the good," I whispered.

Uncle Gregor pulled me away from him again, his eyes searching mine. "Let's make something quick to eat," he suggested. "There's a lot of stories to tell."

I made us sandwiches after that, a peanut butter and jelly with mayonnaise for me and a ham and cheese with mustard and potato chips for him, the chips crushed between the bread. It's funny, actually, that I remember that. For hours, he told me stories, and I do remember them. All of them, but what I remember most was his face, the way his eyes lit up at some and darkened with others. Outside, the sun faded, setting below the trees, turning the limbs into silent, spooky sentinels. A chilly wind pushed against the kitchen's dark panes, the breeze lifting loose tin on the roof. It knocked against the ceiling as if it sought entrance. Maybe it was weeping, too.

Afterwards, when talking became too much for Gregor, when the fatigue settled in, he took himself off to bed. I remained, my hands clutching a mug of coffee. It was the chicory kind. I hated the taste of chicory, but I enjoyed the scent, the reminder that my uncle was still here.

Staring out the window, I realized something. If I'd had a pickup truck right then, I would have wanted to drive. All we had was my uncle's old car, and I didn't trust it not to break down in the dark. And yet, my mind drove beyond the house. My head was suddenly inside a sunlit meadow, winter wind chapping my cheeks as I grinded Heathcliff's gears, the tires rushing over grass, timber rattling in the bed.

It seemed wrong that my heart was yearning for love while grieving a loss it feared.

I was in my bedroom later that night when my gaze slid to my bookshelf, my eyes widening, my body shooting upright as I realized there was a book missing. Where my tattered copy of *Wuthering Heights* had once sat was an empty space, the small hole gawking at me.

Heathcliff had stolen Heathcliff. The irony made me smile. Maybe my uncle was right. It was time for me to spread my broken wings, to let in the fear and the possibility of heartache. My heart knew what it meant to be broken. It wasn't breaking my heart I was afraid of. It was healing.

Chapter 6

Another day at school, another last period English class full of markers and sneakers.

"Plans today?" his shoe asked.

"No," mine answered.

"Dinner? My house?"

I hesitated, my thoughts on Uncle Gregor, but there was prepared food in the freezer for unexpected things like this, and I answered with, *"Okay."*

The bell rang, and Heathcliff followed me out, his shoes next to mine.

"It's at my house. The dinner, that is. It's kind of a special one. It's for Mams' birthday. She's eighty-eight today," Heathcliff said.

I paused in the hallway. "Are you sure that I should come? Shouldn't that just be family?"

"Max!" a female voice shouted.

My gaze flew to the hall, to the small group approaching us. Rebecca Martin, Jessica Reeves, and Brian Henry.

Rebecca's highlights appeared golden in the dim corridor, her sparkling gaze passing over me before finding Heathcliff's. "Always in such a rush, Max! Did you hear about the party at the creek this Friday? You should come."

"You really should," Brian agreed. "Bring that rusted old heap you call a pickup." He laughed. "We're going to do some mud ridin' before it gets dark."

"After that, it's all about the beer," Jessica giggled.

My gaze remained averted, so that I was part of the group but not the conversation.

"I don't know," Heathcliff hedged.

"Oh, come on," Rebecca exclaimed. "You know you want to! Any chance to show off what that old truck of yours can do." She arched her brows. "There's a lot of memories in that truck."

"Dude," Brian inserted, "she's right. It's bring your own beer, but you and your brother never had any trouble getting that."

"You can even bring your friend here. Hawthorne, right?" Rebecca added.

Brian and Heathcliff's hands clasped in a brief, familiar shake.

"Yeah," Heathcliff finally answered. "I'll see what I've got going on."

"Awesome!" Jessica squealed. "See you two later." She smiled. "Hope to see you there, Hawthorne."

They left, leaving Heathcliff and I standing awkwardly, his hands darting to his blue jean pockets.

"Yeah, well," he cleared his throat, "I really want you to come tonight. Family or no. My Mams really likes your uncle. Talks about him all of the time."

My silence was long and heavy, the interruption from his friends leaving me uncertain. What was I doing?

"And the party Friday," he added suddenly. "They're right. You should come. They're really okay people just looking to blow off a little steam like the rest of us. And you know," his feet shifted next to mine, "you should come to it with me. If you want to that is."

I stared at his shoe. "I'll come tonight."

I didn't mention the party, and he didn't push it.

"Great," he replied. "Need a ride home?" My head shook, and he coughed. "Okay, well … pick you up in a few hours?"

He left, and I used the walk home to clear my head, my shoes crackling over brittle leaves and pinecones. The ever present scent of smoke snaked through the air. There was always something burning this time of year, voices rising and tires crunching over gravel. I made it a habit to stay on well-worn paths to avoid hunters.

My uncle was lying on the ground when I stepped into our yard, and I started to rush toward him until I realized his chest was rising and falling, his eyes on something in the trees above him.

His head turned when he heard my shoes. "I could have sworn I saw a new species of bird," he called out. "Want to join me?"

My mouth twitched. "I'm okay, thanks. I kind of have a dinner date."

Uncle Gregor sat up, brushing leaves from his shirt. He had a tie around his neck, but it was hanging loose and undone. Dark circles marred his eyes, and I knew his illness was eating away at him. "You remember what we talked about last night right, Hawthorne? Give it a chance."

Pushing open the door, I paused and turned toward him. "Uncle?"

"Yeah?"

"If you find that bird, name it after me, would you?"

He laughed. "You've got it."

The door shut behind me, my troubled thoughts chasing me to my room, my closet, and my mirror, my reflection peering back at me. I didn't have much, but I did own a few things that weren't hand-me-downs, and I pulled on a rose-colored V-neck blouse that offset my wild, strawberry hair.

My fingers touched the glass, sliding down my cheek's reflection as if it were Heathcliff's hand instead of mine. Did he think about me like this?

I stepped away from the mirror. This was madness! I felt crazy, my head going around and around in circles but never finding its way to anything sensible. If this was confusion, I'd found it. If it was attraction, then I wasn't sure I liked it.

Sitting on the edge of the bed, I stared at the wall, listening as the door opened and closed downstairs, my uncle's feet carrying him through the house. He was humming an old song, the classic *Have a Little Faith in Me*, and I grinned. Uncle Gregor had a way of telling me things without ever saying a word.

Outside a truck revved, and I stood, my sweaty palms sliding down the sides of my jeans.

"Hawthorne!" my uncle called.

It was all pretense. He knew and I knew that his playing the protective father was going through the motions for us. Uncle Gregor had always trusted me probably more than he should.

My feet pounded the stairs, my breath coming in pants as I stumbled to a stop at the door. Inhaling, I grabbed the knob, my gaze flying to my uncle. He stood in the hallway, his newspaper tucked beneath his arm, the smell of coffee floating from the kitchen.

"I'm here," he said.

Those two words were devastating and beautiful. I was living my life in dual emotions. My body felt torn trying to process them all. I had to keep reminding myself that he was here now and that's what mattered.

Pulling the door open, I murmured, "It's just dinner."

Heathcliff was on the walk outside, his shoes headed for the house. I intercepted him, and he paused.

"I could have come to the door," he said, amused.

"It's okay."

Taking my hand, he tugged me toward his truck, the work jacket from before sprawled out across the seat. Taking it, I pushed my arms into the sleeves as I climbed in.

Heathcliff's door was barely closed when he said, "About school today." He gripped the steering wheel. "It was kind of awkward after my friends came up, but I just want you to know something." He looked at me now, but I didn't meet his eyes. "I know you don't want to be a part of that scene. I get it, I do, but I don't want to hide this. I'm interested, okay. I want to know you, Hawthorne. Even if it means taking you out of your comfort zone. I want to know the girl behind the stare."

My throat worked as I swallowed, my hands clenching the material of his jacket. "I just hope you're not looking for this really spectacular story. Silence often makes people seem more mysterious than they really are. I'm not really all that mysterious."

The truck moved, the tires bouncing past the crepe myrtles, my words hanging between us. "No," he said finally, "you're not all that mysterious, but you're a thinker. I like that about you."

My gaze slid to his profile, to his neck and shoulders, his words making me uncomfortable. "You stole something from me," I blurted to ease the tension.

He smiled. "You noticed the missing *Wuthering Heights*." A chuckle escaped, and he added, "You highlight passages in your books."

Facing forward, I stared at the road, at the lowering sun and cracked asphalt. "Only stuff that really sticks with me."

The wind brushed my hair, sending it flying. Heathcliff's hand shot out, his fingers tangling in the strands before releasing it. "God, it's like it has a life of its own." He exhaled. "You want to know what my favorite marked quote was in the book? It was highlighted in neon orange, and said, *Honest people don't hide their deeds.* For that to have struck a cord in you, then you must believe it."

"Why wouldn't I?" I asked.

He reached for me, his arm falling across the seat as if he wanted me to move closer. I did, but probably not as close as he wished. "That's why I asked you to come tonight," he said. "When I saw that quote, I knew I needed you there."

Startled, I breathed, "Needed?"

He shrugged. "Remember the paper? My family often uses dinners like this to talk about the future. I'm going to be frank here. I'm not good at being honest with my family, my father especially. I don't want to work here when I finish school. I don't want to stay here."

My heart broke. Just like that it shattered. Before I'd even had a chance to explore the idea of a relationship, it was gone. My uncle's words circled my brain, but the teenage drama queen I liked to pretend didn't exist in my heart rebelled.

She rebelled, she screamed, she punched the insides of my guts, and then she became quiet. She simply quit being anything. My uncle was right. At least I knew before it started that my heart was going to be broken. I either needed to decide that was okay or I needed to walk away.

"You want me there to make it easier for you to tell them you want to leave," I said.

"Yeah," he responded. "I do. Do you hate me for that?"

I laughed, the sound harsher than I intended. "I don't really know you enough to hate you." A shuddering breath escaped, and with it the rushed words, "Actually, I admire you." There it was. I was deciding that his leaving was okay, that I could do this even knowing it was going to end. "If you can't be honest with yourself, then there's no point, right?"

The arm on the back of the seat was heavy against my shoulders, his fingers suddenly gripping my arm through the jacket. "What I want to do one day doesn't change this, you know. It doesn't change the fact that I really *do* want to know you. That I want to be your friend, maybe even more than that."

There was a sudden lump in my throat, but I swallowed it away. "We still have time before school ends."

"You mean that?" he asked, surprised.

My words were more than words, and we both knew it.

Glancing out the window, I replied, "That party Friday … I think I might want to try it."

Another brief pause. "Hold that thought," he said. Braking on the side of the road, he stuck his head out of the window and hollered. Startled laughter bubbled up through my chest as he ducked back inside, his feet hitting the gas. "You don't need a story, Hawthorne!" he cried. "We're going to make one for you."

Despite knowing that whatever story he wrote was going to end, I felt light. Like a feather floating on the breeze, wild and free. Maybe Gregor was right. Maybe love could just be a moment, the kind that teaches rather than robs.

Heathcliff pulled the truck into a driveway lined in solar torches, each one placed before a row of azalea bushes. When the season changed, the lane would be aflame with color. The narrow avenue ended in a circle drive, a two-level log cabin resting before it. It wasn't a huge home, but it wasn't small either. It was nice, sprawling in places, landscaped yet homey. A barn sat in the back, a wood shop visible from the road.

"From our work on the paper, I know you don't really know what you want to do …" I said, my words trailing off.

Heathcliff parked and turned the key in the ignition. "Yeah, but that's the thrill of it. The unknown is exciting. Not knowing what you really want to do is an adventure. It's a chance to go out there and find out what you want, to learn about yourself. Not everyone has it figured out, you know. The opportunities here are kind of limited."

My gaze traveled to the house, to the lit windows and shadowy figures moving within. I couldn't help but wonder what I would have wanted if my life had been different, if my parents had stayed.

"What's it like?" I asked. "Being a part of a big family?"

Heathcliff stilled, his arm suddenly tugging me to his side of the truck. "There's nothing else like it. There's love, and then there's more. I wouldn't ask to be a part of any other family. Mine's amazing. It's because they're so wonderful that I'm having such a hard time telling them I want out of this town."

His embrace felt way better than it should, and my voice lowered. "It wouldn't be forever though. You'd visit."

His chin fell near my shoulder, and my breathing hitched. "That's not the way they'll see it. You know better than anyone what they'll think, Hawthorne."

"That you're running," I whispered.

Releasing me, he opened his door, slid out, and then offered me his hand. "I have no idea how to make them see that I'm not."

My fingers met his palm, and his hand wrapped around mine as I climbed free, our gazes on the house. My heart clenched. It clenched because I knew exactly how to make them see.

"You have to go in sometime," I said.

Heathcliff sighed and led me to the door, his fingers clutching mine. Grabbing the doorknob, he paused. "Thank you," he said suddenly. "Thank you for coming with me. Most of all, thank you for not running away knowing I don't want to stay. My last girlfriend broke it off as soon as she found out. After a year of dating, she couldn't get out of the truck fast enough. But considering your history, I wouldn't have blamed you."

"Can I be honest?" I asked. For the first time since meeting him, my gaze met his. He'd been candid with me, and that earned a lot.

He sucked in a breath, and my head lowered. Releasing my hand, he gripped my chin, his fingers pushing my face up. "Be honest. Please."

Frowning, I murmured, "I've been left. I don't fear people leaving. I fear the way they'll go."

Pulling away from his touch, I placed my hand over his on the knob and twisted it. The door fell in, revealing a country-inspired entryway. Running deer chased each other on rugs covering a rough hewn floor, and a cushioned rocking chair sat before an antique wash basin and mirror. Stairs to the right of the entry led to the second story with a mudroom tucked next to the stairwell. To my left, a large living space opened up, the kitchen and dining room open to the living area. Other than the wooden entry, the floors were brick.

Heathcliff's family milled around the house. Some of them reclined on dark leather couches while others watched a football game on ESPN on a wide screen television hanging above a large fireplace. Women laughed and called to each other in the kitchen while two children argued over a light-up yo-yo near the dining room, their mischievous gazes darting to the covered plates on the table .

At the sound of the door, his family froze, their gazes lifting.

"Max! Took you long enough!" a middle-aged, merry woman proclaimed, her cheeks flushed from the warm kitchen. Wiping her hands on an apron around her waist, she moved toward us.

"My mom," Heathcliff whispered.

For a small-statured woman, she walked fast. "You're the last one here," she chided, her gaze sweeping her son's face before sliding to mine. "Clare Macy," she breathed. "I'd know that face anywhere."

She offered me her hand, and I accepted it. "Hawthorne, ma'am. I go by Hawthorne."

"It's good to see you again, Hawthorne," Dusty Vincent greeted. The man I'd met at the hardware store approached us, his large hands in his blue jean pockets. He was freshly shaven, his hair trimmed, a black long sleeve tee with *Vincent's* embroidered on a small pocket covering his chest.

"If I'm the last that means we can eat, right?" Heathcliff teased.

His mom swiped his arm playfully. His dad stepped aside so that we could enter, his family's eyes trailing us. The whispers followed me. *"That's Meg Macy's daughter, ain't it?" "Damned if she ain't a dead ringer of her mother." "Except that hair. That wild mass definitely came from her daddy."*

Nodding at the two boys still fighting next to the table, Heathcliff said, "My nephews, David and Hayden."

I smiled, but they barely spared me a glance. The yo-yo definitely trumped the strange girl.

"They're going to end up strangling each other with that thing," a woman hissed loudly.

"My aunt," Heathcliff grimaced.

The rotund, snarling woman grabbed the boys by the ear and escorted them away.

The family filed into the kitchen, each of them taking seats in the dining room. Heathcliff pulled a chair out for me, but before I could sit, blue eyes caught mine from across the table.

"Afraid we don't see many girls with Max," a young man laughed. "So you'll have to excuse the staring." Standing, he offered me his hand. "I'm Chris, Max's brother."

The man was handsome, his tall figure more lithe than muscular, a light goatee covering his chin. He flashed his teeth, and I accepted his hand.

A young woman chuckled from the chair next to him. "Before long, he'll tell you he's the better looking, more talented son." She nodded. "I'm Chris' wife, Samantha."

Taking a seat, I smiled at her.

Faces and names blurred together as Heathcliff pointed out an additional three cousins, an uncle, and a great-aunt. But it was the woman at the head of the table who caught my eye. She was staring at me, her gaze boring into my face, her sharp green eyes bold and harsh.

"Clare Macy," the woman greeted. My lips parted, but her wrinkled hand rose, stopping me. "It's Clare, girl. That's all I've ever known you as, and it's what I'll call you."

"Mams—" Heathcliff began.

"Oh, hush up, boy! I didn't reach eighty-eight by keeping my mouth shut, and I ain't startin' now when I know I'm one foot in the grave." She nodded at me. "Just about raised your uncle Gregor, I did. Good boy, too. He's got a good heart and a bright mind. It saddens me that he's going to be taken so soon."

"Mom," Dusty warned.

She glared at him. "I ain't sayin' nothing she ain't heard. Lawd, y'all act like

I'm skinnin' her cat right in front of her face. Getting down to it, then. I'm right glad to be seeing you among us, girl. You've been awful sheltered up in that big ol' house."

She grew quiet, and I stared. "Um … thank you," I said, my eyes narrowing. "My uncle has told me a lot about you. Said you were the hand of God. A mean spirited witch with a heart of gold."

Faint gasps emanated around the table, but I held Mams' gaze.

She grinned. "I'll be," she cackled. "The hand of God. Did ya'll hear that? You might have got your mama's face, but you sure didn't get her tongue. Right silver that mouth of yours is, and you know when to use it. I like that. I think your uncle got it right calling you Hawthorne." She nodded at me. "Fine then, girl, you've earned the name. Now let's crack open this meal!"

"She thinks dying means she can be meaner," Chris hissed from across the table.

Heathcliff nudged me. "I'll be damned. I've never heard her say so much and mean so many nice things all at one time."

"My table, your tongue," Heathcliff's mom warned.

"You've done sullied the meal," Chris joked.

Heathcliff snorted. "Mams cusses worse than that."

My gaze scanned the table, half listening to the chatter, my mind wandering to the things in life I'd missed. Family mostly. Uncle Gregor had always been enough because he had to be, because his parents, my grandparents, were gone. My other grandparents had never wanted anything to do with me. I'd been a taint by birth, a child born out of wedlock to their wild daughter. It seemed I represented too much and lived too little.

"So, how's the training going, Chris?" one of the cousins asked.

Heathcliff's brother smiled. "Terrific! Not really a whole lot to learn considering I came out of the crib having to know it."

The table filled with laughter, but Heathcliff tensed next to me.

"I got lucky," Dusty declared. "Not one, but two sons to pass on the business to."

Heathcliff shifted, his fork lying next to his plate, his jaw tense.

"Max'll be good at the hardware stuff. He has a knack for putting things together," another cousin added.

Heathcliff cleared his throat and glanced at me, his hand fisting on the table. "I don't really think I want to work in the stores. Chris is much more qualified to run all of it. Better yet, he wants to."

Chris threw his brother a look, but Heathcliff didn't take the hint.

Silence descended.

"Well," Mams said, "if that ain't some bald faced honesty."

Dusty's fork met the table. "What are you saying, Son?"

Heathcliff's gaze slid to his dad's. "I'm not sure what I want to do honestly, but I kind of want to leave here to find out."

If the silence was loud before, it was deafening now.

"Leave," his mother whispered.

"Not forever," Heathcliff amended. "Just to do some soul searching, I guess you could call it."

"That's madness!" Dusty roared.

"Is it?" I asked. My voice was low but firm because I knew what was coming next; the blame. It would all land on me, on the daughter of people with running in their blood. "There's nothing wrong with leaving. I know more than anyone that this town is growing smaller and smaller each year, but it's not going anywhere. There's too much pride, tradition, and strength in this town. There's a difference between running and seeking. There's a difference between running and quitting. If you're running toward something, you're not running away. It's only when you're trying to hide from your failures that you don't come back."

It was said. The words I'd always been afraid to admit hadn't just been spoken, they'd been told to a room full of people. My parents had left, and they would never return because returning meant admitting the biggest failure they'd ever made; their failure as parents.

Discomfort made me push away from the table, my feet carrying me to the door.

My feet. They were soldiers. They fought battles for me I didn't even know I was fighting. They walked me through things I normally wouldn't walk through. It didn't matter where I'd been, I was never the same person when I left. It was this realization that brought the smile. Pain doesn't go away, but it does a lot to change you.

My hand wrapped around the doorknob, my gaze going over my shoulder. "I'm not running away," I said. "I'm going home. And your son isn't running away. He's searching for something. He'll find it, and when he does, he'll come back. Because that's what people who seek stuff do. They find it, and then they share it with the people they love."

Twisting the knob, I left, my grin widening as the door clicked shut behind me. There was that irony again. Heathcliff was looking for something beyond our hometown, and in the process was helping me find myself.

The wind kissed my face as I stepped toward Heathcliff's truck and climbed in. The seat was uncomfortable, the cracked leather cold against my jeans. It's funny how life unveils itself, choosing the oddest moments to say *open your eyes*.

"Hey," Heathcliff called, his voice breaking me out of my reverie. He stood outside the truck, his hands on the open window. "You okay?"

"Yeah," I answered, smiling. "I think I am."

He gave me a funny look, his hand pulling at the truck door. "You aren't leaving yet," he told me.

I glanced at the house. "I'm fine right here until you're done. Seriously. You need to go back to your family."

"That's kind of hard when it was the birthday woman who ordered me to leave." He chuckled. "I think she likes you." Pulling the door open, he held out his hand. "Come on, I want to show you something."

My fingers met his palm, and he tugged me from the vehicle hard enough I stumbled into him, my free hand going to his chest. His sudden wink was proof that it'd been on purpose.

Tucking me close, he led me over the lawn to the backyard. Solar lamps threw dim light over his features, the shadows making his cheeks look sharper, his eyes fierce. He was an interesting mix of masculine and boyish, tall and muscular but vulnerable in a way that wasn't noticeable at first.

"You aren't a failure," he said abruptly.

My gaze shot to his profile. "I know that, but I am *their* failure. It's crazy, right? Where they failed, Uncle Gregor succeeded."

Heathcliff's hand tightened on mine. "I don't think I would have seen it quite that way. You see things differently, Hawthorne. You take things and cast a whole new light on them."

"You do, too."

Releasing me, he shoved his hands into his pockets, the gesture reminding me of his father.

"Not the way you do." He glanced at the house. "Thank you for what you did in there. I'm not sure how they're taking it, but I don't think they would have even considered my feelings if you hadn't spoken."

I shrugged. "It's fear. Everyone has it. They love you enough it hurts. This is probably going to sound stupid, but I … I think that if love didn't exist fear wouldn't either. You have to love something to be afraid of losing it, whether that's simply loving ourselves or someone else. They love you, and they love this town. They fear losing both."

He stared. "You're an old soul."

I smiled. "No, I just think people could use a dose of realism. Do you know what I want to do? You have to promise not to laugh though."

He nodded, his lips twitching.

I chuckled. "I want to cook, but I want to fill whatever I make with philosophy, with life. We're from the South. For our ancestors, food was often hard to come by. We needed it to survive. Now, we use it to live, to congregate, to express love, pain, grief, and comfort. I want to make cooking a philosophy."

Heathcliff grinned, but he didn't laugh. "The Philosophical Chef. That could work. It'd be an interesting brand."

I shrugged. "I'm sure it's been done before, but everything's been done before. The key is to make it your own. To take whatever you choose to do and make it yours."

He nodded at the barn, and we walked toward it. "That's kind of deep, isn't it?" he asked.

My gaze found the woodshop within, landing on handmade benches, chairs, tables, furniture, and sculptures. It was beautiful, the scent of the wood as compelling as the artistry.

"I guess it is. Does that make me less appealing?"

He shot me a look. "If you think being deep makes you less appealing, then you must not think highly of me."

My gaze caught his, my pulse quickening. "This shop," I stuttered, "is it your dad's?"

Heathcliff nodded. "It's his, and it was my grandfather's before him. I guess you could say that's what makes a Vincent, timber and land. We respect nature. It's been our survival, so we give as much as we take."

"You've heard that quite a bit in your life, haven't you?"

"I believe it, too." He pulled his hand out of his pocket and entwined his fingers with mine. Tugging me toward the back of the shop, he led me to a ladder leading up to the barn's loft. "My brother and I spent a lot of time up here as kids. We'd watch my dad and uncles in the fields or whittling at wood. Sometimes they'd be doing something on the tractors or haying. We'd work, too, but we'd also hide and dare each other to jump from the loft to the piles of hay or leaves we'd stack on the ground below before our dad found the heap."

Climbing the ladder ahead of him, I scanned the dark loft, the only light coming from a security post in the yard, the soft yellow glow surreal where it splashed over the barren area. Stray straw littered the floor, and a few pieces of completed woodwork sat propped against the walls, leaving the area before the large double doors open.

"Did y'all jump?" I asked.

He followed me into the loft, his soft laughter surrounding us. "More often than not, we chickened out. We got bolder as we got older though. I've made that jump plenty now. It's kind of like a rite of passage I guess. I found my nephews up here one afternoon daring each other to do the same." He walked over to the open doors and looked out into the night. "After that, Chris talked Dad into keeping one of the work trucks parked beneath the doors, the back full of hay. The drop isn't as far that way, and it reduces the risk a little."

"Why not just forbid them from coming to the barn?" I asked, joining him.

He grinned. "You're talking about full on country boys here. We've got a lot of common sense, but we don't always use it. Especially when it comes to adrenaline or acts of nonsensical bravery. Besides, this isn't a big barn, not like the large working ones on the Parker farm. The drop isn't that bad. With age, the fall looks less and less daunting."

My gaze found his in the soft yellow light. "Now who's being deep?" I asked with a smile.

He gestured at the night. "You should jump."

My eyes widened. "What?"

"Jump," he said. "Here, I'll even go first."

Without another word, he was gone, his body taken by the night. There was a light thud, a quick laugh, and then, "Your turn."

Hesitating at the door, I glanced over the edge to find Heathcliff standing on a pile of hay in the back of a truck, his dimly lit face full of amusement. He was right, the fall wasn't far, but it also wasn't sensible.

"We're not kids," I called down.

He threw his hands up into the air. "We're not quite adults yet either, Hawthorne. Embrace that. Jump. Don't be afraid to fall."

With his palms up, his hands suddenly seemed as important as his feet. It was like I hadn't really met him, I'd met *pieces* of him, first his shoes, then his hands and face, each of them adding up to become something larger than they would have been had I noticed them all at once.

"Jump, Hawthorne," he insisted, his voice gentle.

Inhaling the night air, I looked out over the yard, over the security lit and moonlit fields, and I did the most irrational thing I'd done in my life up until that point. I followed him down.

Air rushed toward me as I jumped, my feet hanging in the sky one moment and then standing in hay the next, my breath coming in laugh-induced pants, Heathcliff's hands spanning my waist.

He laughed with me. "That's the first unplanned thing you've ever done, isn't it?" he asked.

My giggles tapered off, my head lifting to meet his. "And if it was?"

His gaze became serious, his eyes studying my flushed cheeks. "I like being part of your firsts," he whispered. "It's more exciting than jumping from barns. I'm seeing the world all over again, and in a whole new way."

His head lowered, and my lips parted, more prepared this time for the warm press of lips that followed. His fingers slid up my back from my waist, bunching my shirt in his fists as he went, the cool night air brisk on revealed skin.

My hands found his shoulders, my fingers digging into the long-sleeve T-shirt he wore, my short nails pressing into the tense muscles beneath. His tongue invaded my mouth, gently sweeping against mine, insistent but slow, as if time had stopped.

It was cold outside, but in the back of that truck, it was warm. The hay dug through my jeans to irritate the skin on my ankles. It should have bothered me, but it didn't. The only thing that mattered was the moment. The only thing that mattered was that I'd jumped, that I'd bridged some strange gap between my childhood and my future.

A voice called out from the house beyond, and Heathcliff pulled away, his chest rising and falling as he glanced up into the darkness.

"I think I should probably get you home," he breathed.

His actions belied his words, his mouth suddenly capturing mine again. His hands released my shirt and dove into my hair, his fingers tangling in the waves, his lips firmer than they had been before, more desperate. My arms wrapped around his neck, my mouth as insistent as his, our breaths mingling in the night, fogging up on the winter breeze.

"Okay," he gasped, pulling away, his eyes on mine. "I should really get you home now."

My arms fell away from his neck, and he released my hair, his hand finding mine as we moved over the hay to the edge of the truck bed. He climbed out first, and then assisted me, his hands spanning my waist briefly as my feet found the ground.

Neither of us spoke. We simply walked across the yard to his truck. The silence seemed important somehow, as if the kiss spoke for itself, the emotions in it too big for words. I wouldn't call it love. It was more like discovery, like an uncharted journey into a confusing mix of emotions. Forget the cup half full or half empty thing. My cup was a little bit of both. One moment it felt too full, and the next it didn't feel full enough.

Heathcliff drove into the night, the windows down, the wind rushing around us. The sky was clear, the stars bright. Pine, wood smoke, and freedom. That's what the night smelled like. It smelled like grass and pond water, like beauty and harshness, and we breathed it in.

The tires crunched over gravel, dirt, and then asphalt, over open roads and tree-lined dirt paths, from highway to back road. We were on the lane leading to the plantation when Heathcliff glanced at me. "What was better?" he asked. "The kiss or the fall?"

He pulled to a stop in front of the house, and I smiled, my face averted. "Aren't they the same thing?"

Those words hung in the air as I climbed free of the vehicle and ran for the house before he could even think about walking me to the door.

My fingers found the unlocked knob. The door fell in, and I closed it quickly behind me, locking it before settling against it, my breath coming in gasps.

There was a light on in the kitchen, and I knew my uncle had remained up. It wasn't too late, but it was for him, and I knew it.

The chair in the dining room scraped against the floor, Gregor's shadow falling over the hardwood as he paused in the doorway.

His worried gaze found my face.

I smiled. "It's okay, Uncle," I said. "Tonight, I learned how to fall."

Chapter 7

The next two days, I didn't see Heathcliff outside of English class. He was doing work for his father on the Parker farm, but the separation didn't matter. Something had changed between us, and we both knew it.

For two days, we traded glances, his foot hovering between our chairs, his hands fisted on the edge of his desk.

Our shoes spoke for us, color smearing into my sneakers as we wrote, erased, and then wrote again.

"Friday night?" his shoe asked.

"I'm in," mine answered.

It was corny using our shoes to speak when we could have just as easily used paper, but there was also something really special and unique about it. I didn't own a cell phone because my uncle and I had just never thought it a necessity, but now I wished I did. Maybe it would have eased the uncomfortable feeling in my gut as I lay awake at night staring at the ceiling. It wasn't that he consumed my thoughts—he didn't—but there was no denying that I felt his absence more keenly than I should.

I found myself wondering things as I lay awake, questioning myself and my feelings. Fear ate away at me. It was good that I was letting my heart fall, but was I doing it because I truly cared about Heathcliff on a primal level, or was it because I needed someone to help me through the pain of my uncle's illness?

For two days, Heathcliff worked, and I accompanied my uncle to three separate appointments, two of them for lab work and another with his oncologist.

Each time I saw Heathcliff's shoes in English class, my heart stuttered, my body heating. Each afternoon, that same heat was doused by chilling grief.

In all honesty, I think my uncle would have preferred to do his appointments alone, but my heart wouldn't allow it. So, I sat next to him, our feet fidgeting against tiled floors and plastic chairs, the smell of antiseptic assaulting us. There was little conversation, just a lot of hand holding and swallowed worries.

Gregor was patient and understanding, but the doctor's words washed over me garbled and loud. The cancer had spread, beginning first in his pancreas. They could give him something for pain, could do treatments to prolong life, but it was all very perfunctory. In the end, the cancer was too progressed. In the end, there was no saving him and no telling how much longer he'd live.

I wanted to scream and cry and fight, but I didn't because Gregor wouldn't want that. There's nothing more confusing than knowing you're going to lose someone you love and there's nothing you can do about it. I felt like an egg with a fractured shell, the crack growing larger and larger until I was sure the insides would fall out, scrambled and undone. I wanted to ask Gregor how he felt, but I didn't. I think he needed that semblance of calm strength, as if he needed to be strong for me to be strong for himself.

There were questions he did answer. He wanted to die at home, and the doctor discussed the care he was eligible for, the palliative nursing he may need as the pain progressed and his body became less able to function. For now, he'd continue as he always had until he just couldn't anymore.

It was the second day that I asked to drive home. It wasn't that I didn't know how to drive, I'd just never really had to before. There were a lot of things that were going to have to change. Driving was the least of them. I had a driver's license, had taken both the written and hands on test when I was sixteen, but I'd rarely been behind the wheel.

Climbing into my uncle's dented Ford Tempo, I took the steering wheel and stared as he stooped to get in, his face creased.

"I love you, Uncle Gregor," I said suddenly.

I'm not sure what made me say the words just then. We'd said them plenty of times before, but this time was different. I needed him to know that someone loved him, that someone cared enough about him to change the way they lived to be there for him. He'd always been there for me.

Uncle Gregor shut the door behind him, his fatigued smile wide when his gaze met mine. "I love you, too."

He settled back against the seat, and I began to drive, the road speeding beneath us, the trees outside blurring into one long line of green and brown, like a stroke of wild paint.

With one unreliable vehicle, I'd always walked while Gregor used the car, so it kind of surprised me that Heathcliff was right. Driving felt good.

"Why don't we roll the windows down, Uncle?" I suggested.

He didn't seem loathe to the idea, his eyes on the world beyond the metal body, and I opened the windows, the air rushing in around us. It smelled cleaner and wetter than the closed interior.

"Feels good, right?" I asked loudly.

Uncle Gregor glanced at me, his lined eyes crinkling. "I like you this way," he replied.

My hands tightened on the steering wheel, a smile forming on my lips. "You look funny with the wind messing with your hair."

He chuckled.

We passed a line of chicken houses, the foul odor rushing through the car, and Uncle

Gregor threw me an amused look.
"Hawthorne, how could you?"

"That was totally you," I teased.

My laughter joined his, and it felt good.
Outside, the world was pressing in on us, but
it didn't matter. Life wasn't about the world
beyond anymore. It was about moments.
Little moments.

Something caught my eye outside, and I
pulled the car over on the side of the road.

"Remember this?" I gasped.

Uncle Gregor sat up, his gaze finding an
old silo. It was empty and rusted, the grain
long gone. Beside it was a path, a trodden
trail leading down to a small lake.

Gregor's hand went to the door's
handle. Pushing it open, he stepped out, his
fatigued face lifting to the bright sun above.

I joined him. "Gosh, I think I was
maybe thirteen the last time we came here."

My uncle had brought me here often
when I was growing up. It was his thinking
place, he'd told me. We'd play hide and
seek in the silo, then trek down to the lake.
He'd search the shallow water near the edge
for things to study, and I'd fish.
Occasionally, we'd take a boat out on the

water, letting it float as we ate sandwiches or talked about things; books, people, school, or the future. We'd even fought on the lake's edge. The first time had been about a cat. I'd had a list of reasons why we needed one, and Uncle Gregor had an equally impressive list of reasons why it wasn't practical.

Then came the year I turned thirteen, the last year we'd come together. It had been a bad year for me. It was the year I started my period, and the year I found myself resenting Gregor for my parents' absence. It was normal, he'd told me then, to hate him. It was my hormones, my repressed rage. At thirteen, I hadn't cared about any of that. I just wanted someone to resent other than myself.

"I hate you!" I'd yelled, tears rushing down my cheeks.

Memories assaulted me as I stared at the silo and the path beside it.

My hand found my Uncle Gregor's, my fingers wrapping around his. "I didn't mean it, you know."

He leaned against the car, his foot tapping. I think he wanted to walk to the

lake but was too tired to attempt it.
"Children often never mean it. I never
thought you hated me. We all say that to the
people we love at some point or another."

Despite the winter month, the
temperature outside wasn't frigid, though
it'd drop when night fell.

"Did you ever love anyone?" It was
something I'd never thought to ask my
uncle, something I'd never stopped to think
about. "I mean, other than me. A significant
other kind of love?"

Uncle Gregor smiled. "I did. It was
remarkable, too. The kind you never forget."

My startled gaze found his profile.
"Where is she? Why didn't it last?"

He sighed. "It wasn't a she, Hawthorne.
It was a him."

I stared, his words and their implication
sinking deep. "What?" My hand tightened in
his. "Why didn't I know this? Why didn't
you tell me?"

His smile was somewhere between sad
and content. "Life happens. I guess I was
worried about what my relationship would
have done to you at the time. You were so
little when your parents left, so young to be

surrounded by the stigma their abandonment caused you. I didn't want to add to that. By the time I realized I was wrong, that I was being selfish, I'd lost him."

I gasped. "He found another partner?"

Gregor shrugged. "Maybe. He'd left the country for work, and it was impossible to follow him. I was tied up in court finishing up the paperwork for legal guardianship of you. You needed me, Hawthorne. I don't regret the decision to stay."

"Court?" I whispered.

He glanced at me. "There's something you need to know. It's time, and this is the perfect place to say it." He took a shuddering breath. "Your parents planned to leave. I knew they were going. I figured it was easier on you believing that they'd just up and left one day rather than knowing they knew they wanted out. They decided to sign away their rights, and I went through the adoption process. Legally, you're mine, Hawthorne. You've been mine for a long time."

A lump formed in my throat, a tear sliding down my cheek. I wasn't sure which was worse. Being abandoned or having my parents *plan* to abandon me. They hadn't just left on a whim, they'd put a six-year-old child up for adoption. "Why didn't you tell me?"

He studied my face. "Because everyone needs hope. At the time, I thought it was better for you to hope your parents would return than to hate us all. Because if you knew they'd planned to leave, then you'd realize that they never planned to return." He blinked, and for the first time, I noticed the moisture in his eyes. "What you've got to remember, Hawthorne, is that despite what your parents did, there was someone who wanted you."

The tears came fast and hard now, my chest heaving with the force. He hadn't just wanted me, he'd sacrificed everything to keep me. Me.

It was in that moment I realized something. No matter how small the family, the love we shared was bigger than the lack of people in our home. Love built on sand is shaky, but love built on rocky shores can endure the strongest of storms.

"Do something for me," I whispered. "Quit fighting. It's okay to let go now. It's okay to rest. For my sake."

It was the hardest thing I'd ever had to say.

Chapter 8

It was Friday night, and I'd just climbed into Heathcliff's pickup truck, my hands reaching for his familiar blue jean work jacket when he leaned over the seat and asked, "What's your all-time favorite memory?"

My eyes came up to meet his in the dimming light. "Why?"

He shrugged. "Because the best nights should always begin with happy thoughts, and I figure you need those after the last two days."

I stared, my pulse quickening. "You've given this some thought."

He gripped the steering wheel, his eyes on the rearview mirror as he backed up and turned to pull out of the drive. "What? You couldn't possibly be on my mind." He glanced at me and winked. "You know, I think one of my all-time favorite memories is kissing you in a pile of hay."

A laugh escaped me, the crisp night air blowing against my cheeks. "And now you're fishing for compliments. I see how it is." Pulling his jacket closer around me, I murmured, "It was one of mine, too."

He grinned, his lips parting, but whatever he was about to say was cut off by my sudden words. "I was ten-years-old, and I wanted to fly. I was obsessed with books about airplanes, and I'd lie for hours in the fields next to the house and stare at the sky. One morning, my uncle woke me up early, babbling something about seeing the world before bundling me up and ushering me out of the house. He had a friend who owned a small private plane, and he'd arranged a flight. It was an amazing experience. We were so high, and I was looking at the world in an entirely new way. Everything below seemed so small, so distant and far away. From that far up, everything seemed so trivial. I wasn't Hawthorne. I wasn't wearing a glaring red "A" on my chest that screamed abandonment. I was just me, and I was flying." My gaze jumped from Heathcliff's profile to the window. "That night, my uncle took me to a small county fair on the outside of town, and we rode the Ferris wheel at least a dozen times because I didn't want to get off. I'm not sure if it was because I wanted to see the lights in town or because I wanted to pretend to touch the stars. It was a magical night."

Heathcliff turned the truck onto a dirt lane, the bumps making the Toyota bounce. "That's a good memory, Hawthorne." His hand dropped to the seat between us. "Come sit next to me?"

I scooted to the center of the truck, the feel of his arm as it fell across my shoulders cozy in the dark. Night made everything easier, made things that would seem awkward in daylight less uncomfortable and more certain.

"I like it when the power goes out," Heathcliff said suddenly. "You know, during bad weather when the wind or lightning knocks out the electricity and plunges everything into darkness." He swallowed, his Adam's apple bobbing. "My family is so large. There's always more than just my parents and me at home. We've always got cousins, nephews, aunts or uncles staying. There's so much noise. Sometimes it's like music, a comfortable sound, the constant laughter, the cheers during a football game or talk about work.

But storms are a funny thing. When they knock out the lights, no matter how much noise there is, it's like everyone just exhales and then there's silence. Mom lights the candles she keeps around the house, and no one says anything. We just stop and listen to the rain. In those moments, I feel closer to my family than I do when we talk."

There was silence after he spoke, and somehow I knew he'd never told anyone else that before.

He cleared his throat, lifting his arm from my shoulder long enough to pull the truck over on the side of the lane. There were other pickups, the sound of country music loud through the open windows. Headlights glared onto grass, sand, and dirt before landing on a creek beyond, the beams swallowed by the muddy rushing water. Laughter filled the air, quick shouts and ribald jokes.

Heathcliff glanced down at me. "Is that why your uncle calls you Hawthorne?" he asked abruptly. "Because you have an invisible "A" for abandonment across your chest?"

I sighed. "Honestly? I don't know. I've never asked him. He reads a lot of classic novels, and I guess I've just always assumed … I mean, he has all of Nathaniel Hawthorne's work, including *The Scarlett Letter*."

"I think you should ask him," Heathcliff said. "For what it's worth, I don't think that's why he calls you that."

My gaze found his, his hazel eyes black in the darkness. "Maybe I should."

He smiled, his teeth flashing. "You ready for this?" He nodded at the creek. "Even quiet people fit in here, Hawthorne."

He pushed open his door and climbed out, his hand finding mine as he assisted me down after him. My shoes had barely hit the sand when Jessica Reeve's giddy voice washed over us.

"Oh, my God! You came! Look who the cat drug in, Rebecca!" she cried.

Heathcliff's hand tightened on mine as he tugged me across the sand into the glare of the headlights toward a crackling bonfire, the flames lifting from a large, rusted fire pit. Someone threw a crushed beer can into the blaze and sparks flew.

"Well, I'll be!" Rebecca Martin called out. She approached us slowly, her gaze raking my form as she paused before Heathcliff. A belted tunic hugged her figure, the true color lost to the bright lights. Tan leggings paired with cowgirl boots adorned her legs, and a longneck beer bottle dangled from her manicured nails. "Max Vincent, I've been inviting you to these things all year, and this is the first time you've deigned to join us. Makes me miss last year when you were a regular."

Heathcliff smiled. "I've been busier this year."

"So I've heard," she replied. "How's Mams?"

"Good. For now."

Rebecca nodded, and then glanced at me. "Glad you could make it. Ya'll grab a beer if you didn't bring any of your own. There's plenty to go around."

Brian Henry stumbled forward, two bottles in his hand. "It ain't a party if you haven't popped a top." He laughed at his own joke, the beer shoved in our direction. Heathcliff accepted his. I did, too, but more slowly.

"I don't think we've ever seen you at one of these," Jessica said suddenly, her gaze on my face. Like Rebecca, she wore a long shirt but hers wasn't belted, and it hung over a pair of skinny jeans, her boots resting against her knees. My black long sleeve shirt, jeans, and tennis shoes suddenly felt inadequate. Couple that with Heathcliff's bulky work jacket, and I felt less somehow.

The tops had already been removed from the beers, and I took a steadying swallow. "I've actually never been out here," I responded. "Not this creek anyway."

Rebecca giggled, and for the first time I noticed how red her eyes were. It was obvious she'd had more than just beer. She kept glancing at her feet as if she wasn't sure the sand was still there. "You should totally come here more." She tried pointing at me, but her finger poked at Heathcliff instead. "I bet you look utterly awesome under all of those clothes," she told me. "I know I do, but I'm totally all enhanced." She giggled louder. "I know you know my mom. Pageant director and all around perfect Southern Belle. I've been under the knife three times already, and that's not counting the boob job I have lined up when I turn eighteen in a few months."

She turned up her beer, and Brian leaned in to support her as she stumbled.

Jessica laughed. "If ya'll want something more than beer, we've got that, too. Obviously."

"We're okay," Heathcliff said. "The beer is plenty."

A slow country song came on, and Rebecca gasped. "I love this one! Come on, Brian, let's dance!"

She jerked him into the middle of the circle of pickups, her body undulating with the beat, her arms coming up to encompass Brian's neck. He stood behind her, his eyes bright as she clung to him, her movements bringing them indecently close. For a moment, conversation lulled as people watched them dance, pulses quickening. More beer cans hit the fire. Other couples joined Brian and Rebecca, most of them immodest, their lips melded or their hips grinding.

I swallowed more alcohol.

"Is that your first beer?" Heathcliff asked.

He took a long swig of his, and I watched as he sighed, his gaze going to the couples on the sand.

"No," I answered abruptly.

Surprised, he glanced at me. "No?"

I grinned. "It's true that my uncle and I haven't spent a whole lot of time in town, but I'm not that sheltered. Gregor has always had an adventurous spirit. He likes science, and does some consulting work for a company near New Orleans. He's taken me with him occasionally. I've been in bars, and I've had beers. Plus, my uncle has a liquor cabinet in his office. He likes adding a splash to his coffee or a coke sometimes, and I'll usually have a little with him."

"Well, you're full of surprises." He snorted. "So if I can't have that first, how about a dance?"

Grabbing my beer and setting it on the ground with his, he nodded at the sand, his hand tugging me gently. I followed because I couldn't think of a reason not to.

"I don't really know how to dance," I admitted.

He smiled down at me. "You don't have to know how. Just follow me."

He pulled me into his embrace, the gesture more like a hug than a dance, my body flush with his.

My blood filled with fire as his hands slid inside the work jacket, his fingers splaying against my back.

He bent, his head lowering, his lips finding my ear. "I won't lie. I was kind of hopin' this was your first beer." He laughed, his breath fanning my neck, and I shivered. "Better yet, I would love to see you smashed."

His head lifted, and my eyes met his. "I think I'm drunk now," I whispered.

There were other ways to be inebriated other than alcohol. I certainly felt unsteady.

"Oh, God," Heathcliff groaned. "Don't look at me that way, Hawthorne."

We were so close now that I could feel his heart beating against me. His hands slid beneath the hem of my shirt, his chilly fingers caressing my back.

The slow song ended, a faster one replacing it, but instead of quickening his pace, Heathcliff pulled me aside, tugging me into the darkness just beyond the circle of headlights. My back was suddenly touching someone's truck, Heathcliff's hands falling to seize my hips.

He didn't kiss me. That was the first thing that surprised me. The second was the feelings that swamped me when he lifted me, using his hands to guide my legs around his hips. His breath mingled with mine as he pressed against me, awareness building as our hips danced.

My eyes adjusted to the dimness, my gaze meeting his. His face was only inches away from mine, but his head didn't lower. He simply stared, one of his hands remaining at my hip while the other swept into my hair. This seemed more intimate somehow than kissing, his eyes on my eyes, his tongue darting out to moisten his lips. My gasps were swallowed by laughter and loud music. My hands didn't know what to do with themselves. My fingers had a sudden mind of their own, finding different parts of Heathcliff's body to grip and then release; his waist, his arms, and his shirt.

My world became our winded breathing and his bright eyes. Everything else was temporarily gone; school, my uncle's cancer, his grandmother's cirrhosis, and an impending summer I didn't want to think about.

Heathcliff's forehead fell against mine. "Be alive, Hawthorne," he insisted. "Just be alive."

Our lips hovered but never touched, his hips grinding against mine, the movement creating sensations that seemed mildly pleasant at first before turning into something desperate and reaching.

"Let it come," he whispered.

I broke, the sensations so strong they tore my body apart, his lips suddenly crashing down onto mine to capture the scream that would have followed. His hips stopped moving, and his body trapped mine against the truck, the hand that had been in my hair resting now against the side of the pickup, his fingers gripping the vehicle. There was desperation in his kiss.

I wiggled, and his lips tore away from mine, his hand tightening on my hip. "Don't move. For God's sake, don't move, Hawthorne." He laughed, the sound tense. "I can't. Not here." His forehead fell against mine once more. "If you were thinking about anything other than that right here right now, then your mind is decidedly more busy than mine."

On an exhale, I breathed, "I'm flying."

There was nothing else I could have said in that moment. Maybe another girl could have come up with something less revealing. Maybe she could have teased him, enticed him with her flirting wit, but I had nothing. Nothing except blunt honesty.

He chuckled, the sound so low I felt it rather than heard it. "I'm right there with you."

My feet hit the soft ground as he suddenly released me, his hands finding my waist, his fingers tracing the waistband of my jeans, dipping below them just enough to entice but not enough to startle.

Voices tore us apart, laughter rising as feet stumbled into the trees. "Try aiming your piss at the ground, dude," a guy hollered.

"Just shut up, man," a male voice answered.

A third voice, a female one, giggled, "Did you guys see Max Vincent tonight? I can't believe he managed to drag the Macy girl out here."

Heathcliff stiffened, his hands gripping my waist.

The pissing boy snorted. "Bound to happen in my opinion. That girl's been holed up too long."

"I bet she's secretly a wild child," his friend replied. "I mean, you've heard the stories about her mom, right?"

My hands found Heathcliff's on my waist. "I want to go home," I hissed.

I was pulling away from his hold when another voice stopped me.

"You people don't know shit," Rebecca Martin interrupted suddenly, her tone smooth and even despite being high. "I like her. She's as genuine and patient as molasses. The rest of us certainly can't say the same. Look in a mirror, dimwits. Or have you even attempted Callahan's assignment?"

"I like you better when you ain't lit, Becca," the unnamed girl complained.

Rebecca laughed. "No, you don't. Ya'll like what my looks and my mother's position in the county can get you."

"She's got a point," Brian Henry called into the darkness. "Stop whining. You ain't got a chance in hell gettin' in Vincent's pants, Kaitlyn. I like the Hawthorne girl, too."

I wasn't sure what was more startling. The crudeness of it all, or the fact that I suddenly had friends. People I'd never attempted to get to know who'd noticed me. A moment I thought had been destroyed was suddenly saved.

"Still want to go?" Heathcliff asked against my ear.

I swallowed hard, my hands releasing his. "Maybe one more beer."

The plane ride when I was ten suddenly invaded my memory. Right now, just like then, I was flying. Even with my feet firmly against the earth, I was soaring high, my eyes on the ground. Everything below me seemed so small, so trivial. There was only my uncle and the time I had left with him, potential friends I'd never thought I'd have, and a young man who was keeping me in the air. He was introducing me to emotions and sensations that seemed too big. Too big but manageable. Because I knew even if this ended now, I wouldn't regret it. Love could just be a moment, an amazing moment that could teach a person to breathe. It didn't have to hold a person back.

Chapter 9

Heathcliff and I didn't speak much on the way to my house after the party. I sat next to him, my head on his shoulder. It wasn't safe, but it didn't seem to matter. It was as if having distance between us that night would have been wrong.

We had pulled into the drive, and I was climbing free of the pickup when he said, "Hawthorne … wait."

Pausing, I glanced at him. His brows furrowed, the words he wanted to speak caught somewhere between his head and his mouth. He didn't need to say them. I could see them in his eyes.

"I'll … uh … I'll be around tomorrow," he promised.

I smiled because I knew he'd return. I'd wake up to the sound of an ax, a drill, or the smell of fresh paint, and it would become one of my new favorite memories, a new favorite sound and a new favorite scent.

Pulling his jacket off, I threw it into the truck. "Be careful."

The pickup backed out of the drive, his taillights disappearing into the darkness. He'd come back because I'd seen in his eyes what he'd probably seen in mine. He was going to break my heart. Somehow I knew that, and instead of running, I was waiting for the pain.

The thought followed me into the house, tracked me to the kitchen past the faint scent of chicory, and chased me into the living room. Uncle Gregor was sleeping on the couch, the light switched on next to him, a book resting open on the arm. Pulling an old afghan over his prone form, I checked his breathing, my lips brushing his forehead, before moving up the stairs to my room. One quick glance at my flushed cheeks in the mirror on my dresser, and I was lying on the bed, my gaze on my window. The moon was visible just beyond the bare trees, and I stared at it.

There was no rain outside, but it was coming. It'd be more than a downpour. A hurricane was approaching the plantation, and it was going to rip through my world. I didn't welcome it, but I also wasn't running away. I was going to board up my windows and wait it out.

Sleep took me before I made it out of my clothes, restless energy keeping me bound to wakefulness just beyond the world of dreams.

A pounding hammer woke me, the sound pasting a smile on my face. It pulled me out of the bed and into the shower before guiding me downstairs. My feet found Uncle Gregor, Heathcliff standing next to him on the landing, staring at a pail of fresh paint the color of a robin's egg. The blue reminded me of the sky on a sunny, cloudless day. It was a happy color, full of possibility.

"Well, what do you think?" my uncle asked me.

Glancing up, I found them perusing me. Gregor's gaze was filled with curiosity while Heathcliff's was hungry, his intense eyes trailing down my damp hair to the oversized navy blue, button up shirt I wore.

"It's perfect," I murmured.

Gregor sipped on a cup of coffee, his gaze falling to the paint. "Well, then. Perfect timing, I suppose. There's no rain in the forecast for over a week."

"It's waiting." The words escaped before I'd realized I'd said them. My mouth was often as bad as my feet, saying things I'd never meant to say.

Heathcliff's eyes shot to my face, searching it.

Clearing my throat, I mumbled, "The paint is waiting, I meant. Maybe we should start?"

"We?" Heathcliff asked.

I smiled. "Did you think you'd get to have all of the fun?"

Snorting, he lifted the pail. "Maybe I've been looking at painting all wrong. Fun isn't exactly the word I would have used."

Gregor laughed. "I'll stick to coffee, paperwork, and bird watching." He glanced at me before letting his gaze slide to Heathcliff. "I invited your Mams out to the house this afternoon. She and I have a lot of catching up to do, I think."

"And she said she'd come?" Heathcliff asked, his startled words surprising us. He shifted uneasily. "I mean, she doesn't leave home very often these days."

Gregor winked. "It's strange how life works, son. We tend to put things off when we know we have plenty of time to do them. Then when there isn't much time left, we start to realize what we should have already done."

He left us with those words, whistling as he ambled toward his office.

For a moment, I stared at Heathcliff before letting my gaze fall to the pail in his hand. "The house won't paint itself."

Heathcliff watched my uncle's disappearing figure. "Is he always so perceptive?"

"Eerily so," I laughed. "Which begs the question, what haven't you done that you should have done?"

His gaze found my face. "Go to the prom with me."

The demand was so unexpected I leaned against the foyer wall, my eyes widening. "What?"

"The prom," Heathcliff repeated. "I'd really like it if you came with me."

My head spun. "Are you serious?"

Turning toward the door, he smiled and gestured for me to follow. "Were you not expecting to go?"

"More like I wasn't expecting you to want to."

Our feet took us outside, to his waiting pickup truck, the bed full of painting supplies and surface preparation tools.

"I hadn't planned to," he said. "Until now." Putting the paint in the truck, he handed me a scraper and a dust mask while he grabbed an arm load of other supplies. "Seems like an appropriate way to end the year."

My shoes followed his, my eyes on his back. "A proper way to say good-bye, you mean?" He slowed, but I kept walking.

"Hawthorne—"

Pausing next to the house, I glanced back at him. "It's a good way to say good-bye." I smiled. "I'd love to go."

His gaze searched mine, his eyes narrowing. "Really?"

"It'll be a great farewell," I emphasized.

"Hawthorne—"

"This house really won't paint itself."

I was still smiling, and he took his cue from me, his lips curling upward. "You're a strange one," he murmured. Placing his stuff on the ground, he looked up at the house, his gaze searching the exterior before falling back to me. "I didn't expect you, you know." His hands found his blue jean pockets. "I mean, I did and I didn't. I noticed you watching my shoes this year, and it fascinated me. I'll admit I tested it, moving my feet closer to see what you'd do. You never shied away, but you also never spoke."

"Until Sylvia Plath," I supplied.

He chuckled. "Damn poetry. You totally walked into that trap, you know."

We both stared at the house.

"I didn't expect you," he repeated.

Something about his words made my pulse quicken. "I'm guessing no one's ever told you that some moments don't have to last forever." I felt his gaze on me, but I didn't look at him. "There's a long road ahead of us in life, Heathcliff. This is just a moment."

He snorted. "Heathcliff … I'm never going to live that name down." He stepped closer but didn't touch me. "What kind of moment are you looking for? I'm only asking because I'm worried I'm going to disappoint."

"What ..." My gaze moved over his face, his expression startling me, and I gasped. "You're afraid."

His eyes fell away from me. "Now look who's being funny."

"No," I accused. "You are." My arm shot out, my hand finding his arm. "You're afraid I'm going to ask you to stay."

His jaw tensed. "No, I'm afraid I'm going to feel like I have to."

My arm dropped back to my side. "Do you want to know what made me look at your face?" I asked. "I finally *really* looked at you because you told me you wanted to leave this town, and you were honest about it. I didn't look because I expected you to remain here. I looked because you weren't afraid to tell me you were going. I'm not looking for a forever moment."

He leaned forward, his face peering down into mine. "Then what—"

"I want to make love to you," I blurted, my cheeks reddening.

Heathcliff froze, his lips parting as he stared. "Did you really just say that because I'm pretty sure you did, but I'm also pretty sure I might still be having the same vivid dream that woke me up this morning? Only maybe I didn't wake up because I'm pretty sure I just heard you say—"

"Make love to me," I insisted, swallowing hard.

I was being forward, and I knew it. Uncle Gregor's illness was changing me. In some ways, it was an oddly good change. In others, I was simply confused, afraid that life would end before I even had a chance to live it. I felt desperate to do, feel, and see it all. It helped that Heathcliff's words confirmed he thought about me the same way I did him when we weren't together.

Heathcliff's hand lifted, his fingers running through his hair, mussing it. "You really said it." He studied me, his gaze searching mine. "That's an awful big leap from marked shoes, poetry, hand holding, and dry humping against a pickup. And yeah, I know I'm being crude, but you do realize you're asking to have sex with me?"

His hand found his hair again, and I found myself grinning. "I'm pretty sure that's what I said."

He laughed, amusement mixed with disbelief. "You're like this really strange painting. One of those crazy abstract things where someone just threw paint at the canvas using every color known to man. Because there's no way to pin down just one color, no way to pin *you* down. Stare at you too long and a man could lose his mind."

Swallowing, I whispered, "Yet you keep coming back."

"My mind's already gone."

I was lost in a stormy sea of words where nothing I said next would be right or wrong. It would just *be*. "I guess I need you right now."

He ran his hand through his hair yet again, his gaze skirting the house before returning to mine.

I knew what he was thinking—my uncle, the cancer, the impending summer and fall—and I leaned forward. "If it was any other girl standing here in any other situation, would you stop and think about this?"

"No," he answered honestly.

"Then don't think."

Leaning down, I picked up some sandpaper and handed it to him.

He accepted it. "You mention sex, and then ask me not to think." He laughed. "Hawthorne, you're going to be awful lucky if I can remember you have a face now." To prove his point, his gaze fell to my chest.

"Mams will be here soon."

Heathcliff groaned. "And with those words, I'm reminded of my humanity."

Together, we approached the wall, the sound of scraping and sanding replacing chaotic thoughts and racing heartbeats, the work becoming more tiring as time passed. The monotonous movements grew into a chant in my head, the mantra working to convince me that I wasn't being foolish.

Hours had passed, and my muscles were cramping when Heathcliff climbed down from a ladder he'd pulled from our old shed and paused next to me, his shadow looming over mine.

"Do you want to be with me because of your uncle?" he asked.

Standing slowly, I stared up at him. "It's because of Sylvia Plath," I answered. "Because when I look into a mirror one day, I don't want to remember your shoes in English class and wonder why I wasn't brave enough to be with the person behind them." I shrugged. "When you leave, do you honestly want to look into a mirror and ask yourself the same thing?"

He frowned. "What makes you think I would?"

Smiling, I picked up the supplies we'd finished with and walked toward his truck. The sound of tires on gravel met our ears, a car materializing on the drive.

My gaze went over my shoulder. "Because you came back. Because you dropped me off after the party at the creek, looked me in the eyes, promised you'd be back, and then you came. Life can be that simple. If you let it."

He scowled at me, his gaze going to the drive. "I'd throttle you if I could," he groused. "Mams is about to climb out of her car, and I'm too busy wondering about things I shouldn't be wondering about when my grandmother is present."

"The prom?" I asked.

He threw me a look, and I chuckled.

"I'm losing my mind," he mumbled.

"Better than your heart, right?" I asked.

Rolling the sleeves up on his work shirt, he glanced at me. "Yeah … maybe."

The pause in his words said it all. The pause made all the difference. The pause gave my shoes wings.

Chapter 10

"You've got a right nice place here, Gregor. It's a shame you've let it rot into this bag o' bones," Mams groused as she exited my uncle's office.

Heathcliff and I stood waiting in the foyer, the painting temporarily trumped by curiosity.

Gregor laughed, his spectacled gaze flicking to mine. "Guess with just the two of us here, we didn't need much."

Mams glanced up, her aged face lifting toward the light. Her lined skin had a decidedly yellow hue to it. Her steps were slow, but she didn't falter.

Her sharp gaze passed between Heathcliff and me before settling on her grandson. "There a reason you still hangin' around here, boy?"

Heathcliff's hands went to his blue jean pockets. "I thought maybe I'd follow you home."

"Oh, I know that tone." She laughed. "You're upset with me for gallivantin' around town in my car. Not supposed to drive, the doctors say." She wagged her finger at him. "I've got a little bit more time left in me, Max my boy."

Heathcliff's brows rose. "I think I'll follow just the same."

Mams approached us, Gregor on her heels, her short stature making her more intimidating rather than less. "It's too pretty a day to leave just yet." She glanced over her shoulder at Gregor. "Got some sweet iced tea in this place? Or have you turned into a barbarian?"

He chuckled and nodded at me. "Hawthorne's the brilliant one in the kitchen. I just live here."

Mams' gaze passed to me.

"There's some in the fridge." I replied, ducking my head.

"Well, what are you waitin' for?" She waved her hand. "Go and fetch it, girl. Bring it outside. A little January chill and sunshine ain't never hurt anyone."

She led the way to the door, the guys following, Heathcliff's sympathetic gaze finding mine over his shoulder. Mams had a domineering kind of personality no one argued with.

My lips formed a smile, a small laugh escaping me. Truth be told, I admired the way she waltzed into an area, commanded it, and made it hers.

Rushing into the kitchen, I collected four glasses of sweet tea and ice on a tray before making my way into the yard. A makeshift picnic area had been cleared on the lawn, an old mildewed chair from the porch pulled out into the sun for Mams. She perched on it, her back ramrod straight, her gaze on my uncle where he lounged against a tree in the shade.

"Sun's good for you in short stretches, you know," Mams admonished.

My uncle nodded at her. "That it is, Mams. That it is."

Heathcliff met me halfway, his hands accepting the tray of tea before offering glasses to Mams and my uncle. I sat on the grass, and he handed me a glass before taking the final one. Setting the tray on the ground, he spread out next to me, his long legs commanding the space.

It was strange sitting there with Heathcliff at my side, his grandmother above us, my uncle across from us. Two young people sipping tea with their elders like a setting from an old antebellum novel. Ice clinked against glasses beaded with condensation. The old-fashioned scene, however, was nothing compared to Mams. It would have been obvious even to the most absentminded person that she had an agenda.

Her eyes fell to her grandson before swinging to me. "I don't mind admittin' I was more than a little shocked when Max brought home the daughter of Jack and Meg Macy. Like a ghost from the past, you are."

"Mams!" Heathcliff hissed.

My uncle chuckled. "It won't do any good, son. I've known your Mams a long time, and when she's got something to say, it's best to let her get it out."

Mams cleared her throat, throwing a look at Gregor before turning back to me. "My grandson's a wanderer. I've known it since the day he ran off into the woods when he was a child. His parents had to call the police to sweep the trees and ponds. He's like a warm breeze in spring, the kind that promises warmth and then leaves you empty."

"Mams—" Heathcliff began, his voice low.

She cast him a look. "Don't be shushin' me, Max Vincent. I didn't say I loved you any less, boy. I'm just pointin' out that some things can't be pinned down. Not hereabouts anyhow."

"Look," Heathcliff said, starting to rise, "I don't know why you're here or what this is—"

"I've always liked the wind," I interjected. "There's this thing about warm spring breezes. They may vanish to be replaced by the heat of summer and the cold months that follow, but they return, and when they do, their simple, brief touches are enough. They don't make promises. They simply change you."

Heathcliff froze, his startled gaze flying to mine. My eyes were locked on Mams', my gray gaze captured by her piercing hazel one. Heathcliff had gotten his eyes from his grandmother.

She blinked. "I see so much more of your uncle in you than I ever will your parents, girl. Take comfort in that." She glanced at Heathcliff. "You follow a girl home, start disappearin' and takin' stuff from the store to help fix up the house she lives in, and expect no one to interfere? Boy, you'd best be prepared. I'm just the referee. Be glad I put enough cash in the store to replace the stuff you snuck out."

Heathcliff lowered himself back to the ground, his lips parting before closing again. Plucking a blade of dry, brittle grass, he fiddled with it.

"There's rough times comin'," Mams added. "For both of you. Maybe I seem like a meddlin' old fool for gettin' involved in somethin' that ain't none of my business, but I happen to care about both of you in different ways." She looked at Gregor. "You turn eighteen in a few months, Hawthorne. School will be endin', and there will be decisions to make. I've had some discussions with your uncle over the years, and I've put back money in a fund to help pay for an international culinary internship once you finish college should you choose to do it. Your uncle tells me you have a thing for cookin'."

My pulse began to beat wildly, my eyes widening. Heathcliff leaned forward, an expression of astonishment crossing his features. My uncle simply smiled.

"Why are you doing this?" I whispered.

Mams' knowing gaze searched mine. "Your mother's mom, your grandmother, was my best friend. It never sat well with me that Gayle renounced Meg, her only daughter, for being pregnant. When your grandparents refused to acknowledge your existence … let's just say there were a lot o' angry words between us. But I ain't doin' this for you. I'm doin' this for your uncle. He's garnered a lot o' respect from the older set in this town over the years for pickin' up his brother's responsibilities. There's more than just my money in that fund, girl. I'm just the one to head it."

My heart suddenly felt like a water balloon with too much water. Squeeze too hard, and it would explode.

Uncle Gregor sat up. "Sometimes it takes a village."

My gaze passed between them, my thoughts racing to moments I'd always worked to block from my memory. Town visits with people whispering behind my back. It reminded me of Kenny Parker and

his wife in the sideview mirror after
Heathcliff helped unload lumber, their eyes
trailing his disappearing truck. The way
Kenny's arm had snaked around his wife,
his gaze full of compassion.

It hit me then why Mams had wanted
Heathcliff to leave when she'd seen us in the
hall. This conversation hadn't been meant
for him.

Shame reddened my face. "I'm a town
project."

Mams snorted. "You've proven yourself
smart up to this point, girl. Don't go gettin'
daft on me now. You ain't no more a project
than the rest o' us. I've had a lot of time on
my hands over the years. Truth be told, I've
got a fund for half the younguns in this
town. Seemed a right good thing to do.
There ain't a way to save the world all at
once, but there's a way to change lives."

Heathcliff started to rise again, then sat,
his stunned gaze on his grandmother's face.
"I didn't know."

She laughed. "Course you didn't. Your
daddy would have put me away for senility.
You got your good heart from me, boy.
Don't you forget it. I ain't selfish, but I

admit to wantin' a little pat on the back from my work before I die." She winked. "You've got a fund, too, Max. Enough to explore that wanderin' heart of yours. Come back if you want or don't. It makes no nevermind to me. I always thought it a right shame the men in our family thought it necessary to tie down every capable child to the business. There's plenty of Vincents here for that."

Heathcliff stared at his grandmother.

My head spun, my gaze falling to my uncle. He was watching me, his head nodding. I'd been wrong about so many things over the years. All the whispers I'd thought had been about me and my parents … some of them had been, I'm sure, but my uncle hadn't remained in this town because it was where our home was. He'd remained here because it was full of big hearts—not always open minds, that took some work— but there were a lot of open hearts. He was right. Sometimes it took a village.

"I'm feeling a mite tired," Mams said abruptly.

Standing, Heathcliff rushed to her side. "Why don't I drive you back?" he asked. "I can walk here tomorrow and take the truck home then."

It was a testament to how fatigued Mams actually was that she submitted to him so easily. With a quick glance in my direction, Heathcliff left, his arm supporting his grandmother as they moved to her spotless black Buick.

The car doors slammed, the driver's side window rolling down.

"I'll be back," Heathcliff called.

Tires crunched on gravel.

My gaze swept to my uncle to discover he'd moved to the grass, lying with his back against the ground the same way he'd been laying when I'd returned home from school days back.

I joined him, my head falling next to his, my eyes on the sky. Above us, white fluffy clouds meandered across a bright blue expanse before disappearing behind tree limbs.

"What are we looking for?" I asked.

"Nothing," Uncle Gregor answered. "We're just watching."

The world was suddenly upside down. I could feel the grass beneath me, but I was walking on blue earth, my mind wandering with the clouds. "Why does she do that?" I asked.

He knew what I was asking, and he exhaled. "She needed to feel like she was doing something for others. Some people thrive off of that. They see life differently than the rest of us. The euphoria they get from seeing someone happy or better off because of something they did is hard to come down from. They need to keep feeling that high. We all need something, you know. Mams has always been that way. She started her first fund in a mason jar over thirty years ago to help a boy injured in a car accident. Since then, she's led fundraisers and opened dozens of accounts to help support many local families. Most of it has been done anonymously." He lifted his hand toward the sky. "See that?"

My gaze followed his fingers to a group of buzzards flying in the distance.

"Nasty creatures, many say," he murmured. "Those are Turkey Buzzards. Mostly associated with death and disease, they aren't looked upon kindly. However, there's an old Native American legend, a

Lenape one that tells how the Turkey Buzzard saved the world. How it pushed away the encroaching sun to protect the Earth from burning, and in so doing, went from being a beautiful bird to having its awful, modern appearance. No animal wanted anything to do with it again, but it didn't matter. The buzzard had saved the world. He didn't need the attention." His hands formed a goal post shape to frame the flying buzzards. "Everyone has their place in the world. Sometimes that place is full of people and laughter and noise. Other times, it's found in silence, in being different."

I stared at the birds. "I guess that would make Mams the town saint, huh?"

Gregor chuckled. "Saint Mams sounds about right."

Heathcliff's words in the truck the night before struck me, and I let my head fall to the side. "Why do you call me Hawthorne?" I asked. "Do I remind you that much of *The Scarlett Letter*?

Uncle Gregor's astonished gaze met mine. "Is that what you think?" I nodded, and his gaze softened. "You're not named after a book. You're named after the Hawthorn tree."

Startled, I gasped, "A tree?"

He smiled. "The Hawthorn tree is cloaked in legend. Some say it brings evil powers into the home. Some say it's a gateway to the Otherworld. Some use it to invite spirits in while others use it to keep them out. Still more say that it protects from storms. My favorite is the one that says it brings clarity, patience, and stillness." He reached for me, his hand finding mine. "You brought those things to my life. You brought clarity and patience, and because of that, I called you Hawthorne."

My gaze returned to the sky. "The Hawthorn tree," I whispered. "I like that." A smile overtook my features. "You know something, Uncle?"

"Hmm ..."

"We don't need forever. You've already given me that."

My words hung between us. I didn't look at Gregor because I was afraid I'd see the thing I feared most from him; tears. We remained on the ground, our gazes on the sky until the blue began to change, overtaken by pink and purple hues, the clouds graying. The temperatures dropped, the chill too much for my uncle, and he stood carefully. Shooting me a gentle smile, he walked to the house. Sitting up, I gathered the glasses from earlier and followed him in.

Uncle Gregor stacked wood in the living room fireplace while I branched off into the kitchen to fix supper. We ate together in companionable silence, ending the night with a quick game of checkers before heading to bed.

Then I did something I hadn't done since I was a child. Once my Uncle Gregor was asleep, I climbed into bed with him, lying on my side on the corner of his mattress, my gaze on the wall. This is how I wanted to remember him, the father who'd protected me during bad weather and slayed the demons that haunted my nightmares. The man who'd listened to me cry and patiently decoded my dreams.

His breathing was deep, and I listened to it, the sound lulling me to sleep.

A few hours later, I woke cold and shivering. Climbing quietly from the bed, I

snuck out of the room and up the stairs, my
bare feet silent on the carpet. My bedroom
door creaked as I opened it, my hands
grabbing automatically for the cocoa-
colored afghan that sat at the end of my bed.
Pulling it around my shoulders, I stumbled
across the floor to my window seat, my gaze
going to the silver-bathed yard beyond.

Heathcliff's pickup was visible from my
perch. It looked black in the dim light, the
decay and rust hidden by the night. The dark
transformed it, turning it into something
beautiful and different.

Beyond the truck, a shadow moved, and
I squinted. Cats and raccoons were common
visitors at night, but this shadow was longer
and broader.

It moved again, and I stood, my knees
on the window seat, my eyes wide. The
security post in the yard barely threw off any
light, but it was bright enough for me to
make out the shape of a man.

People didn't steal things in my small
town. It just wasn't done. At least not at my
uncle's plantation, but there was a first time
for everything.

Heart pounding, I pulled the afghan tighter around me, my feet rushing for the stairs. At the bottom, I sped to the front door, my hand finding the knob just as it turned. Soundlessly, I backed away, my eyes wide, my mouth parting as the door swung inward.

A face appeared, a startled gasp whooshing from the intruder. "Hawthorne?"

I yelped. "Heathcliff?"

"Shh," he hissed, his hand covering my mouth as he pulled the door shut behind him.

I stared. He was still dressed in the same clothes, his shirt from earlier wrinkled and streaked with dirt from the yard. His hair was mussed, dark circles marring his eyes.

"What are you doing here?" I whispered.

His gaze met mine, and I saw in his eyes what often shone from mine; grief. He'd spent the afternoon with his Mams, with a woman who hadn't raised him the same way Gregor had raised me, but who played a major part in his life anyhow.

"I keep remembering what you said this afternoon," he responded.

I stepped closer. "About making love?"

He exhaled. "No ... I mean, yes, but not that exactly."

"What?"

His gaze searched mine. "The part where you said you needed me." He stepped forward, our feet meeting in the entryway, foot against foot.

Glancing down at my bare toes and his tennis shoe, I had a déjà vu moment to the first time our feet touched in English class, to the first time I'd wondered about the boy next to me, the one who reminded me of brooding, gothic romance novels.

"Yeah," I breathed.

He leaned close, his breath feathering the top of my head. "I need you now."

It's kind of funny how moments collide. From the first time our feet met in the aisle between our desks to this moment, to our ever touching feet.

Taking his hand, I led him up the stairs.

Chapter 11

"Did you walk here?" I asked, my gaze trailing Heathcliff's work shirt and jeans. He wore no jacket.

His hands hovered over his blue jean pockets as he sat on the edge of the bed, his gaze coming up to meet mine. "I needed the walk."

It was well past midnight, but I didn't point this out.

Sitting next to him, I glanced at his hands before letting my gaze trail up to his face. He was watching me, his hazel eyes brown in the dim light. I'd switched on a small lamp, and the soft yellow glow made everything softer, more intimate somehow. I knew by the look in Heathcliff's eyes that there was a lot on his mind.

"Did you mean what you said today?" he asked. "About … you know?"

A lump formed in my throat. "Why? Do you mean *now*?"

"God, I don't know." The words fell from his mouth, his gaze sharp and uneasy. "Do you have any experience?"

"No." It seemed counterproductive to lie and say I did.

"I should be sticking with beers and racing my truck." He was speaking to himself, the mumbled words tumbling forth unchecked.

My brows rose. "Is that what you did? Before you came here, I mean?"

"Not really ... well, sometimes. With a few people from school. We've got bets run, and a makeshift track past Hazard Hill."

"Oh," I managed, deflated. "Do you run the Hill?"

Heathcliff snorted. "Not since they shut it down after the last accident there."

My chin fell, my gaze falling to my lap. "You don't have to be here."

The bed dipped as he shifted, my hip falling against his. "Yeah, I do. I can drive that truck all night long, throw back the beers with Brian and Marshall, and still not feel the understanding I do here. Rough rides are smoother when you've got a passenger who understands the road."

His hand suddenly cupped my face, and my gaze flew to his.

"Kiss me, Hawthorne," he demanded.

Our lips met, moving in a slow dance that was different from the frenzied passion we'd shared at the creek. He was taking his time, his tongue seeking entrance, his mouth exploring mine. My insides turned to liquid, my pulse quickening.

Pulling back suddenly, he stared at my kiss-swollen mouth. "Are you sure about this?"

"No," I exhaled. "Are we supposed to be sure?"

He smiled. "No."

I backed onto the bed, my eyes locked with his. He followed me, his body hovering just above mine, his arms holding him off of the mattress.

Slowly and efficiently, he began unbuttoning his work shirt with one hand, his other hand keeping him above me. "I'm not going to make love to you tonight," he said abruptly.

His words were like a bucket of cold water, dousing the flames he'd ignited. "What?"

The last button was undone, and the shirt fell open, revealing a lean body and cut abs, his jeans slung low on his hips despite the black belt at his waist. His body was molded by work, the kind of build I knew would grow even broader and muscular as he got older.

"Not tonight," he responded. "Not with your uncle downstairs. Not until you're a little more comfortable." He rolled to the side and removed his shirt, throwing it on the floor before kicking his shoes off. "Lay with me."

With a deep breath, I sprawled out next to him, our heads sharing the same pillow. The large T-shirt and cotton pajama bottoms I'd put on after the game of checkers with Uncle Gregor felt suddenly inadequate.

Heathcliff's hand found mine, his fingers lacing through my fingers, his lips sweeping my forehead before trailing down my nose to my mouth.

"If you ever looked at me once with what I know is in you, I would be your slave," he recited suddenly.

A surprised laugh escaped me. "Quoting Bronte?" My amused gaze swept his features. "You don't have to be Heathcliff, you know."

"Oh, I know." He grinned. "What I'm wondering is why you didn't highlight that quote in the book? I kind of dig it."

"You dig it?" I laughed again.

His gaze cooled, his sudden serious expression killing the humor, turning it into something else entirely. "I do," he let slip. "Your eyes keep bringing me back to you. Like two isolated tornadoes waiting to be unleashed." His gaze searched mine. "The quote makes sense to me."

I swallowed hard. "This feels too big somehow."

He must have agreed with me because his eyes fell closed before reopening. "I'm leaving, Hawthorne."

I grimaced. "You keep telling me that."

"I feel like I have to."

Pulling my hand free from his, I touched his chest. "You don't need to stay. I like the idea that there's more to you than just this town. It's like I'm touching the wind."

"You say that now," he huffed, frowning. "This is moving too fast, and I can't think. I don't want this to go too far only for us … for *you* to regret it later."

It's amazing how uncomfortable a person can be with another person until they've gotten to know each other. If you'd asked me weeks ago if I thought I'd ever hear the brooding guy sitting next to me in class quoting Bronte, I would have said you were crazy. He'd chosen me to open up to, and now he was afraid that what he wanted to do in the future was going to push me away. Honestly, I didn't want to let go of this feeling. I hated the idea that he was leaving, but I hated the thought of not feeling this way even more.

"We're a lot alike, you and me," I said. My hand came up to smooth the furrows between his brows. "Maybe we chose a bad time to do this considering what our wants for the future are, but the truth is, we're here. Now. The later will come. You don't need to stay."

His hand captured mine, his fingers trailing down my arm before skipping to my waist. There, he gripped the hem of my shirt, pulling it up to expose the plain beige bra I wore beneath.

Inhaling sharply, I rose, letting him remove the shirt. The garment met his on the floor, the room's chill hitting my bared flesh. Goosebumps dotted my skin.

"I thought—" I began.

His mouth cut off my words, his lips slanting over mine, his fingers playing with my ribs before his hand rested against my back, splayed just beneath my bra straps.

"We're not," he murmured against my lips.

We rolled, his chest pressing against mine, our mouths dancing. His weight should have been uncomfortable, but it wasn't. It felt safe.

After a moment, his lips pulled away. "Shit," he muttered, his forehead falling against mine.

Inhaling sharply, he rolled us again. He landed on his side and pulled me against him, moving so that my back rested against his chest, his arm falling over my hip.

He played with the waistband on my pajama bottoms. "I start some work on the Parker farm next week. They're building a new barn before spring gets here. It's going to make it hard to come out in the afternoons."

I gasped as his fingers ran along my skin. "That sounds promising."

"I've been saving up for later," he replied. "For after graduation." He paused. "Will you be okay? With your uncle and all?"

I smiled. "I'll be fine."

His fingers dipped beneath my waistband, gripping the material. "I spent more time with my grandmother today than I think I've spent with her since I was a kid. She's more fun than I remember."

"She's definitely one of a kind," I offered.

He chuckled. "So is your uncle. You're lucky to have him, Hawthorne."

My heart sank, reality crashing down on me. "I am." My breath caught, tears choking me. "I'm afraid of watching him die. I'm afraid I won't be strong enough to let go."

Heathcliff froze. "I don't think you're meant to be strong in that kind of situation. I think you're just supposed to be there."

"Maybe."

Releasing my pants, he touched my bare stomach. "My grandmother told me today that the only thing she wants when her time comes is a quick good-bye, a hug, and a smile. Even if there are tears. Because she doesn't want to be sent off with a frown."

Smiling softly, I said, "I like your grandmother. I like her honesty."

Heathcliff's gentle fingers spread across my skin, his palm over my belly button. "She likes you, too. That's saying a lot." His hand continued to wander. "I want to come back," he whispered against my ear. "At night when I'm done with work. Here. I can park in the fields and walk the rest of the way."

My breath caught, my mind racing. "Won't your family find out?"

He leaned closer. "Just tell me you want me to come, and I'll figure out the rest."

There was silence, our breathing loud. After learning of Uncle Gregor's illness, the dark had become a scary, lonely place full of heartache. I'd begun dreading going to bed. I'd begun dreading being alone. He was offering to fill that void. I was taking a chance if I said yes.

"I want you to come," fell from my lips, rushed and low.

He relaxed behind me, all of the tension leaving his body. Until that moment, until his relieved breath, I hadn't realized how much he'd needed me to say yes.

Chapter 12

The morning brought no Heathcliff, his missing truck a stark reminder that he'd been in my house, my bed, and—I was beginning to suspect—my heart.

A hasty shower and a quick change, and I was downstairs, my hands hugging a hot mug of cream-filled coffee. Uncle Gregor joined me, his gaze on the yard beyond our kitchen window.

"Max was here early, I take it?" he asked.

The mug hid my expression as I sipped my coffee. "Looks like it."

"Mmmm," my uncle mumbled. He took his own sip of coffee. "Do me a favor, Hawthorne. If you're going to let him stay, at least let him join us for supper occasionally. Don't suppose he's any good at checkers?"

My gaze shot to his. "What?"

"I'm not sleeping well these days." He smiled, the grin quickly followed by a grimace. "The pain is worse at night." He glanced at me. "I might have seen more than one pair of feet disappearing up the stairs last night."

The next swallow I took was too large and too hot, but the burn felt good. "You know, you make it awful hard to be ... I don't know ... a teenager!"

He chuckled. "That's the point, dear Hawthorne."

"You really aren't angry?" I stared. "No lectures? No plans to buy me a chastity belt?"

Uncle Gregor choked on his coffee. "A chastity belt?" Patting his chest, he threw me a look as he fought to recover. "We really need to get a TV. I think you may be reading too much."

My brows rose. "Seriously, you aren't angry?"

He grinned. "Honestly, I think you two are good for each other right now. That doesn't mean I don't want you to be careful. I just think people are often brought into our lives for a reason, and I'd rather you have someone you can lean on when I go."

His easy manner should have comforted me, but a wave of unexpected anger swept over me instead, cross words tumbling out of my mouth. "How can you be so nonchalant about it all? You're dying! Shouldn't you be angry! Something! *Anything*!"

My tirade surprised me, and I froze, the words shocking me, my heart swirling with emotions.

Uncle Gregor's mug paused halfway to his mouth. "Angry," he said slowly, his eyes falling to his coffee. "I can't allow myself to be angry, Hawthorne. Or sad."

"Why?"

He sighed. "Because I'm afraid if I get angry, I won't be able to get out of that place."

Tears trekked down my cheeks. "I'll be angry for you." The whispered words were broken by sobs.

I hated myself for the tears, hated myself for the anger. I didn't want to be that person, the one who broke down when she needed to stay strong. The one who didn't even know she was angry in the first place, the one who exploded in moments when she shouldn't.

My body shook, so I set the coffee mug down, my fingers trembling.

Uncle Gregor's hand found my back. "Do you think I haven't railed? Do you think I haven't yelled at the skies, haven't cried and asked myself why?"

My tears came harder. "You should have told me sooner."

"And there's the crux of it," Uncle Gregor whispered. "That's what you're really angry at, Hawthorne. Not the illness. You're mad at me because I haven't let you carry it with me, but I didn't want you to stop living."

I couldn't remain standing any more. My feet simply couldn't hold me up. I fell into a chair near the kitchen table, my nose and eyes running, my chest burning with the pain.

"I would have liked to try."

Uncle Gregor sat in the chair across from me. "Look at me and yell. Scream at the top of your lungs. Be angry. Grieve. Do it all, Hawthorne."

He was dying, and yet despite the fact that it was *his* body suffering, *his* body racked by pain, he was giving me permission to be upset about it.

"What would that help?" I sniffed.

"It won't," he answered. "It won't help, but it gives you a voice. That's the hardest part about all of this. Cancer is a silent enemy, but the people affected don't have to be quiet."

"You are."

My hand rested on the table, and his hand came up to cover it. "Because I'm okay living the rest of my life watching you be happy."

Some tears can't be held back. Some tears destroy you. My tears were a flood, never ending. My chest heaved, each intake of breath harder than the last.

"This is okay," Uncle Gregor promised. "It's just hitting you, and that's okay."

My swollen, red eyes met his clear ones. "It's okay that I yell?"

He squeezed my hand. "Yell, Hawthorne. Yell loud."

I did. I screamed and screamed, the shrill, eerie sound tearing through the empty house. It was a shaky yell full of tears, a rage-filled shriek releasing all of the anger, frustration, and fear I'd been holding in without realizing it. The scream tore me apart.

A door opened and shut, but my uncle and I didn't move.

Pounding feet tore through the house, stopping just short of the kitchen alcove where we sat. "I heard screaming—" Heathcliff's winded voice began.

"There's nothing we can do, is there?" I asked.

Uncle Gregor shook his head. "Nothing except yell, rail, and shake our fists, releasing all of the anger so that we can move past it to something different."

My gaze remained locked on his. There was a whole world in my uncle's eyes. So many memories etched into his skin. He'd walked me through so much in my life, through so many firsts, through so many emotions. Each tear that trickled down my face was a memory. A tear. *Eight years old. It was twilight, and Gregor was teaching me how to catch fireflies in mason jars.* A tear. *Ten years old. My first ride on an Amtrack train, the world passing the windows in a blur.* A tear. *Eleven years old. Playing Bingo at the legion with my uncle and his friends. I won twenty dollars and used every bit of it to buy candy on the way home.* A tear. *Thirteen years old. My first real cookbook, a grocery trip, and my first failed attempt at making a pineapple upside down cake.* So many tears ... so many memories.

"Leave your heart open, Hawthorne," Uncle Gregor murmured, his gaze flicking to a fidgeting Heathcliff behind me.

"I'm just going to go and paint," Heathcliff blurted.

The tears kept coming, trickling one after another as Heathcliff's feet moved back through the house.

"Do you still need to scream?" Uncle Gregor asked.

I shook my head. There was no anger left, only sadness.

He stood, his tired gaze on my face. "We all say good-bye at some point in our lives, Hawthorne. Let's laugh, skip, and holler our way to the end."

Swiping my cheeks with the back of my hands, I laughed and stood with him. "Okay."

He led me through the house, our coffee forgotten, and into the yard beyond. Heathcliff was there, the back of his truck open, a paint pail hanging from his hand. He glanced up at us as we joined him, his sympathetic gaze flicking over my face before meeting my uncle's.

"You must have left early this morning to be back so soon," Gregor said.

Heathcliff faltered, the pail in his hand swinging. "Sir?"

Uncle Gregor chuckled. "Come in for supper and a game of checkers next time. I'll get Hawthorne to make a cherry pie. You've never tasted anything like it, I can promise you that."

He walked away then, still chuckling, a murmured, "It's so easy ruffling those young ones' feathers these days," under his breath.

Heathcliff glanced at me, at my tear-stained, spotty face, and said, "I take it last night isn't a secret?"

In response, I grinned. "He's a perceptive man."

His answering smile was quick, the crestfallen expression that followed just as rapid, his sullen gaze searching my face. Stepping forward, he touched my cheek with his free hand. My face felt sore from the tears, my body drained.

"You okay?" he whispered.

For some reason, I hated the way I looked after I cried, hated the idea of anyone seeing me that way, and I pulled my face away. "I'm fine."

His gaze flickered with something I couldn't quite catch, but before I could figure it out, he turned and grabbed a couple of paint rollers. "There are brushes back here, too. Want to help?"

"Yeah." Work was something I liked doing. Labor of any kind exorcised demons.

Heathcliff didn't say anything after that. He simply walked to the house with me on his heels. Occasionally, he glanced at me as we worked, but we didn't speak. There was nothing except the smell of paint and the sound of our movements.

The sun was setting, and most of the house was finished when we quit. Heathcliff rolled up the drop sheets he'd laid out when he first arrived, and rinsed off brushes with the water hose coiled up on the side of the house.

"I'm supposed to help load a few things for the work at the Parker farm this week," he murmured. "Be back later?"

The last words came out as a question, and I glanced at him. "Cherry pie and checkers."

He smiled. "No need to park in the fields I take it. I'll be back."

I watched as he finished gathering up the supplies before loading them up in his truck, the back of his shirt sticking to him despite the chill. He was closing the tailgate and about to climb into the pickup when I stopped him.

"Hey," I called out.

He froze, his hand on the open driver's side door, his gaze swinging to mine.

"I'm not okay," I told him. "I will be, but I'm not right now. I think … maybe we should start feeling comfortable enough with each other to share that kind of stuff."

His head inclined, and a smile lit his eyes. "Checkers and cherry pie," he said. "That pie sounds like a really good idea."

As he drove off, the twilight swallowing his truck, I found myself laughing. Such a strange leap in emotions, from a rage-filled scream to laughter.

Maybe Heathcliff was good for me.

Like cherry pie and checkers.

Chapter 13

Heathcliff was really bad at checkers. Or maybe Uncle Gregor and I were just really good. Either way, Heathcliff had lost three games against Gregor and two against me, a whole cherry pie demolished, before the night caught up to Uncle Gregor. His weary eyes met ours, an unspoken apology written in his gaze.

Standing shakily, he teased, "I think I can admit defeat when I need to."

Heathcliff stood with him, the empty pie tin on his lap falling with a *clang* to the floor. "Let me help you."

Uncle Gregor started to wave him away, but then paused, a pained expression pinching his features. "You know, I think I would like some assistance." He glanced at me. "Hawthorne, there are some pills on top of the fridge in the kitchen. It's the only bottle there. Can you bring those to me?"

Heathcliff offered Gregor his arm, leading him carefully through the living room and into the hallway as I scurried to the kitchen. My hands shook as I reached for the bottle on the fridge. The pills were for pain, and my heart hurt as I carried them to my uncle's bedroom, a glass of water in my other hand.

"These?" I asked upon entering the room, even though I knew the answer.

Uncle Gregor sat on the edge of the bed, his head hanging. He accepted the bottle, shaking a pill out into his palm before swallowing it with the water I'd brought.

"That should do it," he said, his voice cheerful.

Lying back, he pulled the blanket over himself before rolling to his side, tensing as he pulled his knees into his chest.

"Do you need me to stay?" My voice shook despite every effort to keep it level.

I was beginning to see a change in myself. Days past, I'd sat at the table with Uncle Gregor and talked about my fear of his dying. Today, I'd been angry about it. Now I was determined to help him through it. Fear, anger, and the need to nurture. Maybe they were steps in the grieving process, maybe they weren't, but they were changing me. I was seeing life differently.

Uncle Gregor peered up at me, his lips thin. "Go on to bed, Hawthorne. I'm okay. I promise." His eyes pleaded with me. "There's going to be a point when I'm going to need you," he added. "Right now, I think I've got this." He winked, trying for his usual offhanded, debonair manner, but his closing eyes ruined the effect, his brows furrowed with pain.

Heathcliff touched my arm, his eyes sad. Together, we left, the sound of the door shutting behind us too loud in the hallway, as if it were cutting me off from Gregor in a way I was afraid to admit. Cancer, I was beginning to learn, didn't just rob a person's voice, it often took away a person's ability to understand things about the people he/she was losing.

"Come on," Heathcliff soothed.

Taking my hand, he led me to the stairwell, our feet soft on the stairs as we made our way to bed. The shutting door was just as loud in my room, the sound an echo in my heart. Two shut doors, too little time.

"You want to talk about it? Cry maybe?" Heathcliff asked, shifting awkwardly. He looked so out of place in my room, his uneasy stance endearing. He didn't have to be here. He didn't have to keep coming back, but he did. He'd made an investment in me, and he was keeping his promise.

Maybe that's what made me do it.

"I've cried too much. There have been too many tears lately," I whispered, my hands going to the hem of my shirt. Slowly, I pulled it over my head and threw it down, my eyes on the floor.

Heathcliff inhaled sharply. "What are you doing, Hawthorne?"

I swallowed hard. "Do you have any sort of protection on you?" My cheeks flushed, but I fought against nerves and embarrassment, my gaze coming up to meet his. He was staring at me, his eyes flicking from my face to my chest and back again.

"Hawthorne ..." His words trailed off, his forehead creasing. "What are you thinking? Because I'm having a hard time trying to process your thoughts."

My hands fell to my jeans. "Honestly? I really do want to make love to you. Maybe it's crazy, especially now of all times, but I think about it more than I should."

Heathcliff stepped toward me, his hand diving into his pocket to pull out a faded leather wallet. "My parents own a gas station." Flipping the wallet open, he tugged a foil packet free. "I always have protection on me. Easy access." Throwing the condom onto the bed, he pocketed the wallet and took another step forward. "Are you sure?"

"I think so."

"I need more than that," he said.

My eyes searched his. "Have you done this before?"

He nodded. "Twice."

It was the honesty in his gaze, the easy way he told me the truth about his experience that made my decision for me. Fumbling with the button and zipper on my jeans, I pulled them past my hips and stepped free of them before I lost my nerve, my underwear and bra the only thing left.

"I'm sure," I told him. He stared, and I fidgeted. "But I don't know what I'm doing."

His gaze softened, and he closed the distance between us until his feet met mine. Neither of us wore shoes. They'd been discarded before the checkers and cherry pie, and there was something oddly thrilling about our bare toes touching.

He'd showered and changed after our work that afternoon, his work top replaced by a T-shirt. His hands went to the hem. With one swift motion, he threw it onto the floor next to mine. His jeans followed, leaving him in a pair of black boxer briefs.

"Now we're even," he said.

His hands cupped my face, his head lowering, his lips meeting mine. There was something different about this kiss. It was rushed and hard, full of passion and frenzy, but also nervous and careful. Our tongues clashed, and my hands came up to cover his.

Our bodies were touching now, his height and build shadowing mine, one of his hands falling to grip my hip.

The back of my legs hit the bed, and I realized we'd been moving toward it, his lips working their magic on mine, clouding my thoughts. My entire body burned, a roaring inferno of raw nerves and sensation.

Heathcliff's hand found my back, his fingers undoing the clasp of my bra. It fell open, and he worked the straps down my arms, his lips never leaving mine, as if he knew baring my breasts for the first time would be embarrassing for me.

"Last chance," Heathcliff murmured against my lips, pulling away so that he was looking down into my face. "Last chance to say no."

In response, my hands fell to his waist, my fingers tugging at his briefs. My hands shook, and he helped me, his hands joining mine as he stepped free of the underwear. I couldn't make myself look past his chest, my eyes locked on the muscles there.

Gently, he pushed me down onto the bed, rolling over just long enough to tear open the condom he'd thrown onto the comforter. Then his hands were on my waist, working my panties down past my hips and knees until I could kick them free.

Once again, his lips met mine, his hands roaming my body, pausing at my breasts before dropping lower.

"It's okay to touch me," he breathed against my mouth.

Embarrassing heat infused my face, my hands coming up to grasp his shoulders before moving lower, my fingers gliding over his biceps to his chest and down his stomach before stopping at his hips.

He was touching me now in places no one had ever touched, and I squirmed, gasping against his mouth.

"That's it," he breathed.

Sensation racked me, and my body rose up off of the bed. His tongue tangled with mine, growing more demanding as my body pressed against his hand. His fingers picked up speed, and I cried out.

"It's too much," I whimpered, my lips pulling away from his.

"It just feels that way," he promised, his eyes on mine. "Just wait."

And then it hit me, a tidal wave of sensation that had my fingers digging into his waist, my breath catching.

Heathcliff shifted, his weight settling between my thighs, using the indescribable moment to push inside of me.

I tensed, and his hand slid up to my cheek, cupping it, his eyes capturing mine. "Give it time. If we were in a hurry this wouldn't work."

It was such an odd sensation being joined with someone, his body easing into my body, warm and uncomfortable at first, like a large hand trying to squeeze into a too small glove.

"It hurts," I admitted.

He inhaled, his bare chest pressing against mine, his jaw tensed, and I knew he was holding himself back. "You tell me when you're ready," he whispered.

His lips fell on mine once more, our mouths and tongues dancing, his hands cradling my face before sliding into my wild, tangled hair. My hands skimmed his sides and back, my fingers gliding over ribs and corded muscle. The kiss deepened, and my body responded, his hips pressing further into mine as I writhed beneath him.

Pleasure and pain. That's exactly how I'd describe my first clumsy attempt at lovemaking. Heathcliff took it slow, never forcing me into a rhythm I wasn't comfortable with, his moans low against my ear with each agonizingly beautiful, yet painful inch forward.

His head rose, his damp forehead resting against mine, his breath fanning my face. He was making this about me, and the sudden realization slammed into me hard, firing my blood.

Inhaling sharply, my almost murmured, "This isn't going to work" came out as, "I'm ready."

He exhaled shakily, one of his hands falling to grip my bare hip, his body slowly retreating from mine only to return to it, one thrust after another, each one easier than the last. At first, it wasn't magic, it was simply skin against stretched skin, painful and uneasy, wet and uncoordinated. We kept trading laughter and gasps, from humor to cover the embarrassment to winded pants from unexpected pleasure.

I can't say exactly when it changed from that to something more, but it did.

He'd pulled himself up onto his arms— his biceps bulging, his forehead creased, the new angle applying pressure where there hadn't been any before—and I gasped, my lips parting. The pain was still there, but there was also something more.

His gaze found mine, his eyes reading the desire there, his hips moving faster, harder. My hands found his arms and gripped them, as if holding them would ground me somehow.

Sensation built, waned, and then built again. We were both reaching for something, our gazes falling to where our bodies joined, the sight making it more strikingly real, his body rising and falling into mine.

"Clare," he breathed.

He shifted again, the friction so painfully sweet it was almost unbearable, the sensations building until my body came apart, muscles clenching where they'd never clenched before, and for the first time, I found myself calling out, "Max."

With one final thrust, he joined me, his gratified exhale meeting my cry. He collapsed on top of me, keeping his weight distributed enough that he wasn't too heavy, his damp skin resting against mine, our bodies still joined but cooling. Our mingled breaths were rushed and uneven, our chests rising and falling.

"God, Clare," he gasped, rolling so that I was resting now on top of him, my cheek falling against his damp torso, my ear against his heart. It thudded loud and quick.

The moment seemed both too awkward and too perfect for conversation, as if words would spoil it somehow, making something so unique and beautiful into something clumsy and wrong. I didn't want it to be either of those things. I wanted it to remain special and different and new.

Heathcliff must have felt the same way because there was nothing except the sounds of our ragged breathing as our pulses slowed.

Silence stretched for so long, I thought Heathcliff had fallen asleep when he suddenly asked, "Are you okay?"

His voice startled me, and I inhaled. "I'm okay." Sore, but okay.

Silence, and then, "You called me Max."

My lips twitched. "Yeah ... I guess I did."

"Do it again," he demanded, his voice low.

My head lifted, so that my gaze met his. "Max."

The way he stared at me made me uncomfortable, and I let my fingers splay across his chest, pressing gently. "You know, I think people look at sex all wrong."

Heathcliff grimaced, the moment broken but not forgotten. "Now is really not the time to get all philosophical on me, Hawthorne." He shifted, and I moved so that he could roll to the side of the bed, his hands dropping to his waist. I knew he was discarding the condom, and I kept my gaze averted.

"Seems perfect to me," I said.

He laughed.

"Really," I insisted. "People make it all about love. I'm not saying it's not important to love. It's just that sex is kind of special on its own, too." I was babbling, but I couldn't seem to make myself stop. "Like this really incredible mind meld, only with bodies rather than minds."

Heathcliff rolled back onto the bed, his arm pulling me against him. "Okay, first, are you really comparing sex to a mind meld?"

I flushed. "I read a lot of my uncle's old *Star Trek* books growing up. Think about it, though. It's an incredible connection even if affection isn't involved."

He froze. "Are you saying you don't love me?" he asked.

An odd expression crossed his face, and I stared. "No, that's not what I'm saying. It's just … wait. Are you saying that you do?"

Our gazes locked. There was no reply from Heathcliff, but I didn't need a response. I saw what I needed to know in his eyes, and the pulse that had begun to slow, picked up speed again.

He cleared his throat. "So sex is kind of like a mind meld, huh?"

He stumbled on the words, and I jumped on them. Anything to dispatch the uneasiness between us. It was another lesson I was learning. Feelings are fast. Try to outrun them, and they catch you.

"More like a body meld," I amended.

He chuckled, his fingers running down my arm until they met my hand. "Did you read comics, too, growing up, or just books?"

His fingers laced with mine, and I glanced at our joined hands. "Oh, I read comics. All kinds. I might have a thing for Captain America and Thor. I also have a girl crush on Rogue."

"Ugh!" Heathcliff groaned. "Whatever. The real badass superheroes are definitely the Hulk and Superman."

"The Hulk?" I snorted. "Let me guess. You chose him because he's big, mean, and green?"

"Two words for you." Heathcliff's face was suddenly nose-to-nose with mine. "Hulk Smash!"

I grinned. "Two words. Anger management."

Heathcliff chuckled, and then fell silent. After a moment, he inhaled. "Hawthorne—"

"You don't have to say anything," I interrupted.

His fingers tightened around mine. "You do realize this is going to change things between us?"

My gaze fell from his. "We have until the end of the year."

"Yeah," he murmured. I couldn't see his face, but I could tell he was weighing his words and thoughts carefully by the way his fingers clenched and unclenched around mine. "My family gets together a lot on the weekends, especially now." He paused, and then blurted, "I'd like it if you came. Not all of the time. I haven't been going myself these last few weekends." He shifted so that my body leaned heavily against his. "I wouldn't quit doing the work I started here. It would just be a family gathering or two. Maybe more time at the creek?"

My heart did odd somersaults in my chest. "It depends on my uncle ... but I'll come."

Our fingers fell apart, and his hand found my face. Lifting my chin, he searched my gaze before dropping a gentle kiss on my lips. "Just remember, Hawthorne. Rough roads are often easier to travel with someone who knows the road."

I frowned. "At some point the road is going to end."

He didn't disagree. "Yeah ... it will."

Chapter 14

By morning, Heathcliff was gone, the empty place in the bed next to me and my sore body a reminder of something new, incredible, different, and scary. I'd had sex with Max Vincent. I'd shared more with him than I'd shared with anyone, and the fear was creeping in, doing its best to convince me I'd been wrong to trust him. My gut told me my fear could screw itself.

Outside, the sun sparkled on frost—January quickly dissolving into February—and I stumbled out of bed, blushing at the sight of the blood on my sheets before rushing to the shower. Clean and dressed for school, I tore the linens from my bed, rolling them up before replacing them with the spare sheets I kept in the top of my closet. The soiled ones I took to the laundry room, pushing the white fabric down into the washing machine before pouring in bleach.

"A little early for chores, isn't it?" Uncle Gregor called from the kitchen.

I jumped, the top of the washing machine slamming shut, the sound too loud in the still morning.

"Do you ever sleep anymore?" I called back.

His chuckle followed, the laugh stopped short by a groan.

I made my way to the kitchen, my feet stopping just beyond the alcove, my gaze finding my uncle's stooped back. He sat at the table, his head bent, a hand rubbing the back of his neck. Dark circles marred his eyes. A steaming cup of coffee sat in front of him, the smoke curling upward like wicked fingers ready to strangle him.

"Do you need me to stay home?" I asked.

Uncle Gregor glanced up at me, a weary smile curling his lips. "It's going to get worse, Hawthorne. Much worse."

A lump formed in my throat, and I swallowed past it, my hand falling to the table. "I'm here," I promised.

His grin remained, his hand patting mine. "Always and forever. Now go to school. I'm going to make some phone calls about the care the doctor talked about before I can't anymore."

His strength humbled me, his perseverance something I'd forever strive to match.

"For my sake," he added, saying the three words I'd never be able to say no to. *Our* words. "Go."

"Call the school if you need me," I demanded.

He nodded, and I left, my feet carrying me into the frosty morning, the air crisp and wet. It clung to me, the clean feel of it on my skin and tongue heavy and rejuvenating.

Birds pushed through the trees, their calls a heavy cry in my ears. My feet kept moving forward, never stopping. If I paused, they'd turn back.

My body actually sagged with relief when I caught sight of the school, my thighs and body more sore than I thought they would be, my mind an exhausted mess of emotions. I spied Heathcliff's truck in the parking lot, my heart jumping at the sight of the dull red vehicle.

"Hey, Hawthorne!" a voice called out as I entered the building.

My head shot up, my eyes meeting Rebecca Martin's curious gaze.

She fell into step next to me. "So, you and Max, huh?"

"Me and Max?" We'd reached my locker, and I pulled it open, grabbing two books and a binder.

She watched my hands before glancing at my face. "I mean, after he came with you to the creek, we all just assumed—"

"We're together," Heathcliff's voice interrupted. His shadow loomed over me, a protective mountain at my back. "In case anyone was wondering," he added.

Rebecca's eyes twinkled. "I thought as much. You know me. Nosy Rosy and all that." Her gaze flicked from his face to mine. "If you ever get tired of him, you should think about joining me for a trip to the mall or something. It's kind of nice having someone new around."

Her words were kind, her eyes equally serious. I kept searching for the malice in her tone but found none.

"Yeah … okay," I replied.

She grinned. "Well, I'll see you second period," she said before glancing at Max, "and you in last."

Her boots clicked on the floor as she left, an occasional glance over her shoulder the only sign that she had more questions. Lots more.

My gaze went to Max, his clean shaven jaw, damp hair, and clothes a reminder of his upcoming work at the Parker farm that afternoon.

"I figured it'd be easier to go straight from school," he said when he caught my stare.

A long-sleeve black T-shirt with *Vincent's* on the front covered his chest, the top hanging over old, sturdy jeans.

"We're together?" The question slipped out of my mouth.

His eyes searched mine. "Aren't we?"

Shifting my books to one arm, I slammed my locker door closed. "I think so?"

"I'd like to be," he rushed to say.

I stared. "Me, too."

He grinned. "Good. Are you okay? I mean after … you know."

Daylight had cut out our tongues, making it harder to be frank.

My cheeks flamed. "Yeah, I'm good."

Without another word, Heathcliff took my books, gently extracting them from my arms. "What's your first class?"

It seemed weird that we didn't know each other's schedules, our relationship up until now based on our feet, last period, work on the plantation, and the illnesses in our families.

"French."

"French?" he asked, surprised.

I shrugged. "It's my second year taking it. I have a thing for languages. I have a collection of CDs at home, each one teaching a different one."

"Really?" he asked as we walked.

I smiled. "Want me to speak to you in Italian or Portuguese?"

He laughed. "No, I'm good thanks. It's cool though. That you're learning them, I mean."

The door to my first class was fast approaching, and I glanced at him. "What do you do? Something not many people know about?"

He eyed me. "You really want to know?" I nodded, and he threw a look down the hall before meeting my gaze. "Ditch school with me at lunch, and I'll show you."

"Okay."

With a wink, he left me at the door. Curious looks glanced off of me as students passed. The stares didn't matter. Not now. Too much in my life was changing. Too fast. Some of the changes filled me with an indescribable need for speed. Some of them made me wish there were more hours in a day, more months in a year. Others made me wish time would stop altogether. Time was a friend and an enemy.

My distracted thoughts followed me into French, my gaze on the clock, the things running through my head keeping me from focusing. Excited anticipation carried me through the hour to my second class, the one I shared with Rebecca. It was then my preoccupation hurt me, the distraction causing me to say yes to things she asked that I'd probably regret later. There were some murmured words about a trip to town that ended with a slip of paper and my home phone number.

"You don't have a cell?" she asked, startled. My head shook, and she gaped at me. "Everyone has a cell phone. Aren't land lines like mostly extinct?" I'd shrugged, relief flooding me when the bell rang.

The next three classes were a blissful blur, and I rushed from fifth period only to stumble into Heathcliff.

He steadied me with a laugh. "Going somewhere? Not in a hurry are you?"

Taking my books, he deposited them into my locker before leading me to his truck. My stomach churned as I climbed in, mainly because I'd never done anything like this, brash and unexpected.

He climbed behind the wheel, his tires squealing as he backed up and tore out of the parking lot. Wind rushed into my face through the open windows, ripping through my hair and clearing my head.

Heathcliff threw me a grin, his teeth flashing as he sped over blacktop, turning down the nearest back road, the concrete below transforming into dirt. His speed increased, his truck taking turns that had me lost in minutes.

I was on the verge of asking where we were going when he pulled into a short drive, the only thing in front of us a small storage building.

"It used to belong to my grandfather," Heathcliff told me as he switched off the engine. "His hooch, he called it. Some type of military slang. When he passed, Mams gave me permission to use it." Throwing open his door, he climbed out and rounded the truck, his gaze meeting mine as he helped me out. "This was Paps' escape, just a place to go when he needed to get away or wanted a place to play a little poker with his friends."

Overgrown, brown grass rustled against our jeans as we walked to the structure. It was a good size, larger than most sheds, but way smaller than any house. Heathcliff pulled a key from his pocket, using it to undo a padlock before throwing open the door. He hit a light switch inside, a dim glow filling the space, and I gasped.

A lone bulb illuminated a clean room, the building housing an odd one bedroom apartment. On one side was an incredibly small kitchen, a two burner camp stove resting next to a shining, steel sink. Cabinets lined the wall behind it, curtains hanging over the spaces in place of cabinet doors. A tiny, two chair table separated the kitchen area from a small living space. There was a threadbare couch, the kind that turned into a bed, clean sheets stacked on top of it.

"My house is actually just a quick walk through the woods," Heathcliff informed me. "This is all on my family's property. The hooch was Paps' man cave." He laughed. "Mine now, I guess. No one else uses it."

Using a concrete block, we stepped into the building, my eyes landing on a stack of interesting machinery stacked against a wall housing a gas heater and a small window, an air conditioner shoved into it. The smell of sawdust, oil, and cleanser assaulted my nostrils. It was an oddly nice odor.

"There it is," Heathcliff said, gesturing at the machinery. "Doesn't look like much, but I like taking extra parts from busted equipment and turning them into something useful. That small one there," he pointed to an odd scrap of metal that had been welded together and turned into something eerily familiar, "is a toaster. Works great, too."

I glanced at Heathcliff. "This is incredible," I breathed.

He snorted. "Not really. I just like working with parts the same way my dad and uncles like working with wood."

"It's incredible," I insisted, my gaze falling to the couch. The place was clean and well taken care of, the sheets fresh. "You stay here?"

He shrugged. "Sometimes. Started my junior year, and as long as I kept my work up and didn't disappear too often, my parents didn't care. I come here, do a little work with the parts, and walk through the woods to shower in the morning. It's not every night, just off and on. All boys should have a hobby, my Mams says."

My gaze remained on the couch. "That's how you've gotten away with coming to the plantation."

He shifted awkwardly, and I realized he'd ditched his hobby a lot lately to spend time with me.

Touching his arm, I asked, "Could I come here sometimes and watch you work?"

"Really?" His gaze found mine.

"Sure. I could bring a few books."

He smiled. "Yeah, I'd like that."

Releasing him, I moved further into the room, my gaze alighting on an object leaning against the couch cushions.

"Is that a guitar?"

Heathcliff stepped next to me, his hands going to his pockets. "Another habit I picked up from my grandfather. I'm really not all that good, but I like picking at it."

For some reason, the idea that he played music intrigued me. "You'll have to teach me."

His eyes brightened. "I'd like that, too." Pausing, he stared at me, his gaze roaming over my face. "Thank you," he waved at the building, "for being interested in this. Or pretending you are anyway."

"No," I blurted, "I really am."

Leaning close, he captured me by the waist. "You could bring those foreign language CDs. Probably wouldn't hurt for me to learn some culture."

A laugh rose up in my throat, the sound cut off by his lips. I should be getting used to his kisses by now, but they kept stealing my breath, turning my insides to liquid lava. My world narrowed to his lips, his tongue, and the feel of his arms clutching me.

When we broke apart, I gasped, "I think we're getting better at this."

"You know what they say about practice."

Heat pooled in places too sore to even consider what his words implied, and I grimaced despite the wave of desire.

Heathcliff's lips brushed my forehead. "No hurry, remember. We have to get back."

Stepping free of the building, we stopped just long enough for him to switch off the light and lock the door before climbing back into the truck. We sped down the back roads toward the school, the wind a beast inside the vehicle, tearing at us as if it were trying to keep us in the woods. I didn't want to go back. Going back meant returning to reality. It meant facing the future. I wanted to give in to the wind, let it pull me backward.

The walls of my heart were caving in, and they were going to crush me.

Chapter 15

Life is made up of a bunch of hurdles and a lot of routines. It's getting up in the morning to redo what you did the day before. Occasionally, there are changes or obstacles, but mostly it's the same. Love stories usually focus on the hurdles, leaving out the repetition because repeating something over and over again doesn't seem necessary or entertaining enough to mention.

My relationship with Heathcliff fell into a routine, a comfortable one. He worked a lot, doing things for his father or taking jobs at the farms nearby. The only real time I had with him was at night, some afternoons, and on the weekends when we alternated between his family, the plantation, and the small building on his family's property. But we made the most of it.

Days fell into each other, blurring into one, my time with my uncle growing shorter and shorter. He started losing weight, his bright eyes growing dull and full of pain. Each day was a battle for him, but he wouldn't quit fighting. Every morning, he woke up, took his coffee to the kitchen, and sat down with me to talk about life, school, and the many ways he could beat Heathcliff at their next game of checkers. He needed the conversation, and I needed to talk.

I'd gotten better at talking. I'd even gotten better at making friends. Rebecca Martin particularly. For all of her looks and popularity, she was a lonely girl.

"I'm looking for a genuine friendship," she told me one morning, her eyes glowing as she leaned back in her chair. "Something that doesn't involve pageants, surgery, and clothes. You get that, right?"

I'd nodded and that had been enough. After that, she'd found ways to catch up with me in between classes and after school when Heathcliff was working. One nod, and we were suddenly friends, as if she'd decided telling me she wanted a genuine person in her life was an invisible contract of comradeship.

"You need a mentor," she said. "Someone who can teach you something about hair. Makeup, too, if you want. And let's be honest, I need you because the only time I get to cheat on this ridiculous diet my mother always has me on is when I'm somewhere she can't watch me."

With Rebecca, I never had to do a lot of talking, just a lot of nodding, smiles, and car trips to places I didn't care a whole lot about. The mall for one. And yet, being around Rebecca felt good. She made me smile and filled a lonely place in me I'd never realized was missing.

"Skinny jeans. That's where it is. You need skinny jeans," she murmured one afternoon.

No matter how many times I told Rebecca no, she found a way around it. Clothes appeared in my locker, coupons appeared on my desk, and packages appeared at my house. I kept trying to return them, and Rebecca kept bringing them back. It was a never ending cycle that concluded with me telling her I couldn't take anymore, and her agreeing to stop if I kept what she'd already sent.

Truth was, I began to count on her need to be there. Rebecca was living a lie, and I was living in the shadow of death. Somehow, we met in that strange place

between the two, clinging to the
companionship we found there.

She drove me home after school every
afternoon, coming in to meet my uncle
before sitting in the kitchen nibbling on
whatever I'd baked that week. I came to
depend on her and on her friendship. It was
nice, really, being close to someone who
didn't share any interests with you, but who
enjoyed being in the same room with you
anyway.

"When you become a chef, I'll totally
help you open a place," Rebecca said. She
loved to eat as much as I loved to cook. It
worked, our friendship.

Strangely enough, I had Heathcliff to
thank for Rebecca. I had Heathcliff to thank
for all of it. He was the reason my life was
changing. In a quiet, almost imperceptible
way, he was repairing my relationship with
the town and with me. He was taking me
places, encouraging me to talk, and helping
me grow. He was teaching me to trust
myself and to trust others. He was teaching
me to be a part of something and yet still be
unique.

Every spare moment we had, Heathcliff and I spent it together, his building in the woods our favorite destination. It was the only place not filled with grief and the threat of graduation. There among the trees, there was only love and long conversations.

One afternoon, he pulled out his guitar. His couch had been turned into a bed, and I was reclined on it, reading. Heathcliff had been working on a new "parts" project, turning a bunch of scrap metal into a grill for the creek. The parties there were few and far between in the winter, but they grew more frequent with warm weather. There wasn't much to do in our small town other than crowding together in fields, barns, or at the creek, the pickups circled and the tailgates down.

"You can't laugh," he said as he sat opposite me, tugging the instrument across his lap.

I set my book aside. "I won't."

Taking a pick, he strummed the guitar, testing the strings before falling into a familiar rhythm. He didn't sing, he just played, the tune a mix of blues and country.

Outside the sun grew lower in the sky, but it didn't matter.

The music waned, and I leaned forward. "I didn't take you for a country music guy."

He shrugged. "I'm not really. I listen to a little bit of everything, but when I play … well, country is kind of in the blood whether I want it to be or not. All that crap about love, drinking, pickup trucks, and hard living is the way it is here."

"I like country," I offered. "Some of it better than others. A lot of it's sad."

He picked at the guitar again. "There's a lot of truth in sadness."

My gaze searched his face, my chest tightening. Time was my enemy. Like with Uncle Gregor, I was losing Heathcliff, the far off look in his eyes full of dreams he'd never be able to fulfill here. January had melted into February and March, the weather outside warmer than it had been, green foliage starting to sprout among the brown.

"Do you ever sing?" I asked.

He grinned. "Sometimes. Mostly, I just play." He motioned for me to join him, and I slid toward him. "We could write a song," he suggested. "Put a twist on Callahan's assignment."

I laughed. "We could, or we could just write a paper."

"There's that, too." Laying the guitar aside, he reached for me, pulling me into his embrace, my back against his chest, his lips finding my neck.

Our relationship wasn't based on sex, but I won't lie and say we didn't spend a lot of time making love. We spent more time talking, driving the back roads, and visiting with family, but there was also sex. There was an underlying current of heat that drew us together, simmering just beneath the surface, a strong need to be as close as we could to each other.

Each time we made love was different. Like kissing, the sex got better. It was more intimate and less embarrassing. We could talk about things that would have horrified me before. We discussed what we didn't like and what we did, what places on our bodies felt better than others. Whispered words often mingled with gasps, occasional laughter and clumsiness mingling with pleasure.

That afternoon, I turned in his embrace, my lips crashing with his, passion turning something gentle into something heated and desperate. It was as if our bodies knew we were running out of time, our clothes gone as quickly as we could shed them, the protection pulled out and slid on, his body joining with mine.

"Look at me, Clare," he demanded.

My gaze locked with his, his body thrusting into mine, sensation building between us. When we were together, we weren't Hawthorne and Heathcliff, we were Max and Clare, everything stripped away except the vulnerability in our eyes, the things we'd never be able to say written in our gazes. In many ways, we let our bodies speak rather than our mouths.

His fingers fell between us, working their magic, his gaze never leaving mine. "You first," he said.

I writhed, my breath coming in pants, my cheeks flushing. My eyes started to close, and he touched my face.

"Don't you dare," he breathed. "Look at me."

My eyes met his, my brows furrowing as the sensations grew, my body coming apart. His orgasm followed mine, his lips parting on a groan.

"You're so beautiful, Clare," he murmured afterward. "Especially when you're falling apart."

"You, too," I replied, the words embarrassing but right. "I see you, Max."

His embrace was a safety net, full of things I'd never thought I'd experience, emotions and feelings and sensations that tore me apart and put me back together again.

"Eight weeks until prom," he mumbled against my ear, his lips continuing to drive me wild despite our exhaustion.

"I know," I answered.

Prom was good-bye. My birthday came first.

Two weeks after the night in the woods, I turned eighteen. It was a Saturday. By then, Uncle Gregor was unable to move around without help. Nurses came in to assist him, helping him into a wheelchair in the mornings, his wasted body still smiling.

I cried. A lot. My heart was a shredded mess, my time with Heathcliff and Rebecca my only ties to the living world beyond the threat of death.

The day of my birthday, Uncle Gregor's wheelchair met me at the table. "I've got something for you," he said, his eyes bright. "I've given it a lot of thought actually."

A door at the back of the house opened, a winded breath calling out, "Am I too late?"

Heathcliff's face materialized around the corner, a smile plastered on his face.

"Wait for me!" Rebecca's voice joined his. She skidded into the hall, her grin as big as Heathcliff's.

From my place at the table, I stared, my gaze flicking from face to face. "What is this?"

My uncle glanced at Heathcliff. "Max, bring it in."

Heathcliff disappeared, returning a few minutes later with his back to me, something long and heavy dragging behind him. Rebecca turned, her back united with his, their stances a joined effort.

"Uncle Gregor—" I began.

"I think this plantation needs a name," he interjected. "I don't know if I'd call it official, but we do have a marker now."

Heathcliff and Rebecca turned, a wooden sign dragged before them. Designs were carved into the surface. Birds flew across the top, storms clouds on one side being chased away by the sun, a line of crepe myrtle trees hanging over the words, *For My Sake Plantation.*

My eyes burned.

"What do you think?" Uncle Gregor asked. "The Vincents worked on it for me. They'll be here later."

"We're having a party," Rebecca exclaimed, her eyes finding my face, her gaze sobering instantly when she noticed my expression. "Oh, but just a small one. Max's family mostly."

My eyes were frozen on the sign. *For My Sake.*

A single tear escaped, the lone explorer forging a trail for the ones that would follow.

My gaze swung to Gregor's. "I love it."

For the first time since he'd been diagnosed, a tear rolled down my uncle's face. "It seemed right."

Standing, I brushed a kiss across his cheek, my arms wrapping around his frail neck. "For my sake, Uncle," I whispered.

Behind us, Heathcliff and Rebecca snuck away, Rebecca's murmured, "I'll just go get the cake," a distant echo in the hallway.

I barely heard her. There was only Uncle Gregor's hard breathing, and his dear, beautiful face. His strong, enduring face.

My heart hurt. It hurt so bad, I could barely breathe. I didn't know where to put the emotions, where to place all of the grief so that it didn't feel like it was crushing me.

"For my sake," my uncle whispered. "You can do this, Hawthorne. For my sake."

The tears burst forth, and they never stopped coming. They followed me throughout the day, a constant threat despite the laughter Heathcliff's family brought when they joined us, their cars crunching up the gravel drive. His family had become a regular in my life. I think they saw me as their lifeline, as a way to keep Heathcliff from leaving town after graduation. I didn't want to disappoint them, but I knew I would. Because holding Heathcliff back was the same thing as losing him.

Mams was the only one who understood.

She cornered me in the yard, her wise eyes on the festivities. "Happy birthday, girl!" she cackled.

She was faring better than my uncle, her days numbered, but longer than most. A new no salt diet, dialysis, and occasional surgeries to relieve the pressure in her abdomen kept her on her feet and moving. Oh, it was obvious she was hurting. There were times when the fluid in her body built up enough she even lost her wits, but she was surviving.

"You should be laughing," she scolded me.

I glanced at her. "I'm scared to do anything," I admitted. "I'm scared I'll cry instead.

"Pish posh!" Mams admonished. Startled, I stared at her, and she grinned. "I'm not goin' to tell you to be strong today. That's a little much to ask, but I am goin' to tell you to be resilient. You're a good girl, Hawthorne. You've got good blood in your veins, and a right head on your shoulders. You ain't gotta have everythin' figured out. That comes later, but your heart is going to take you in the right direction." Her gaze flew across the yard to Heathcliff. "Otherwise, my grandson wouldn't have seen something in you to save."

My gaze followed hers, my brows furrowing. "Save?"

Mams laughed. "Oh, you young ones really like to hide your heads in the sand." She shook her head. "I know you've heard the story about my dog, Rat. That boy just seems to know when to pull something out of the gutter. He knows how to fix things, he does. I've got faith in him. Just remember something for me, would you, girl?" Her gaze returned to my face, and I saw the ferocity there. "That boy spends so much time saving everyone else that he doesn't even realize he needs it, too. When I'm gone, save him for me, Hawthorne."

Shocked, I whispered, "He's leaving."

She snorted. "Oh, I know. He needs to, but the world is a crazy place. It jades a person, and when he comes back, he's going to need to remember the boy he was to make him the man he needs to be." Her gaze fell to my feet. "He's got a way of tellin' a story, you know. Told me all about you and your shoes." She chuckled. "Funny way to meet if you ask me, and yet ..." She searched my gaze, her eyes digging into my soul. "Shoes can tell a lot about a person. The journey they take you on can tell a lot about how they'll hold up."

With that, she walked away, supported by a cane. Her words didn't leave with her. They echoed, joining the myriad of thoughts and emotions swirling around in my head.

That night, when everyone had left and the house was quiet, I climbed into bed with my Uncle Gregor. It wasn't his regular bed. That had been replaced by a hospital version, an IV stand next to it. I didn't know enough about medicine to know what the nurses came to do to him, but they helped, and for that I was grateful.

Squeezing in next to my uncle, I listened to his breathing. It was harsher than it used to be, but it was there.

"The sign looked good hanging up, didn't it?" Uncle Gregor asked suddenly.

His voice startled me, and I glanced up at his face. His eyes were closed, his lips curled in a weary smile.

"It did," I answered.

The Vincent men had helped place the sign at the end of the lane, marking the *For My Sake Plantation*, the sporadic work Max had continued to do on the property turning our home into something glorious rather than miserable. We'd used a Polaroid camera to snap a picture of the sign and the house before taking it to Gregor.

"I'm so proud of you, Hawthorne," my uncle murmured. "So very proud."

The tears I'd been holding back all day flooded down my face. "You did it, Uncle Gregor. Everything I am is because of you."

"No," Gregor rasped. "No, it's because of you. People can guide you, but they can't make you into the person they want you to be. You took your own paths, and I'm proud."

There were no more words, only the sound of his breathing as it deepened in sleep. I remained with him, my head next to his. He was dying. His time was coming, and I was afraid to leave.

"For my sake," I whispered as I drifted off to sleep.

Chapter 16

School became my nightmare, every second I had to be away from home full of fear. I was so afraid that I'd miss my chance to say good-bye to Uncle Gregor that the fear ate at me, making me anxious. The hospice nurse promised she'd call me if there were any changes, but there was always the fear that I wouldn't make it in time.

My nights with Heathcliff grew fewer and further between. He came to the plantation after work, staying with me for a few hours before going home. It wasn't that I didn't want to be with him, I just wanted to be near Gregor, listening to his breathing, saying things I should have said over the years. It's hard trying to fit a lifetime of sentiment into a few weeks.

Rebecca continued to drive me home after school, coming in to sit with me despite the sadness. She brought laughter into the room, using the visits to munch away on any snack she could get her hands on.

The Vincents came, too, each of them leaving with kind words and warm hugs. Mams visited more than any of them, her hand clutching Gregor's, her old eyes full of memories. She never spoke much, just sat there, as if she knew words didn't mean as much as touch.

Heathcliff always followed, his strong arms embracing me, keeping my heart anchored until he had to leave. Every night after he was gone, after Uncle Gregor fell asleep, I cried. I cried, until one day, the tears just wouldn't come anymore, as if my body had been wrung dry.

Time passed, March dissolving into April. Trees and flowers bloomed, carpenter bees buzzed, the smell of honeysuckle wafted on the breeze, and yellow pollen dusted everything.

At school, everyone was preparing for prom and graduation, Mrs. Callahan's mirror project a looming deadline. I was apart from it all, spending time between the classroom and the plantation.

When I wasn't with Gregor, I cooked. A lot.

I'd just begun preparing a pecan pie when Heathcliff found me one afternoon, his large frame leaning against the open kitchen door.

"You're stressed," he said.

I glanced up at him. "What?"

He smiled, the gesture soft. "That's the fourth pecan pie in two days. Either there's a bake sale I'm not aware of, or you're worried."

My hands paused, the knife I was using to chop pecans growing still. "It *is* a lot of pies, isn't it?"

He entered the kitchen, moving so that he was standing behind me, his hands falling on mine. "Finish. I can take the extras home. Mom can use them in the café."

His hands fell away, and I started chopping the pecans again. "It's just that cooking takes my mind off of things, you know."

He remained behind me, his gaze on the bar. "I still want you to go to the prom with me, Hawthorne," he said suddenly.

I froze, the knife falling to the counter. "I can't—"

"Just wait," he said. "You'll see."
Turning, I stared up at him, and he leaned
forward. "Trust me."

"I do," I whispered.

The words brought a smile to his lips, a
whispered promise to return, and a quick
exit, leaving me to finish my fourth pecan
pie in two days.

It's funny, really. Food is often linked
with memory. For example, the smell of
chicory would always remind me of Uncle
Gregor and our kitchen table. Cookies and
pralines would always remind me of marker-
covered tennis shoes and a mirror
assignment. Cherry pie would, ironically,
always remind me of the first time I ever
made love. All good memories, all beautiful
moments.

Pecan pie, however, would always
remind me of good-byes.

Chapter 17

The day of prom, I stayed home from school and sat with Gregor, a book open in front of me. I'd taken to reading to him, and he often nodded in approval, his gaunt face turned toward my voice.

A knock on the door interrupted a chapter of *Crime and Punishment*, and I set the book aside, my gaze swinging to the nurse in the room beyond.

"It's for you," she called.

"Go," my uncle rasped.

In the foyer, Rebecca waited, a garment bag hanging over her shoulder, her gaze searching the room before finding my surprised face as I entered.

A grin lit up her features. "Okay, so I'm not staying or anything. I'm just dropping this off." She lowered the black bag, and I stared at the plastic uneasily. Rebecca chuckled. "It's not going to bite. Here." She handed it to me.

It was lighter than I expected. Lifting it, I threw her a look. "What is it?"

"You'll have to wait until I leave before you find out. That way you can't take it back." Rebecca winked, watching me a moment, her gaze searching mine, before turning back the way she'd come. She left, no more words passing between us.

She'd barely closed the door when I laid the garment bag on the floor and unzipped it. Inside laid a simple, strapless gray dress. It wasn't poofy or long, probably knee-length at most, the skirt subtly tiered. The only embellishment was a thin black, satin bow at the waist that tied on the side. A note was pinned to the top, Heathcliff's handwriting etched across the paper.

Put it on and wait for me. The dress will bring out your eyes.

Standing, I lifted the gown, my gaze going over my shoulder to the nurse waiting just beyond the room. She turned when she saw me looking, her auburn bun facing me, the grin I'd caught on her face dissolving.

Even though she gave me her back, she cleared her throat, and said, "It's very pretty."

The nurse's name was Susie. She'd been with us for weeks now and was a sweet, middle-aged woman who always smelled like eucalyptus.

"I'm not sure this is a good idea," I said.

Susie turned to face me again. "Never hurts to put it on."

After a moment's hesitation, I took the dress and climbed the stairs to my room, discarding the clothes I had on to step into the gown. It hadn't look like much in the bag, but when I turned toward the gold mirror on my dresser, I gasped. The dress was so simple, it was spectacular, hugging my frame and highlighting things I never would have noticed about myself before. Especially my hair. The strawberry-blonde mess always confounded me, reminding me of a dandelion right before someone blew it to make a wish. The dress made my hair look different, like a red-gold halo right before the sun sets. Also, Heathcliff was right about the eyes. My gaze was suddenly filled with stormy clouds, emotions swirling.

Downstairs, a knock sounded on the door, and I jumped, rushing to run my fingers through my hair before heading to the stairs.

Voices met me.

"She's getting ready," Susie said.

Heathcliff's laugh met her words. "And here I thought I'd have to force her into the dress."

There'd been no shoes in the garment bag, and so I didn't wear any, my bare feet quiet on the stairs as I descended. Heathcliff stood at the bottom with Susie, his broad frame enfolded in black dress pants and a suit jacket over a white dress shirt. There was no tie, and the top two buttons on the white shirt were left undone.

"You know I can't leave," I said, my voice breaking through their discussion.

Susie glanced up at me, her eyes widening before she backed into the house, leaving us alone.

Heathcliff's head lifted, his lips parting as his gaze met mine, his eyes roaming my hair before dragging down the dress to my feet.

"That," he said, gesturing at my frame, "looks so much better than I imagined."

He stared, and I glanced down at myself. Silently, I wondered if he'd picked out the dress, but I didn't ask it aloud. That didn't matter. Him being here mattered.

A lump formed in my throat. "I can't leave," I repeated.

Heathcliff smiled, leaning over to remove his shoes—his sneakers of all things—leaving only a pair of dress socks. "I wasn't really planning to go anywhere."

My feet paused on the bottom step. "You want to stay here?"

Straightening, he glanced at me. "It's better than the prom, really. I'd rather be all dressed up here with the family we love than in a room full of people sweating because of the completely inadequate air conditioner in the school gym."

My heart swelled, my breath catching. "Heathcliff—"

He didn't let me finish, his inscrutable gaze catching mine. "Take my hand, Hawthorne." He offered me his palm, and I stepped toward him, my fingers curling around his. "Let's go show your uncle what that dress does for his niece."

Swallowing sudden tears, I followed his lead, our feet moving through the house until they rested at the end of Gregor's hospital bed. His eyes were closed, but they opened when Heathcliff cleared his throat. My uncle's dull gaze brightened when he caught sight of the two of us.

"I thought maybe," Heathcliff glanced at me, and then at Gregor, "that you'd like to chaperone your niece's prom, sir."

For a long moment, Gregor stared as if it were the first time he'd ever laid eyes on me, tears filling his gaze. "God, when did you become a woman, Hawthorne?" he breathed.

My eyes watered, my smile meeting his abrupt grin.

"Susie!" Gregor called, his raspy voice breaking on the words. "You've got to come see Hawthorne. Looks like an angel, she does!"

Susie appeared in the doorway. "That she does," she replied, grinning, her gaze flicking over us before moving to my uncle, a peculiar look passing through her eyes.

Heathcliff glanced down at me and winked. "Now, all we need is music."

Susie shook herself and clapped. "I'll turn on the radio!"

Heathcliff's hand rose, stopping her. "No, it's okay. I've got it." Fishing in his pocket, he pulled out an iPod. "I've got some stuff on here that will work."

Stepping away from me, he set it on the table next to Gregor, pausing just long enough to press a few buttons. Music spilled out of it, the first song an old, slow one.

Offering me his hand, Heathcliff breathed, "Dance with me."

I glanced at Uncle Gregor. He was watching the entire scene, his cheeks flushing. There was something odd about his eyes, and I ignored Heathcliff's hand. Stepping toward the bed, I leaned over it, my gaze on Gregor's.

"Are you okay?" I whispered.

Gregor blinked, his eyes finding my face. He seemed to have a hard time focusing, his breath coming heavy when he said, "Dance, Hawthorne. I'd really like to see you dance."

My lips brushed his forehead, his skin so fragile now I was almost afraid to touch him. "I love you, Dad," I murmured.

I don't know why I said it. I'd said it before, and then fallen back into the routine of calling him Uncle because the word was less awkward for us after all these years, but now Dad just seemed more appropriate.

"I love you, too," he answered, grinning. "Now dance."

I turned, and Heathcliff met me at the side of the bed, his arms embracing me. The music on the iPod had changed, the song an upbeat one, slow but full of amusement, and Heathcliff pulled me into a series of twirls. My feet stumbled, and we laughed, my gaze coming up to meet his.

"I'm not going to be good at this," I said.

Heathcliff shrugged. "You don't have to be. You just have to smile and enjoy it."

And we did. We danced, and we laughed, the music carrying us across the floor. Uncle Gregor laughed with us, and then fell silent, his bright eyes watching as we circled around the room, my bare feet spending more time stepping on Heathcliff's socks than on the floor. He twirled me so that my feet lifted, rising in the air. The shock of it made me giggle, the music cocooning us. For the first time in weeks, the room was bursting with happiness, with smiles and beauty.

It was a moment I was never going to forget. I'd always remember how much, in that instant, I loved Heathcliff. I'd remember how handsome his face looked lifted in amusement.

The music played, songs Heathcliff sang along to while I hummed, and we danced. We danced until our feet were sore, and the sun started to set, sending golden rays through the windows to light up the room.

It was then, while we danced and while our laughter rose to the ceiling that Uncle Gregor passed into a coma, his spirit ready to depart on gold, music, and joy.

Chapter 18

There are no words big enough to describe grief. It's an incredibly lonely, empty place, a large hole that swallows your soul and threatens to destroy it. It's a dark place with no light that blinds you, deafens you, and crushes your spirit. It's a place full of memories you're afraid to lose.

I was in that place. No amount of tears washed away the loneliness. No amount of screams chased it away. There were simply memories, an avalanche of memories that I desperately needed to hold onto.

There was so much that death didn't prepare me for. It didn't prepare me for the storm that would break my will. Uncle Gregor's passing sent me to my knees and left me there.

The day he died, it rained. It rained so hard that the yard turned into a muddy mess, the vehicles that pulled into the drive sloshing through water, their metal bodies highlighted by lightning. The air screamed with me, thunder rolling, crashing over me like a bowling ball of pain.

It was twenty-four hours after my impromptu prom, and I was still wearing the dress, my hair wild, my feet glued to the wooden floor next to Gregor's hospital bed. His body had been taken, and there were people surrounding me, people helping clean the room while others worked in the kitchen, making food and conversation. I knew most of the men and women who came through, but I didn't see them. The tears blurred my vision, my heart stuck in a strange limbo between needing to live and wanting to join Gregor.

Sometimes, I stood. Other times, I knelt. Most of the time, I cried, silent tears trekking down my cheek. Mams' voice circled me. After a phone call from Heathcliff, she'd arrived just after Gregor's death, her commanding voice taking over where my voice had ended. She didn't try to console me. She didn't even approach me. She just took over, guiding people to where they needed to be.

I think she knew I was lost.

This part of my life wanted to destroy me. It's true that death finds us all at some point, but the heart doesn't care about that. It simply grieves.

I felt like a tornado. I'd grown up being afraid of the kind of storms that brought funnel clouds. There's nothing more terrifying than hiding in a basement, bathtub, or closet wondering if Mother Nature's enraged thumb would land on your house. Grief kind of felt like that.

My entire body was a maelstrom of funneling emotions that imprisoned me. There was nowhere for them to go. Somewhere inside of me, there was a calm place, a quiet center, the eye of the storm, but I couldn't find it.

People came and went, but only one presence truly stayed with me. Heathcliff. Mostly, he stood next to me, sometimes kneeling on the floor when I couldn't stand. At first, he didn't even attempt to hold me, but then I reached for him. I'm not sure why. In many ways, I didn't want anyone. I just wanted to hurt, to spend my grief the same way I'd lived my life, with just Gregor and me.

But at some point, I did reach for Heathcliff, and he embraced me, his arms tightening.

"You're not alone," he said against my hair.

He never left. He, along with his grandmother, stayed at the plantation with me, their comforting presence surrounding me. Mams made phone calls, talked to the funeral home, and set up things I wouldn't even have known how to set up. All I had to do was sign papers.

"He had everythin' lined up," Mams' told me that first Gregor-less night. "His insurance covers everything. All you have to do is help me make a few selections and sign a few papers."

I was getting good at putting my signature on paperwork through a haze of tears.

Vaguely, I remember showering and changing, my heavy, tear-drained body falling onto my bed. Downstairs, people moved around, Heathcliff's voice mingling with his family's. They'd taken me under their wings, but all I could do was stare blankly at the window above my window seat, my fist clutching my stomach, my knees drawn up to my chest. The tears made my body too hot for blankets and too cold to be warm.

The light from my window started out dull and full of threats, changing with the day, the gray crawling across the floor, up my walls, and then back across the floor again before being snuffed out by scattered storms. Lightning flashed.

This was grief. This was pain.

Outside, it rained.

"For my sake," I sobbed. "You've got this, Hawthorne. For my sake."

Downstairs, music played, the sound of Heathcliff's guitar both sad and healing. He made more mistakes on the instrument than he got right, but it eased the pain some, filling the screaming silence in my head with something more.

"Be brave, Hawthorne," I told myself.

I wish I could say that I was able to pull myself together, to make it through my uncle's passing with poise and grace, but there's a huge difference between knowing you're going to lose someone and actually experiencing the loss. There was no grace in my tears, no poise in the way I walked, and no beauty in the way I ranted at my walls.

In many ways, I think people need to be angry before they can be accepting. I was angry, so very angry at death and life and people who had the kind of happiness that had been robbed from me. It didn't matter how unfair that sounded, how selfish it seemed to make me. I was angry, and so I yelled at the invisible people in front of me, blaming my missing parents, happy people I respected, myself, and even Gregor.

I yelled, swore, and punched my bed.

Outside, it rained.

The day of the wake, Heathcliff stood in front of my open bedroom door, his gaze on my sprawled figure.

"It's okay to fall, Hawthorne," he said. "Sometimes it takes hitting rock bottom to find the strength to climb back up the mountain."

Sitting up, I stared at him, my hair even messier than usual, my face swollen, my head pounding from too many tears.

"You don't know," I scolded. "You don't know how it feels."

He leaned against the open frame. "No, I don't. I wasn't very old when I lost my grandfather, and I certainly haven't lost a parent, but the words sounded good in my head." His gaze traveled down my rumpled sheets. "I'll be here to help you though. I may not understand, but I'll help hold you up while you're in the process of falling."

I didn't think there were any more tears left in me, but a few trickled down my cheeks any way. "I can do this, Heathcliff. I can."

The smile he gave me was a soft one. "I know you can. For his sake and yours." He entered the room and offered me his hand. "It's better to let it all out than to keep it in. Come on, I can't keep you from stumbling, but I can certainly cushion the fall."

My tear-filled eyes found his face before falling to his shoes. He had on his sneakers, the old shoes going well somehow with the jeans and dress shirt he wore. It should have clashed, but it didn't.

Another tear fell. "You have good shoes, you know," I said.

It amazed me how close I'd become to Heathcliff. All because I'd noticed his shoes, and he'd followed me home from school one day.

"Yours aren't so bad either," Heathcliff replied.

There was no more room in my heart for heartbreak. "Can you promise me something?" I asked.

Heathcliff kept his hand held out toward me. "Anything?"

My gaze moved up to his. "When you leave, wear a new pair of shoes. Don't walk away in these."

He froze, but his hand never wavered. "I promise."

My fingers met his palm, and he pulled me effortlessly to my feet, his shoulder supporting me. In retrospect, Heathcliff was always offering me his hand, his fingers pulling me from the darkness. Death was making me poetic, opening my eyes to things I wasn't sure I would have noticed before.

Heathcliff stayed with me, helping as I changed clothes before walking with me to the stairs and the cars beyond the house. His family waited on us, their vehicles following us to the wake.

There wasn't much that could be said about my uncle's viewing, the funeral that followed, and the procession to the cemetery. There was an incredible show of support, most of the town coming out to wish me well, some of them following us to his gravesite while the rest either went home or to the plantation to set up a small meal.

To be honest, I kept searching the crowd. It would have been a dramatic occurrence, an interesting story to tell I suppose, if my eyes had fallen on the two people I was looking for. But, despite the faint hope and fear, I never saw my parents. They wouldn't have known to come, and in truth, I would have hated to see them there. Maybe I hoped they loved Gregor more than they'd cared to stay with me.

In the end, when the day was finished, I found myself grabbing Heathcliff's hand, my fingers squeezing so hard I was sure my nails left impressions in his skin.

"Don't go," I whispered.

"I won't," he promised.

Outside, it started to rain.

Chapter 19

My love story sort of ended with
Gregor's death. I remained at the plantation,
and I returned to school, finishing out my
senior year the way my uncle had wanted
me to. Heathcliff often spent the night with
me, coming in after working with a duffel
bag slung over his shoulders. I'd have
supper ready because cooking was
something I was used to doing, something
I'd always done for Gregor and me.

Every night, Heathcliff and I would sit
at the table and eat before doing school work
and heading to bed. There was a distance
growing between us. It was natural I guess,
and I think in many ways, I'd always known
it was coming.

Life had a funny way of separating
people. Uncle Gregor's death had changed
me, and Heathcliff's dream for the future
was building a wall between us. People
change. Relationships change. We were
changing, and our relationship wasn't
moving forward with those changes.

I was learning something about being broken. Like a shattered dish being glued back together, I didn't look or feel the same way I had before I'd fallen apart.

In a weird way, mine and Heathcliff's relationship ended a lot like it began. In silence. We drifted apart, and one day he just quit coming to the plantation. The only thing keeping us together were our shoes and last period English class. Our feet often touched in the aisle, even after our relationship ended. It was as if we'd never quit being a couple, we'd just returned to that beautiful, quiet place where we'd first met.

There was no animosity between us. The truth was, he was leaving, and we both knew it. He didn't want to hurt me, and I didn't want to hold him back, so the only place we could go from there was back to the beginning. To silence and touching shoes.

Graduation day loomed. I learned through Rebecca, who'd started staying with me not long after Heathcliff quit coming, that Max Vincent had enlisted in the military. It should have surprised me, considering Heathcliff's love for working with metal and parts, but it didn't. It made sense actually. He liked saving things, he liked piecing stuff together, and he'd always wanted to see the world. He also looked up to the grandfather he'd lost as a child. I'd discovered that while spending time with him in the building in the woods, and his grandfather had quite the military career.

I was proud of him.

Two weeks before school ended, Mrs. Callahan's mirror assignment was due, and I spent the night before its deadline sitting on my bed, my hair pulled up and a notebook splayed open before me. My mirror sat next to it.

Heathcliff and I had spent a lot of evenings talking about Mrs. Callahan's assignment, even writing pieces of it for each other, but tonight it was just me. Me and a piece of paper, the empty blue lines staring at me with bated breath.

I looked into the mirror, my stormy eyes meeting my reflection, my upswept wild, strawberry-blonde hair turning me into a human dandelion, a few freckles sprinkled over my mostly clear complexion. My appearance didn't matter. I suddenly understood Sylvia Plath's poem more than I'd ever understood it. No one interprets a poem the same way. That's the beauty of poetry, but this assignment wasn't about a poem. It wasn't even about the mirror. It was about how we viewed ourselves, and how that view can change with time.

Picking up my pencil, I started to write, my heart bleeding down my arms and into my fingers, the words that formed becoming a sprawling mess of gray lead blood. I wrote and I wrote until there was nothing left in me, nothing except a clean slate ready to be re-written on.

The next day, when last period English class came to an end and Mrs. Callahan called for the assignments, I stood with everyone else, my hand going to Heathcliff's arm. He'd stood next to me, and he froze.

In the front of the room, students were placing the papers on Mrs. Callahan's desk and leaving, but I held Heathcliff back, my gaze finding his shoes.

"I've got this," I told him. My words broke the silence we'd once again come to depend on.

"What do you mean?" Heathcliff asked.

"Trust me," I said. "It's time for you to trust me. Just go. I've got this." There were two copies of the paper I'd written the night before, my fingers still sore from writing it once and then re-writing it, and I handed the extra one to him. "Take this and go."

He accepted the paper, and I walked away, approaching Mrs. Callahan's desk without tripping despite the sudden trembling in my body knowing Heathcliff watched.

The rest of the students were gone, and the teacher looked up at me, an expectant smile on her face. She started to speak, but I held out the assignment in my hand, the paper shaking visibly.

"I know this wasn't a group project, but Max Vincent and I worked on it together," I said, clearing my throat. "Well, I did the actual writing, but we've worked most of the past semester working on bits and pieces of it."

Mrs. Callahan took the paper, her gaze going over my shoulder before glancing down at the assignment. The title on the first page caught her off guard, and she threw me a look. "I admit I'm intrigued," she said. Throwing one final glance over my shoulder, she added, "I'll take it. Whatever grade you get, Max will get, too."

Nodding, I left, passing a stunned Heathcliff where he stood just inside the classroom door. He was staring down at the paper, his eyes moving over the words. I didn't stay to find out what he thought. I knew what he and Mrs. Callahan were reading, and my lips curled into a smile as I pushed through the door at the end of the hall, my feet bursting out into a sunny day. A new beginning.

Inside, Heathcliff and Mrs. Callahan were reading this:

Clare Macy
Mrs. Callahan
Date not important

Hawthorne and Heathcliff

Forget poetry for a moment and look at life. Looking into a mirror isn't really about seeing a reflection, it's about seeing change. It's about the passing of time, and time doesn't need a mirror. It just happens, which means we must carry a figurative mirror with us and learn to look at ourselves without needing a looking glass.

This year, I changed.

This year, I met a shoe. It wasn't a remarkable shoe. It was worn, the black trim that once lined the white turned gray. The white part of the sneaker had turned, too, stained by dirt and time, but it was a clean shoe. It was well kept, and I knew by looking at it that it had also been repaired numerous times.

That shoe belonged to a boy, a young man whose feet became a lifeline for me in a world of angry silence. My shoe, equally old and worn but not as well kept, rested next to his. It belonged to a girl, a young woman full of bitterness and distrust.

Shoes are kind of like mirrors. They lie more than a mirror does. They carry people to places they shouldn't go, and because they can't speak, they can't say where they've been. Yet they also take people to places they should have gone, making them try things they've always avoided.

The boy belonged to a shoe that always tried. The girl belonged to a shoe that hid. He belonged to a shoe that was well put together. She belonged to one that didn't care.

His shoe changed hers.

It seems funny that I'm writing about shoes, but not so funny I guess since we're talking about poetry. Plath saw something in her mirror that made personifying the looking glass important.

In these shoes, I saw the same thing. I saw a journey. It was an amazing journey, a story of love, trust, and loss. This boy and his shoe changed the girl and her shoe. He taught her that it was okay to fall. He taught her it was okay to trust.

While she was falling, she learned something. She learned that she'd been hiding so much behind her own pain, her own childhood abandonment issues, that she'd missed her life. She'd closed herself off from the people she loved, the ones who'd loved her enough to stay behind when everyone else left. She learned about her uncle.

The boy's shoe helped her see her uncle. It opened up a line of communication between the girl and her uncle that might have remained closed otherwise. It would have been sad if she'd never met this boy's shoe. It would have been sadder if she'd never realized how much she was truly loved.

Let's be honest, it would have been sad if this girl, me, had never been woken up. I, Clare Macy, found a boy's shoe, and it made me a better person, a better daughter, and a better friend.

That's what this assignment is really about. It's about meeting people and going places that changes you. It's about going through things that leave you scarred and broken but stronger.

Max Vincent's shoe—because it was Max's shoe after all—took me down an amazing road. When I was finally able to look at Max's face, to look beyond his shoe, I fell in love with the boy. My heart fell, and I'm glad it did. Because love, whether it lasts or not, changes you, too. It transforms you into something different. For me, it was a good different.

I've now loved two men in my life, and I've lost them both. Losing them hurts, but their lives taught me so much about living that what they taught me somehow overshadows the loss.

I have a long journey ahead, but where my eyes were closed before, they are open now. All thanks to a shoe. All thanks to a boy my heart called Heathcliff. Some love stories end. Others start your life over.

His jumpstarted mine. For that, I will always be grateful.

So, in short, I don't have to look into a mirror to see the changes in me. I just need to keep walking, and I need to care enough about my shoes to stop occasionally and think about where they've taken me.

Shoes can tell a lot about a person. The journey they take you on can tell a lot about how they'll hold up.

Chapter 20

For two weeks, I spent most of my afternoons with Rebecca preparing for graduation. I didn't see Heathcliff after the day I turned in the mirror assignment. School had mostly ended for seniors, the roll no longer taken in class. Because of that, there wasn't many who went to school. Summers and celebrations started early, but I kept going. I went because sitting at home would have been worse. The plantation didn't feel the same without Gregor, even when Rebecca stayed.

It was because of this that I decided to take the fund Mams had started for me as a child, and the savings Gregor had marked as *school account* in his will, and apply for college. I wasn't a bad student, but I also wasn't the top of my class. While I was eligible for some financial help, most of the costs were left to me. My main interests lay in the culinary field.

For two weeks, I filled out applications and made phone calls, alternating between searching for colleges and shopping for graduation dresses with Rebecca. In truth, she shopped, and I watched, though I did grab a pair of black slacks and a fitted red top in one of the shops, trusting the size rather than using the dressing rooms.

Rebecca despaired of me. "If you want to become a business woman one day, you really need to dress better."

I shrugged. "My career will mainly consist of aprons and chefs hats."

"You don't know that."

"I'll take it as it comes," I said.

She quit trying after that, only throwing a few cursory comments my way later while reclining at the table in the plantation kitchen, her feet propped on an empty chair.

"Are you really going to leave?" Rebecca asked.

Standing at the kitchen counter, I glanced up, my gaze finding hers. I was baking. Ever since the day I made too many pecan pies and Heathcliff took them to his mother, she'd come often to the plantation to see if I had any baked goods she could sell at the Vincent café. It earned me a little extra money. Not much, but I liked the idea that I didn't have to depend too heavily on the funds Uncle Gregor had left behind. He'd had two savings accounts, one for my college education, the other to help keep the plantation running.

"I guess it depends on the college I go to. I think I'd like to do a foreign internship, too. But I couldn't stay away. There's too much of me here," I answered.

She smiled. "Good. I don't think it'd be the same without you."

"You're not leaving?" I asked, surprised.

She snorted. "Of course not. Where would I go? Besides, I'm not cut out for town living. It's kind of nice being a big fish in a small pond. If I leave here, that changes."

I laughed. "Now who's using her mother's reputation?"

She threw me a look, but grinned nonetheless. My relationship with Heathcliff may have ended, but my friendship with Rebecca was growing.

Standing, Rebecca marched into the kitchen and snatched a cookie out of a nearby tin. "Just promise me you won't let me marry the first guy who flashes me his abs."

Smiling was easy around Rebecca. Making promises was even easier. She often used my house to escape her mother, and it became a regular thing finding her at the plantation in the afternoons. So, when graduation day arrived, and I woke up that morning to find her car gone from the drive, I suddenly felt sad.

Tears threatened, but I held them back and went through the motions. There was no coffee downstairs, no comforting smell of chicory, no family anticipations. Just me, my dress pants, my red shirt, and the promise of a new tomorrow. No one expected anything of me, so I had to expect it of myself.

Grabbing my uncle's car keys, I paused at the door, glancing over my shoulder at the kitchen.

"For your sake, Uncle Gregor," I said.

With that, I pulled the door open and walked out into the May humidity, the sun breaking through the trees. Birds flew, diving and rising, their calls loud in the still morning. Across a field, buzzards circled. It brought to mind the Native American story Gregor had told me. No matter what you think of a creature, how ugly and terrible it seems, there's always something worth remembering about it.

"Keep doing what you do," I called out to the buzzards. I was getting good at talking to myself.

I'd just closed the door behind me when I stumbled, my hands catching me before I fell. Glancing down, I gasped, my eyes widening. On the stoop sat Heathcliff's shoes, blue marker marring the side. *Keep me*, they said.

Leaning down, I lifted them, capturing them against my chest, tears pricking my eyes. He'd kept his promise. He may be leaving, but he wasn't taking his old shoes with him.

Re-opening the door, I placed the sneakers inside the foyer before heading to the car, my steps light despite my breaking heart. Uncle Gregor's words swirled in my head. *Sometimes love isn't forever. Sometimes it's just moments in your life that teach you. If it's the forever after kind of love, it'll find you again. If it isn't, don't let a broken heart break you. Let it make you love harder. Love is a mistake worth making.*

Those words followed me down the drive as I drove to school for the final time. They followed me to the fold out chairs sitting before the stage in the school gym. They followed me through two speeches, three songs, and the moment when I accepted my diploma. They rang through my head as I threw my hat into the air, the room filling with flying black caps, the tassels hanging. Cheers, laughter, and clapping surrounded me. Even with Uncle Gregor gone, it was nice.

There was no reason to stay when the ceremony ended, but when I started to make my way through the crowd to my car, I was stopped by a pair of new shoes. These shoes were the same brand as the old shoes that came before them, as if the idea of getting a different pair had never crossed the owner's mind.

"Clare—" Heathcliff's voice began.

His tone was flooded with misgiving, and I glanced up at his face, my hand coming up to cover his mouth.

"Don't," I said. "Don't start having doubts now. My wish for you is that your path leads you to an amazing place. I want it to take you to amazing possibilities and brilliant sunsets. I want it to take you to the moon and back. I want your life to be exactly how you always saw it. Don't look back, Max Vincent."

I removed my hand, and Heathcliff stared at me. He'd gotten his hair shaved since the last time I saw him. It was odd seeing him that way, but it didn't take away from his appearance. If anything, it accentuated his face, making his cheekbones sharper, his eyes bigger.

"You know," he finally said, "I never told you something, and I just don't feel right leaving without it being said." He leaned close. "I loved you, Clare. Truth be told, I still do."

I smiled. "I know. You showed me you did. I just don't want you to stay, and then have you realize later that it wasn't enough. Be happy, Max. That's what I want."

His grin met mine. "I want the same for you. Be that philosophical chef I know you're going to be."

His arms suddenly found my waist, pulling me into a suffocating embrace before letting go, his lips brushing my forehead. Our hands met, clasped, and then released each other.

There weren't any more words after that, and he turned to walk away. My eyes watched his feet.

"Wait!" I called out abruptly. Max paused, and I stepped forward. "Just remember something, would you? Don't forget who you are."

He smiled. "I won't. And, Hawthorne, check your seat before you sit in your car."

He continued onward, the crowd swallowing him. For a moment, I stared after his disappearing shoes before throwing myself into the mass of people, nudging my way to the parking lot. We hadn't been a big graduating class, but where the town was small the families were big, and I was chased to the car by flashing cameras and quick protests.

At my vehicle, I paused, my eyes finding a CD sitting in the seat, the disc kept safe by a plastic sleeve. Opening the door, I picked it up and climbed in. I pulled out of the lot, my speed faster than usual, taking the curves and roads without really looking at them until I was parked once more at the plantation.

Inside, I picked up Heathcliff's shoes, taking them with me into the living room as I placed the CD he'd left me in my uncle's stereo system. The system was an old one, the kind that had a place for CDs and cassettes, a record player sitting on top.

At first, when I pushed play, there was nothing, but about a half a minute in, guitar music started, full of country and heartache, joined soon by Heathcliff's voice. Max was a good singer, not the best in the world, but good, and I sat on the floor, his shoes in my lap.

There's a wild girl, surrounded by hair and dreams.

Her heart is mine, her soul a beautiful beacon.

Her mind is a busy place, full of scars and ripped seams.

Her life is a rough ride.

A potholed mess, no clean straightaway.

But I've got a truck with four wheel drive and too many places to go.

It can handle the strife, can plunge through the broken asphalt.

It's a hard road, baby, and I wouldn't have missed it for the world.

To be a part of that life,

Those dreams, that wild, passionate girl.

There's truth in sadness, no shame in letting go.

We've got a long way to travel. It's easier with someone who knows the road.

A long way to travel, a long way to go.

Hold on, darlin', and quit looking at your shoes.

Look at the road ahead and hang on.

We've got this, one way or another, no matter the dues.

It's you, me, and a world we still need to own.

It's a hard road, baby, and I wouldn't have missed it for the world.
To be a part of that life,
Those dreams, that wild, passionate girl.
There's truth in sadness, no shame in letting go.
We've got a long way to travel. It's easier with someone who knows the road.
A long way to travel, a long way to go.

When I'm gone, and you're alone.
Keep travelin' that road. Keep drivin' over those potholes.
Together, we're great. Alone, you're even stronger.
Own the world, baby. It's yours. Own the world.

There's truth in sadness, no shame in letting go.

You've got a long way to travel. It's easier with someone who knows the road.

But alone, you're stronger. Own the world.

You've got a long way to go.

A long way to go.

The song ended, and for a long time, I simply sat there, the tune ringing in my head. In the end, even in his absence, Heathcliff had left me a gift. He'd left me a song, a pair of shoes, and a reason to fly.

It was enough.

Five years later ...

Chapter 21

"We really need to talk about our uniforms," Rebecca grumbled, stomping into the kitchen, her hands on her hips.

Amused, I glanced at her. "We don't have uniforms."

She frowned. "That's what I mean. We *need* them."

Some things never changed. At twenty-three years old, Rebecca wasn't much different than she'd been at eighteen; the only change her bigger breasts and somewhat jaded opinion of men. Two failed marriages in five years would do that to a person. Her second divorce was still in the filing process. On the other hand, if it hadn't been for the settlement she'd received from her first marriage, *For My Sake Catering* never would have become a reality.

My gaze roamed over my uncle's kitchen, the recent renovations allowing for a bigger oven, cooling racks, and a walk-in freezer area. Strangely, even after four years of college, a year interning in France, and remodels on the plantation, I still had a hard

time seeing *For My Sake Plantation* as
mine. My uncle's spirit felt too big here, as
if no amount of time would ever be enough
to truly overcome the grief. Time brought
healing, but it didn't get rid of the heartache,
the empty place his passing left behind.

"Have you looked at the order I put in
this morning?" Rebecca asked.

I shook myself, my head shooting up.
"What order?"

She sighed. "I know I put it around here
somewhere."

Rebecca and I had remained faithful
friends over the past five years, her local
business degree coming in handy when a
night of drunken celebration somehow
translated into a joint business venture. It
was the last time I ever drank hard liquor
with Rebecca.

"And here you're worried about
uniforms," I said on a laugh.

She threw me a look, knocking over a
stack of ledgers to get to a pack of hot pink
sticky notes. "It was for the Vincents," she
murmured, her gaze flicking from the table
to my face. Pulling off the top note, she
handed it me.

Sucking in a breath, I glanced down at Rebecca's scrawling script, and then exhaled. "Wow. What is this for? A wedding?" There were two cakes on order, both of them with elaborate descriptions, as well as four dozen petit fours.

She shrugged. "I hope not. There's only one unmarried Vincent of age."

The pulse in my neck quickened, the sudden lump in my throat an unnecessary evil. Max Vinent. Heathcliff.

"He's overseas, isn't he?" I asked nonchalantly.

In the past five years, even on visits home, I'd always managed to miss seeing Heathcliff. He was never home when I was, his time in the military keeping him either deployed or working. I'd always made it a point to visit the Vincents, especially Mams, who after all these years was still alive. Somehow, she'd managed to fight the odds, but her time was drawing near, the last few months since my return from France revealing an aged woman whose memory was sketchy at best, her skin more yellow than peach.

The old woman had become an ally over the years, her stoic determination and firm love something I'd come to depend on, and the idea of losing her hurt me almost as much as it did the Vincents. It didn't help that, along with Mams' illness, they all missed Heathcliff. I didn't like to admit it, but I did, too.

It wasn't as if I hadn't dated after Max. I'd been in two relationships the past few years, one in college and the other in France. The longest one had lasted eight months, but there'd always been something missing. Life did that, I guess. Romance born out of hardship and grief was often harder to overcome than romance built out of a shallow need not to be alone.

"He was discharged a year ago, Hawthorne. He's been stateside since then. Quit beating around the bush and just say what you feel. We've been friends long enough for that. Besides, I know you go out to that wretched building in the woods every time you visit his family," Rebecca said, her voice muffled as she popped a newly decorated bonbon into her mouth.

"Those are for the Travis baby shower," I mumbled, my gaze darting to hers. "And I don't go out to that old building."

Rebecca stole another bonbon. "Keep telling yourself that, but the only one you're lying to is yourself. Next you're going to tell me the old pair of sneakers in your bedroom closet isn't his. Though why the hell you'd want to keep a pair of worn tennis shoes is beyond me."

Rolling out fondant icing, I stole a glance at the sticky note. "The shoes remind me to keep trying."

She swallowed the chocolate. "Well, I don't know about you, but I'm pretty curious about what the Vincents have planned, so call them! That's why I invested in this business. I'm nosy, and I'm not afraid to admit it."

I smiled. "It had absolutely nothing to do with the food."

She winked. "Don't tell me France made you sassy."

My snort was answer enough. In many ways, I'd changed. I'd gotten bolder, less shy, and more direct. My wild hair was tamed more often than not, my clothes no

longer my uncle's button-up shirts and
sturdy jeans. My style was a casual one;
loose knit dresses, belted tunics or a blazer
over tanks and jeans. It suited my short
stature. I had a professor in college to thank
for the change, her voice stern when she told
me, "Just because you work in a kitchen
doesn't mean you have to dress like you
never left the house. People don't like to buy
food from trolls."

It had been a rather harsh comment
looking back, but she'd had a kind gaze and
a critical eye, her intentions good. She'd not
been talking about me, she'd been talking
about my attire. Rebecca had been right all
those years before in high school when
she'd told me that if I wanted to be a
business woman, I needed to dress like one.
In truth, I still preferred my uncle's old
shirts, but I kept those for days off. I even
had a few of Heathcliff's he'd left behind
when we'd been together. Those I slept in
occasionally.

Rebecca grabbed her car keys, throwing
me a final glance before heading for the
door. "I'll go get a few things we're out of.
There's a supply order being delivered

today, too. Call the Vincents. I want lots of details when I get back." Smiling, she added, "Don't forget, you've got to make two extra bonbons."

My chuckle followed her out. What she didn't know was that I always made extra because I knew she'd steal them.

Chapter 22

My call to the Vincents was answered on the first ring, a male voice coming across the line, and I froze, the familiar sound crashing over me. It threw me into a whirlwind of emotions and feelings I'd thought I'd learned to let go of.

"Hey, is anyone there?" Heathcliff asked.

Swallowing hard, I inhaled, my voice calm when I inquired, "Is Lynn available?"

There was a pause on the other line. It's weird. The entire time I'd been with Heathcliff, I'd never spoken with him on the phone. Honestly, I'd rarely used the phone. Now, I didn't just have a landline for the business but a cell phone for personal calls. Wonder of wonders, I even texted.

After a moment, I heard, "Hawthorne?"

My hand gripped the receiver. "Yeah … how are you?"

There were so many things I wanted to say, so many things I wanted to ask. When had he gotten back? Did he find what he was looking for? Was he happy?

I could hear him breathing, voices rising in the background. The Vincent house was never empty.

"I'm good," he finally answered, "but you called to talk to Mom, right? Hold on just a sec."

There was static as he pulled the phone away, his voice muffled when he shouted for his mother. There was a distant reply, running feet, and then an out of breath, "Hello?"

"Mrs. Vincent?" I chuckled, "Not chasing grandkids, are you?"

My question was met with a laugh. "Lawd, one of these days, they're going to be the death of me, Hawthorne. I'm guessing you're calling about the order from this morning?"

"I am. You gave Rebecca a really good idea of what you're looking for, but I can usually get a little more creative if I have an idea what it's for."

She pulled the phone away long enough to chastise a child before returning to the conversation. "It's for Mams. You know her birthday was a few months ago. Ninety-three, can you believe it? Anyway, we didn't really do a big gathering because she was feeling a little down, but …" she paused, her voice lowering, "she doesn't have long. We all know it. The fact she's made it as long as she has, and lived to the age she is now is a miracle. We'd like to have one good, last hurrah with her."

There was silence, and then I asked, "Can I change up what you've asked for? I have something in mind."

"Absolutely, child. I trust you. Honestly, I'm so glad you decided to do this … you know, the catering business and all that. It wouldn't have been the same if you weren't the one doing it. Besides, the closest place other than yours is almost an hour away."

I smiled. "It's good to be home. It's even better to be a part of this town."

Again, there was a momentary silence. "We're proud of you, Hawthorne. Your uncle would have been so very proud."

My eyes burned, my throat closing up, my words coming out deeper when I replied, "Thank you, Mrs. Vincent."

"Lynn," she admonished, "and it's the truth."

A few extra details, the date and time (three days), and a few catered meal ideas, and we hung up, Heathcliff's voice still ringing in my ears. He was home.

Despite the two imminent orders waiting in front of me, I ran up the stairs to my room and pulled open my closet, my gaze falling on the pair of tennis shoes sitting just inside. The marker on the side had faded, the words almost gone, but my mind saw them as clearly as my eyes had seen them five years before. *Keep me.*

Chapter 23

For the next two days, Rebecca and I worked hard in the kitchen, filling orders, making deliveries, and clearing our schedule so that we could spend the day on the Vincent order. It was a last minute party, and I wondered if that meant Heathcliff was leaving again. It didn't matter. It didn't even matter that I'd more than likely have to spend most of the night cooking. I'd do anything for Mams.

"What did you come up with for the cakes?" Rebecca asked.

I grinned, taking the sketch pad in front of me and turning it to face her.

She gasped. "Oh, Hawthorne! Wow! There's a lot of love in that design."

Shrugging, I laid the book back down and returned to mixing ingredients. "It's for Mams."

Rebecca joined me in the kitchen, taking over the mixing while I started on other things, my mind occupied. If I was being honest, I'd spent the past two nights listening for Heathcliff's truck, the loud sound of it coming up the drive. It was insane, really, the idea that he'd even have the desire to come out to the plantation. It was even crazier that he'd come to see me. We'd been together during a time I needed him the most. I'd be forever grateful for that, but that didn't mean he needed me. He'd loved me, I knew that, but love and need are often two very different things.

There was a radio in the kitchen Rebecca had insisted we had to have, and she turned it on, dancing to the music, before bumping me with her hip. "Forget he's here for a moment, Hawthorne. You dated a French man, for God's sake. You're cultured now."

I snorted. "If you think that, you don't know me very well."

She laughed. "True. When you finally get a television in this place, then we'll talk cultured."

I threw her a grin, my head bouncing to the music as we worked, Rebecca's lighthearted attitude contagious.

My gaze flicked to her profile. "Have I told you lately how glad I am you're my friend?"

She glanced at me. "You don't have to."

"Yeah," I said, "I do. You took me under your wings years ago when you didn't have to."

She froze, the music droning on in the background. "You did just as much, Hawthorne. You gave me a place to go, and you didn't ask questions. You just let me stay."

Her words surprised me, and I stared. I guess I'd never thought about our friendship and how it happened. It just had. She'd started coming around, and I'd let her. I'd needed the company, and she'd needed the escape.

"Well, thank you," I said finally.

She winked, her hips moving again. Mine moved with hers, our voices rising with the songs, the sound terrible, but we didn't care. Sometimes you just have to sing and dance, whether you're good at it or not.

My mind drifted back to Heathcliff. It's funny how some memories stay with you. I often found myself wondering if I thought about him so much because he'd been my first love or my first lover. Maybe it was a little bit of both. We'd been different things to each other at the time, a way to move forward in a way that we might not have been able to otherwise.

"You know I saw him this morning at the gas station," Rebecca said suddenly. My head shot up, my gaze meeting hers. "Looks mostly the same, I think," she continued. "He seems taller, if that's even possible, and he's definitely broader. Much, much broader. He was wearing a cut off shirt, and there was a scar on his arm. I only noticed it because he has tattoos now. Two of them."

She paused, and I mumbled, "Really?"

"He asked about you."

I blinked, my heart rate climbing. "That's good."

"He had a woman with him, a long-legged blonde."

"Oh."

Rebecca moaned, throwing her hands up. "One thing that will never change about you, Hawthorne, is your ability to stay level-headed even when I want to see some fire."

"Is that what it is?" I asked, chuckling.

She glared. "Give me some fire!"

I shrugged.

"Okay," she tried again, "you want to know what the two tattoos were?" When I didn't say anything, she answered anyway. "One was a quote. Honest people don't hide their deeds, it said. The other was a camouflage footprint with the words 'keep walking' inscribed beneath it."

My hands stilled, and I froze. One was a quote from *Wuthering Heights*, the other a reference I was beginning to understand all too well.

"He still thinks about you, Hawthorne," Rebecca added.

My heart thudded in my ears. Whenever I thought about Heathcliff, I pictured the boy I knew. I wasn't sure I'd understand or even recognize the man.

"I'm a memory, Becca. Memories live a long time, but they don't necessarily stay a reality."

"Maybe not," she replied. "But those are some awful strong memories you two share."

She was right. They *were* strong memories. Time didn't erase memories. They might fade, but they didn't go away. Time made them stronger. Time made them more cherished. There were so many I cherished. Memories of Uncle Gregor. Memories of Heathcliff.

Memories didn't scare me. Seeing them change did.

I was afraid. I was afraid that I'd see Heathcliff and what he'd become would destroy what I'd made him in my mind.

My fear was the elephant in the room, and no amount of music, laughter, or terrible singing could erase it.

Chapter 24

The day of Mams' party dawned bright and beautiful, the sun shining over dew-covered grass and green foliage. It was August, which meant it was warm now, but it would be stifling later, and I rushed to pack up everything we needed to take to the Vincent's, the air conditioner in the van we used for deliveries on high. It was better to keep the vehicle running than run the risk of the food spoiling.

Rebecca was just as harried as I was, her heels clicking as she rushed back and forth from the kitchen to the van. The party wasn't for another three hours, but there was a lot of setting up to do, food that would need to be heated, cakes that would have to be stacked, and more.

"God, I've never even made love to Max Vincent, and I'm nervous. You must be completely sick to your stomach," Rebecca said as she climbed into the passenger seat.

Climbing into the driver's side, I threw her a look. "Remind me never to drink with you again. I obviously talk too much."

She grinned. "You're also wildly hysterical when you're drunk."

I pulled out of the drive, our voices fading as the road blurred beneath us, the nerves eating away at both of us. At Rebecca, because no matter how many events we catered, she always felt like she had to prove something to herself. Mainly because of her mother who'd considered Rebecca nothing except a way to climb up the pageant circuit. At me, because this was the first time I'd see the entire Vincent family all in one place since graduation five years before.

When their driveway came into view, Rebecca exhaled. "We've got this."

My lips twitched. "Shake it off, Becca."

Pulling in behind a slew of vehicles, I parked, my exhale meeting hers.

"Pot," Rebecca mumbled, "calling the kettle black."

Time often had a way of repeating itself. The first time I'd ever seen Heathcliff was the back of my last period English class.

The first time I saw him following a five year absence was in his driveway in a brand new, black F150 pickup that pulled up behind my catering van.

The first thing I ever noticed about him was his shoes.

The first thing I saw when he climbed from the truck was a pair of work boots. They weren't sneakers like the shoes years before, or the same boots he'd worn while working on the plantation, but they were well used and obviously well taken care of.

On my feet were a pair of braided sandals that matched a simple knee-length sundress, and they were glued to the pavement, as if they were afraid to move.

A shadow fell over me, *his* shadow, but I didn't look past his feet.

"Hawthorne," he said, his voice causing goose bumps.

My eyes traveled up his frame, over work-stained jeans, a plain white T-shirt, and a pair of dog tags around his neck, tucked into the shirt. Tattoos peeked out at me from beneath the sleeves of his tee, the scar Rebecca had noticed long and ugly down his forearm. When I finally made it to his face, I had to fight to keep my eyes even. He didn't look different, he just looked older, his face filled out to match his broad chest and thicker neck, his hair short but a little long in the front, his jaw shadowed with the need to shave. It was his eyes that surprised me. They were darker somehow, filled with mystery.

"Heathcliff," I replied, wincing when I realized my mistake.

"Heathcliff?" a female voice asked. A laugh followed, and my gaze slid to a blonde-haired woman, her legs long, a pant suit hugging her frame. She wore sunglasses over her eyes, and they threw my reflection back at me as she stepped next to Heathcliff.

"It's an old mistake," I replied.

Rebecca joined me, her brows raised, her height accentuated by her heels. She pulled herself up to full length, using every bit of her mother's pageant instructions in her favor. It put her eye-to-eye with the blonde.

"It's good to see you again," Rebecca said, offering her hand. "Can you remind me who you are?"

The woman's lips twitched. "I'm Max's girlfriend."

"Ex," Heathcliff suddenly corrected. "Ex-girlfriend."

"A minute detail," the woman added. "I'm Ginger." She offered me her hand, ignoring Rebecca's. "We haven't met. An old high school friend, maybe."

My hand met her palm, the shake brusque and short. "Something like that," I answered.

Rebecca smiled, although there was no friendliness in the gesture. "How did you two meet, if you don't mind me asking? I'm sort of a nosy rosy. Besides, I love a good love story. I've got two marriages behind me to prove it."

Ginger pulled her sunglasses down to the end of her nose, peering over the rim, before replacing them. "My brother was in Max's unit."

"Was?" I asked, my gaze on Heathcliff's.

His eyes searched mine. "We both got out a year ago when our active term was up."

I started to ask another question, but the words wouldn't come, my gaze falling once more to our feet. They'd moved closer while we talked, and I backed away, putting distance between his boots and my sandals.

"We've got to get this stuff unloaded," Rebecca said.

Her words spurred me into action, my feet taking me away from Heathcliff and Ginger.

"Can I help?" Heathcliff asked as we opened the back of the van.

"No," Rebecca answered. "We've got it."

They left us then, their shadows and shoes carrying them into the house, and I slumped against the van, taking a deep breath before leaning in to grab two of the food trays.

"This is going to be fun," Rebecca mumbled.

"Like a trip to the dentist," I responded.

She chuckled, her arms full. Together, we headed for the door. It was ajar, Heathcliff's mom standing just inside, her gaze settling on my face as we entered. There was something interesting about Lynn's eyes, as if she were trying to speak to me without uttering a word.

"We've pushed tables up against the dining room walls," she said. "We thought it might get too hot outside for Mams."

Smiling, I nodded and brushed past groups of chatting Vincents, most of them calling out to me as we pushed through. Only two strangers mingled among the crowd, a young, blond headed man as tall and as broad as Heathcliff, and Ginger. They mostly kept to themselves, lounging near the walls, Heathcliff among them. It was strange seeing so much distance between Heathcliff and his family, as if his time away had created a barrier between them.

Mams, the guest of honor, sat in a wheelchair, her skin yellowed, but her eyes bright and sharp. It was a good day for her. I could tell by the way her gaze assessed me from across the room, following me as I worked.

"Girl!" she called. "You finish that, and then come talk to me." Her gaze flicked to her grandson and his friends, her eyes narrowing. "I'd like to hear about your time in France."

With a subtle nod, I moved back through the room, to the van in the driveway. It took three trips before we had everything laid out. Once finished, Rebecca took the appetizers to the kitchen to heat while I began setting up the cakes. They were simple cakes, elaborate in detail but not in size. They were homes, two houses, one of them a replica of the Vincent home and barn, the other a reproduction of the hardware store and gas station. I'd added trees to the Vincent home, the small building in the woods visible through the foliage. There were tons of tiny details, some of them barely noticeable, but there. A pair of sneakers rested by the front door, and a splayed deck of poker cards rested on a table in the yard.

Heathcliff's mom stepped toward me, peering down at the cakes as I finished, her eyes softening. "This isn't what I asked for," she said.

"I know—"

"It's better," Lynn interrupted. Her hand found my back, her fingers curling into my dress. "I can almost see Mams outside, her hands on her hips, calling out to Paps. Trying to get him back to house for supper from the hooch." She glanced at me. "This is incredible, Hawthorne. Thank you."

"Girl!" Mams cried. Lynn's brows rose, and we both laughed, my gaze going to the old woman's wheelchair. "If you're done, you can come sit with me now!"

Lynn released me, and I pushed my way across the room to Mams' wheelchair. She patted the floor next to her, and I pulled my dress out, arranging it so that I could sit down as delicately as possible.

"I haven't sat like this in years," I told Mams.

I was grossly aware of Heathcliff, his friend, and his ex-girlfriend behind us, their voices hushed. Mams seemed deeply satisfied with her proximity to her grandson despite his obvious need to remain aloof.

"You're lookin' well, girl," she said.

"No different than when you saw me a few weeks ago," I replied.

She grinned, her skin crinkling. "I forgot how that college education gave you a sharper mouth. I like it. Reminds me of me when I was your age."

I laughed. "My tongue is nothing compared to Rebecca's."

She leaned over the side of her chair. "No, yours is just enough, girl. Always remember that. A tongue should be sharp, but it should also know when to grow dull."

I stared up at her. "Someone should write down all those tidbits of wisdom you're always sprouting."

She patted the arm of her chair. "You've made an old woman proud, Hawthorne. I just wanted you to know that in case my mind goes to wanderin', and I can't recall enough to remember to say it."

I'm not sure what made me touch Mams. In all the years I'd known her, I'd never attempted it. Even as wise as she was, she'd never been a duly affectionate woman, but my hand was suddenly over hers on the chair, my gaze coming up to meet her equally shocked stare.

"Say hello to Uncle Gregor for me," I said.

Mams' eyes grew bright. "I'm lookin' forward to seein' that man. You've been through a lot when you were young, girl. I think it's prepared you more for adulthood than those who never went through anythin'. Lean on that."

She leaned even closer, and I moved to meet her.

"Save him," Mams' whispered. "We're going to lose him if you don't."

She sat back, and I stared at her. I didn't have to glance behind me to know who she was talking about.

"How?" I asked.

She smiled. "You'll know."

Heathcliff's dad shouted from the front of the room, and a cheer rose up, claps and celebratory hollers rolling through the space as everyone turned toward Mams. I chose that moment to sneak away, rising slowly and edging along the wall. For the first time in a long time, even as alone as I was in life, I realized how much I was loved. None of the people who cared about me were family, but somehow that made it more special.

My voice rose with the crowd, my laughter joining theirs even as I moved away to stand with Rebecca. Rebecca's hand fell, grasping mine and squeezing before letting go.

There's love, and then there's love. There's the *passionate* kind of love between two people who care about each other, and then there's the *care about you* kind of love. The first kind takes you on an incredible ride, but the second kind is often stronger and harder to break.

Chapter 25

The party was never-ending, the family determined to stay as long as they possibly could, as if leaving meant the end of all of them together with Mams. I knew that feeling. I'd lived that feeling.

When the sun started to set, Rebecca and I began cleaning up despite the milling family. We left the food, wrapped in tinfoil or boxes to be put away, and took our trays and other supplies out to the van. I'd made my last trip to the vehicle when I noticed Heathcliff standing in the backyard, his gaze on the sky. Fireflies were just beginning to light up, the first few stars noticeable in that strange blue heaven, the kind of blue that couldn't decide which shade it wanted to be.

Throwing a quick glance at the house, I turned toward the yard, my stomach dropping with each step forward, my cowardice a monster waiting to swallow me whole.

"Not thinking about jumping into hay, are you?" I teased as I approached.

Startled, Heathcliff's head dropped, his gaze finding my figure. "What?"

I gestured at the barn. "Just thinking about the loft when we were in high school," I replied.

"Oh," he answered, his head rising again. "Seems kind of silly now, doesn't it?"

His words struck me like an arrow, causing my heart to bleed, and I froze. "I don't think so. Everyone's got to learn how to fall somewhere. That way when they have to get back up, they already know how it feels to land."

Heathcliff inhaled, his Adam's apple bobbing as he swallowed. "It was good seeing you today, Hawthorne." His gaze dropped, and I studied his face.

"What happened to you?" I asked, the words slipping out before I could catch them. My words had always done that around Heathcliff. "The man I saw in there today isn't the one I knew years ago."

"It's only been five years," he mumbled.

"I'm looking at you, and I see more than five years etched into your skin."

He didn't expect my reply, his gaze capturing mine despite the encroaching darkness. "You always did see things other people missed."

I glanced at the house. "No one is missing this, Heathcliff. I've seen your mother's eyes, and I've heard the fear in your grandmother's voice. What happened to you?"

He laughed, the sound short. "Heathcliff …"

My cheeks flushed. "I'm sorry … Max."

He took a step toward me. "No, don't apologize. It's okay … call me Heathcliff."

Fear made me want to leave him alone in the darkness, but my memories of the boy I'd been in love with, the one I still loved, moved me forward. "Your family has always meant so much to you," I said. "What's with the distance?"

He stared at me, silence stretching, before he replied, "I wish I'd never left. I know now why my grandfather loved his hooch in the woods. It was the only place he could go that helped him live with his ghosts."

I thought back on the past few years, the pictures Lynn had shown me of Heathcliff in his boot camp graduation photo. I thought back on the tears when Mams told me about his deployments. Honestly, I didn't know where he'd been, how long he'd been there, or what he'd seen, but I knew him. Or I thought I did. Mams had said I'd know how to help him, and in a way, maybe she was right.

"That's the thing with saving people," I told him, stepping forward so that I was next to him, my gaze following his to the sky. "Sometimes you lose some of them."

"Too many of them," Heathcliff muttered.

I was so afraid I was going to say the wrong thing, that I was going to chase him away, but it seemed even more wrong to walk away.

"It matters if you tried, and I know you. I have no doubt you tried, or it wouldn't be eating at you now."

"Hawthorne—"

"Nothing is forever, you know. I don't know what you've seen. I don't know how horrific it was, but I do know something about carrying someone you love around with you. I know what loss is, and what it means to carry those ghosts with you."

"Hawthorne—" Heathcliff began again, but I wouldn't let him finish.

"I found my parents," I told him. "I did. Two years ago. On a break from school, I got curious and did a little digging. My mom is on her fifth marriage, living somewhere in Florida. My dad is dead." Heathcliff's head dropped. I could feel his gaze on my face, but I kept my eyes on the sky. "Drug overdose, the papers said. It happened ten years ago, so I'm assuming Uncle Gregor knew, but like you, he always wanted to save people. He wanted to save them from harsh realities. You know, harsh realities aren't so bad though. Not when you know who you are. Because the key to climbing out of that harshness is knowing the person that climbs free of it; yourself."

"Hawthorne," Heathcliff began. This time I didn't stop him, and I was glad I didn't. "I've missed you."

A door opened behind us, Ginger's laughter following her as she stumbled outside. "It's a party, Brayden. You should really try smiling."

I assumed Brayden was Heathcliff's friend and Ginger's brother, their approaching steps cutting off our conversation.

"Oh, there you are, Max! We've been looking for you," Ginger called.

My head lowered, my gaze swinging to the intruders. Ginger's smile fell when she saw me, but Brayden's eyes filled with curiosity, his gaze flicking from Heathcliff to me.

"Did you ever say your name earlier?" Ginger asked, her eyes on my face, her lips turned down in a frown.

"Hawthorne," I answered, nodding. "Most people just call me Hawthorne."

Another voice rose from the darkness, Rebecca's, and I called out to her, relieved when she stepped into the dim yard behind Brayden and Ginger.

"Are you ready?" she asked me, her suspicious gaze roaming over the siblings before moving to Heathcliff and then me.

I started to leave, my feet moving cautiously backward when I suddenly paused, my gaze going once more to Heathcliff. "By the way, whatever happened to your Toyota?"

He looked at me. "My old pickup? It's parked at my brother's house. Why?"

The smile I gave him was a soft one. "I miss the wind."

With that, I turned and walked away, my hand grabbing Rebecca's arm. She was staring at Heathcliff's friend, and I knew by the way her face was angled, she was looking at the tight shirt he wore over his stomach.

"Don't look at the abs," I hissed. "Just walk away."

Turning, her feet joined mine on our trek to the catering van.

"They're nice abs," Rebecca hissed in return.

"Two divorces," I murmured.

"Damn," she replied. "Throw the bucket of cold water, why don't you?"

We climbed into the vehicle, and as I was backing out of the drive, I rolled down the windows. Somewhere in the darkness, I knew Heathcliff watched, and I wanted him to see them down.

Sometimes starting over starts with a drive.

Chapter 26

I'd taken to running when I was in college, not because I thought I needed the exercise, but because I had a desire to feel the breeze in my face, my body tiring, exorcising things that wouldn't go away otherwise. It was a good way to take off the stress, to strip away a bad exam grade, bad news, or disappointment.

The day after seeing Heathcliff, I ran, letting my feet eat the miles beneath me, my breath coming in pants. Breathe in through the nose and out through the mouth. The run stripped me bare, my thoughts playing over the conversation I'd had with Heathcliff in the yard, the morning humidity causing sweat to seep down my forehead and over my face, like tears.

My feet always sought the back roads, running them until I knew I couldn't go any farther, and then, unlike most runners, I'd walk back, having pushed myself too far to begin with. I kind of saw life that way, I guess. Run, push yourself, but then walk.

Take the time to notice the stuff you missed your first time through.

I was passing the creek, the proverbial summer hang out, when I heard the laughter. Stopping, I leaned over, my hands finding my knees, my chest heaving. The laughter grew and with it so did my curiosity.

Turning down the lane, I snuck among the trees, my feet quiet on the grass as I moved. The sound of rushing water met my ears.

"What's with this place, Max?" Ginger's voice asked.

I froze, my blood running cold at the sound of her voice, at the way she said his name. It shouldn't bother me, but it did.

"I don't know," another voice broke in, a male one, and somehow I knew it was Brayden's. "There's a certain kind of charm in it."

"It's not Hell," Heathcliff answered.

Brayden's short laugh met his words. "You've got that right, brother."

Ginger groaned. "I hate it when the two of you do that! Talk like there's no one else there, like I'm supposed to understand exactly what you mean."

"You didn't have to come with me, Gin," Brayden replied.

His sister snorted. "You know I did."

There was something sad about her voice that touched my heart, a worry for her brother that made my dislike for her lessen. Tone of voice can reveal a lot about a person. Hers told me more than I wanted to admit. She loved her brother, but by the looks she'd thrown Heathcliff at Mams' party, she also loved him. She loved him, and she'd been a part of his life during a time when I couldn't be there.

I'd reached the edge of the trees, my palm resting against the bark on one of the wider trunks. Beyond, sand sparkled in the sun, the muddy water rushing over sandbags and logs, the area around the creek having been cleared by the Parkers, who owned the property, so that the locals could enjoy the swimming.

On the bank Ginger sat, her feet dangling in the water, wearing only a black bikini top and a pair of short blue jean shorts.

"It feels like hell here," she grumbled, her hand fanning her face.

Heathcliff stood behind her, leaning against the tailgate of his black F150. It was down, an ice chest pulled to the edge. Brayden sat beside the cooler. Both of the men were wearing nothing except blue jeans, a longneck bottle in their hands.

My gaze went instantly to Heathcliff, my eyes widening. The tattoos on his arms were just the beginning, the scar on his forearm one of three. A line of scar tissue slashed his stomach just above his belly button, a smaller one starting near his hip and disappearing into his jeans. A tattoo was etched into one side his chest, a coil of thorns surrounding the words, *Be Brave.*

Brayden, who had his own fair share of scars, lifted the beer he held. "It's a quiet place. I don't know why you'd want to leave, Max."

"Because there's nothing to do here," Ginger complained.

Heathcliff smiled, his gaze on the rushing water. "More than you think."

There was silence, the only sound water, wind, and buzzing insects. I'd just begun to inch back into the trees when I heard Brayden ask, "So, what's with the girl at the party last night. Hawthorne, wasn't it?"

"Back off, Brayden," Heathcliff warned.

"Oh, ho!" his friend exclaimed. "There's history there. I knew it." Opening the cooler, he grabbed another beer, and opened it on the side of the truck. "Old girlfriend?"

"She seemed a little odd to me," Ginger mumbled. "And that hair. It's like she's never heard of a straightener."

"That's jealousy talking, Gin," Heathcliff admonished. "Watch it, okay? You're better than that, and you don't know her history."

Ginger fell quiet, her brows furrowing. "I'm thinking Brayden's right. You played a big part in that history, didn't you?"

"Yeah," Heathcliff answered, no apology in his voice. "I did."

My curiosity wanted to stay, but my heart couldn't handle where the conversation was going, so I edged backward. I was back on the road, my gaze on the path ahead of me, when I heard the truck start up, and I bristled. No matter how fast I ran, they were going to pass me as they left. Even so, my sneakers pounded the dirt, moving quicker than they'd ever moved. Sweat rolled down my back and into the loose white tank top I wore over a blue bandeau. My gray cutoff shorts were cotton and short, not the typical running shorts, but they kept me cool.

Behind me, a truck revved, pulling out into the road from the creek path. My shoes kept moving, the sound of the engine at my back growing louder. I stayed to the side of the road, wincing when I realized the pickup was slowing.

"Hawthorne?" Heathcliff called.

I fell into a walk, my breathing labored as he pulled up alongside me.

"Figures," I heard Ginger hiss.

"It's a small town after all," Brayden teased.

Glancing askew at the truck, I threw them a small wave, and then started to jog again. The pickup kept following, the truck so close they might as well have been running with me.

"When did you start running?" Heathcliff asked.

On an exhale, I answered, "Two years ago."

It was getting embarrassing jogging while they followed, my tank top soaked with sweat, my face red from the heat, and I slowed to a walk before stopping completely. The truck stopped with me.

"I'm okay," I said. "You don't have to follow me."

Heathcliff stared, his gaze falling to my legs, to the muscles I'd earned there over the past couple of years. "What made you start running?"

"What does it matter?" Ginger breathed from the back seat. I don't think she knew I could hear her, but with the windows down and the wind blowing, it was hard to miss.

I shrugged. "I don't know. I got talked into it by a friend and discovered I really liked it. He talked me into a few 5K's after that, and it's sort of become a side hobby I guess."

"He?" Heathcliff asked.

If my cheeks weren't already flushed, I would have blushed, and for the first time, I appreciated the heat. Motioning at the road, I took a step back. "Actually, I think I'm going to turn around now. I've got some work I need to do."

Heathcliff patted the side of his truck. "Need a ride?"

"No," I hastened to say, clearing my throat when I realized how harsh it came out. "My favorite part is the walk back."

Next to Heathcliff, Brayden leaned forward in the passenger seat. "Walk back? You don't run both ways? Why?"

My gaze met Heathcliff's friend, noting the genuine curiosity there, and I shrugged again. "I like running because it lets everything go. I like walking back because it reminds me why I ran in the first place." My feet backed up on the road, throwing up red dirt. "Thanks for the offer, but I'd best be going now."

Turning, I walked away, my breathing slower but my pulse quick. Every step I took felt weighted, dragged down by the gazes I knew followed me.

"Come on," I heard Ginger call.

Tires crunched over dirt and gravel, driving away from me. Our town was too small, and with Heathcliff in it, it felt like it was choking me. I was trapped between the girl who'd once loved a boy and the woman who wanted to know what he'd become.

I'd run to rid myself of the conversation I'd had with Heathcliff the night before. On the walk back, I kept recalling it, my mind playing the scene at the creek over and over again.

Something told me Heathcliff was leaving again, and I couldn't risk getting close enough to let it hurt. Uncle Gregor was right. I'd learned a lot from my first broken heart. Weirdly, it had even healed me, but something told me the man Heathcliff had become wouldn't be as gentle as the boy he'd left behind.

Chapter 27

Two days passed with no Heathcliff sightings, my work at home filling most of my days and Rebecca's rambling filling the nights. When I'd first moved back, I'd taken to going with her to town in the evenings, helping out with another business venture of hers, a small coffee shop that sold coffee, tea, and books in the morning before crossing over to beer, appetizers, and karaoke at night. It was an artsy kind of place during the day, a college hangout. But at night, the adults ruled, calling out orders to the bartender before belting out old tunes in terrible, slurred voices.

Most of the time, it was half empty, but on weekends, it was full. It was also my second job. When catering was slow and there were no orders coming in, I worked at *Caffeine's*—I'd had no say in the name— using the money I earned for the plantation's upkeep. I stayed in the kitchen, away from the crowds, cooking whatever order came in, mostly loaded nachos and potato skins with the occasional stuffed mushrooms or pepper wraps. It wasn't an ideal job, but the people were nice. Rebecca had a knack for hiring folks who were down on their luck, giving them a place to stay until things got better.

Kathy was one of those people. She was a merry soul, an older woman with a shock of white hair and thick, large glasses. She'd lost her home to a fire, and with her husband gone and no children, she'd needed the job to pay the rent on a small house on the edge of town. She was a good cook in her own right, and a quick waitress. She also did mean karaoke.

Jerry was the bartender. He was just as merry as Kathy, but his friendly nature was often lost in his massive, bull-like appearance. Bald and thick, he had a constant grimace on his face that didn't welcome conversation, but if you attempted talking to him, it became quickly apparent that his nature opposed his looks. He was terrible at karaoke but could make some mean mixed drinks and was a natural with darts.

I simply made appetizers.

It was at *Caffeine's* that my non-Heathcliff luck ran out. Strange, really. In high school, it was Sylvia Plath who did me in. Now, after a college education that I was still paying for, it was karaoke and whiskey.

On Friday night, two days after the morning run that brought me to the creek, the door to *Caffeine's* opened, bringing in Ginger's loud laughter and Heathcliff's brother's answering, "I told you we had places here other than the creek."

Heathcliff followed, his gaze roaming the room. It was an hour till closing, well past midnight, and the place was mostly empty.

"This is new," Heathcliff said.

Brayden squeezed in behind him. "I'm still laughing at the name."

Chris, Heathcliff's older brother, grinned. "Rebecca Martin runs it. It does pretty well here. Especially during the winter when no one wants to circle the trucks down at the creek, even with the bonfires."

From my place in the kitchen, I heard their voices and my back bristled with awareness. Kathy, who'd been pulling a batch of jalapeno poppers from the grease, glanced at me.

"You okay, honey?"

Nodding, I left the stove, marching to the kitchen door where Rebecca stood, her eyes narrowed on the room beyond.

"*Caffeine's* is a good name," she hissed at me.

I ignored her. "I think I'm pretty much through for the night. If you don't mind, I'm sneaking out the back."

She threw me a look. "Coward."

"You betcha," I replied.

Beyond the door, Heathcliff ordered a beer, Brayden ordered a whiskey, and Ginger asked for a Bloody Mary. Chris searched the café, his eyes honing in on the kitchen door. A bad feeling settled in my gut.

"Hey, Jerry, is Rebecca or Hawthorne here tonight? I have something from Mams I was supposed to deliver to the plantation, and it'll save me the trip."

Jerry threw a towel over his shoulder. "Is this something for Rebecca or Hawthorne?"

"Hawthorne," Chris answered, "but I'm sure Rebecca could deliver it, too."

"I'm out," I hissed in Rebecca's ear.

"Something from Mams?" Heathcliff asked suddenly. "I just saw her this morning. Why didn't she say anything?"

There was a pause followed by Chris' uncertain reply. "Because she wasn't sure you'd be okay with it."

Heathcliff grunted. "I'll take it to the plantation."

Rebecca's fingers curled in my shirt. "You're back in, missy. Unless you want lover boy out at your place."

"It's not the plantation she thought you'd have trouble with," Chris' voice broke in. "It's what she wanted delivered."

The silence that followed was full of tension, Rebecca's gaze flying to my face. Curiosity was a living, breathing being for Rebecca, her nosy nature a naughty child I'd never be rid of.

Jerry's loud bellow broke the tension, his barked, "Hawthorne!" filling the café's interior.

Blowing my cheeks out, I swore under my breath, counting to three in my head before pushing the kitchen door open. Rebecca followed, her curiosity like a fire against my back. At the bar, Heathcliff's head shot up, his gaze passing from his brother to me.

Chris ignored him, a smile transforming his features. He was as thin and tall as he'd been when we were in high school, his goatee a blemish on his chin.

"Hey, Hawthorne, I've got something for you." Reaching into his pocket, he pulled out an envelope and offered it to me.

I stared at it as if it were a snake ready to strike. Mams didn't give me things. Unless you counted the money she'd collected to help with college.

Rebecca stood over my shoulder. "What is it?" she asked.

Accepting the envelope, I glanced at Chris, my gaze troubled. "Thank you."

Rebecca bumped me with her hip. "You don't want to know what's in there?"

My fingers tightened on the paper. "Not here."

"It's okay," Chris said suddenly, causing everyone to freeze. There was something about the way he looked at me that caught me off guard. "You can open it now."

By the way Rebecca tensed, it was taking everything she had not to squeal.

"I don't know," I said slowly. "I'm not sure—"

"Just open it, Hawthorne," Heathcliff suddenly interrupted, his voice full of irritation.

My startled gaze shot to his, a blush blooming across my cheeks. Without another word, I lifted the envelope and ripped over the top. There was something heavy resting within, and I turned it over. A key fell into my palm.

I knew even before I heard the café's door slamming behind Heathcliff's retreating back what the key belonged to.

I'd visited the hooch in the woods quite a few times since returning home, but I'd been unable to enter it, the padlock impenetrable.

Now, I held the key.

Chapter 28

Like the day Heathcliff followed me home from school, I chased him out of the café. He was climbing into his new truck, a scowl on his face, and I ran to the passenger side, my fingers gripping the handle before he could lock it.

"Wait," I called.

Pulling open the door, I stared into the cab, my gaze finding Heathcliff's, his scowl deepened by an overhanging street light.

"I don't want it," I told him, holding out the key. "I don't even know why she'd want me to have it."

Heathcliff's hands gripped the steering wheel, his jaw tense as he gazed out the front windshield. "Don't you?" he asked.

My eyes fell to the truck's leather interior. It still had that new car smell. "Stop," I breathed. "Just stop." My gaze lifted to find Heathcliff's startled eyes staring back at me. "I'm not here to mess your life up. All I did was come home." Climbing up into the truck, I placed the key Mams had given me in his cup holder.

"This," I pointed at the two of us, "isn't up to them. If you want me to be a part of your life, you'll invite me in."

I started to retreat, my descent stopped suddenly by Heathcliff's fingers around my wrist. "Hawthorne …" He glanced out the window again, his jaw tensing and relaxing before tugging on my arm. "Take a ride with me."

It wasn't a question, but it wasn't a demand either. It was an invitation. I should have walked away. I should have said no, but I didn't.

Instead, I glanced at *Caffeine's*. "Your friends?"

"They can ride with Chris. He's parked on the side."

My gaze searched Heathcliff's face, the turmoil there hurting me more than I wanted to admit. There'd been a lot of things between Heathcliff and me in the past, but turmoil wasn't one of them.

My decision made, I settled into the passenger seat and slammed the door behind me, pulling the seatbelt across my chest.

Heathcliff started the truck, his arm going to the back of my seat as he backed out of the parking lot. The proximity filled my body with heat, and I fought not to squirm.

Darkness sped past the window, trees becoming headlight-induced ghosts that sneered at me as Heathcliff drove. Headlights from other vehicles stared at me like angry monsters warning me to turn back.

"Where are you taking me?" I asked.

The surroundings were familiar, and yet they weren't. We passed the city limit sign, driving until we entered the next county.

"Are you scared?" Heathcliff shot back.

My fingers found the door, and I gripped it, my doubts growing with each mile. Lights sparkled as Heathcliff took the exit to the town next to ours. It was bigger than our town, with a shopping mall, restaurants, and entertaining venues that weren't available in our community.

The pickup pulled into a hotel parking lot. It was a nice hotel, the nicest one near our hometown, and I glanced at Heathcliff.

Putting the truck in park, he pulled the keys out of the ignition.

"I've got a room here," he explained.

"What are you saying?"

His gaze rose, meeting mine. "Let's be honest. There isn't a place back home where we don't share some kind of connection." Snatching the key from the cup holder, he waved it around, before throwing it back down. "My family isn't known for its subtlety."

My gaze slid to the hotel, to the lighted lobby just beyond the door. "So, you're bringing me here because no one would expect it?"

He laughed, the sound short. "No, I brought you here because *here* I don't know you."

His words caught me off guard, and I stared at him. "Don't know me?"

"Back home, I know Hawthorne. I know the troubled young girl I met in high school. Her shadow is everywhere, her ghost chasing me from my house to the hooch to the creek. Here, that girl is gone. It's just you and me. You're not that Hawthorne any more, and I'm certainly not that boy. Here, there are no memories, no shadows of what we left behind."

For a long moment, I sat there, my gaze traveling to his side view mirror, my reflection gazing back at me. He was right. I wasn't that girl any more, and he wasn't that boy. We didn't know these new people. We didn't even know if we'd like them.

My hand fell to the door handle. "Show me your room."

Jumping free of the truck, Heathcliff rounded the cab, pulled open my door, and offered me his hand. My fingers met his palm, and for the first time since laying eyes on him, it felt like being with the old Heathcliff.

In silence, we walked through the lobby and into the elevators, the doors closing behind us. Heathcliff pressed the button to the fifth floor, the metal throwing back our distorted reflections as we rode upward, my stomach dropping with each new number.

The door dinged open, and Heathcliff stepped free of the elevator, his hand on the frame to keep it from closing.

"You don't have to come, Hawthorne," he said.

Again, I caught a glimpse of the old
Heathcliff, and it was the vulnerability in his
eyes that pushed me forward.

"I think … I think I need to," I
responded.

My gaze dropped to the floor, my eyes
following his feet as we walked. Shoes.
They told a lot about a person, and
Heathcliff's shoes, while different from the
ones he'd worn in high school, represented
him well. Worn, well used, and repaired.

His boots paused in front of a door, his
hand sinking into his back pocket to pull out
a key card. One swipe, and we were inside.
The room was a big one, a king-sized bed in
the middle of the space surrounded by a
desk, a flat screen TV, and two chairs
flanking a table. A suitcase sat at the end of
the bed, unzipped but closed. It was a neat
room, nothing out of place.

Throwing his key card onto the table,
Heathcliff turned to face me, his hands out
to the side. "This is Max Vincent. A lot of
hotel rooms, and a million demons."

Shifting awkwardly, I forced myself to
meet his gaze. "I vaguely remember a guy

who enjoyed creating things, who spent his life making people happy."

He snorted. "Now I just kill them."

"I beat you to that one, Heathcliff," I breathed. "You're not going to find pity here. Sympathy maybe, but not pity. There hasn't been a person who's entered my life who hasn't either left or passed away, and yet I wouldn't want it any different. Because each person who came into my world changed it."

My gaze dropped to Heathcliff's T-shirt. "Take it off," I ordered.

His hands fell to the hem, his eyes meeting mine. "Déjà vu, Hawthorne. We've done this before."

I threw him a look. "Not this we haven't."

Gripping the hem of his shirt, he pulled it over his head, and threw it onto the floor. I stepped forward, my gaze on the scars and tattoos marring his flesh.

"It's like road a map," I murmured, my arm rising, my finger dragging down the scar on his forearm.

Heathcliff answered my silent question. "Knife wound." My fingers dropped farther to the raised scar tissue on his stomach. "Stupidity," he murmured. "A welding lesson learned." Finally, my fingers dropped to his hip. "Shrapnel. I was lucky. I was far enough away, I only walked away with a mark."

"Be brave," I whispered, my fingers leaving his scars to brush the thorns tattooed on his chest.

Heathcliff's hand came up to cover mine. "I've lost some of my patience over the last few years. I appreciate the curiosity, but …" His words trailed off, fire burning in his gaze.

I pulled away from him, taking several steps back. "You're not that different, you know. Just … dirtier. Like a truck that's been rode too hard in the mud."

Heathcliff's brows arched. "Dirtier? Rode too hard? Honey, you need some better adjectives."

I fought not to smile and lost the battle. "I was trying to be serious."

His expression fell, his gaze roaming my face. "My family talks. A lot. I heard about your four years of college. Your year in France. Why come back? All that education. You're good at what you do."

"Because," I told him, "my heart was here. No matter how far I went or what I did, I couldn't escape this place."

He shook his head. "So you'd rather be catering birthday parties and making greasy appetizers than working in a five star restaurant somewhere?"

I smiled. "Yeah … yeah, I guess I would." Taking a cautious step forward, I asked, "And you? I always thought you'd do something with machinery."

He shrugged. "I do now. I specialized in it in the military, and then got a job in New York soon after discharge."

I was wearing a tank top over shorts, and my fingers fell to the belt loops of my cutoff jeans. "Is that where … is that where Ginger and Brayden are from?"

"Upstate, yeah. Not the city." His gaze dropped to my hands, to the way my fingers fidgeted with the shorts. "I wasn't with Ginger long. I wouldn't even call it a relationship. I'm not good at those."

"You used to be," I blurted, my eyes dropping to the floor to hide the appalled expression in my eyes.

Heathcliff's shoes came into view, stopping just short of mine. "You really think that, don't you?" he asked. "Honey, I was never good at relationships. That was you."

Startled, my head shot up. "What?"

His lips quirked. "Hawthorne, other than short relationships and a few experimental rolls in the hay in high school, I didn't date long. Mostly because they all knew I was leaving. Then you came along. At first, you intrigued me, but then you sort of … kept me. You do that with people."

My eyes widened. "No," I whispered. "No, I don't."

"Yeah," he responded. "Yeah, you do." He closed the distance between us, his face peering down into mine. "Forget your parents. Forget about your uncle's illness for a moment. Those are things that happened, things you couldn't control. Think about afterwards. Think about all of the people who haven't been able to let you go."

I stared at him, my lips parted, my forehead creased. "No—"

"Remember that paper you wrote for us in high school? It was a beautiful paper, by the way, but it was wrong. You taught yourself to trust again. You opened up the lines of communication with your uncle. I just got lucky enough to be brought along for the ride." He leaned forward, his face growing closer to mine. "I do like to help things, but you're the one who saves them." He laughed. "You think I don't know what my grandmother has told you? She asked you to save me because, deep down, she knows I've always needed it. It wasn't you that was lost. It's always been me."

"I don't understand—"

Heathcliff's hand came up to cup my cheek. "Did you know I was a twin?" I gasped, and Heathcliff smiled. "It's tragic, but not as tragic as you're probably thinking. At birth, one of us came out screaming, and the other came out stillborn." He shrugged. "It's funny, you know. I never got to meet my brother, but I always felt like I had to live two lives. It didn't help that I never seemed to fit in with the men in my family. I didn't want to run a store and sit around whittling on wood. I would have done it though … if it hadn't been for you."

"What?" I pulled away from him, backing up until I was against the wall next to the door. My eyes fell to his chest. "So I'm responsible for all of your scars?"

He stared at me. "No, those are all mine. Again, that was my mistake. I wanted to be a part of my family somehow. Following in my grandfather's footsteps seemed like the way to go." He gestured at me. "What you did was encourage me to be different, to embrace the desire to leave, to do other things. Even with the scars, I don't regret going. I regret not being able to do more for the men I spent time with overseas. I regret not being strong enough to go straight to college. I regret not being … not being better at relationships."

My hands flattened against the wall behind me, grounding me. "I didn't expect anything from you."

The smile he gave me was genuine. "I know. You were the first one who didn't." He stared at me. "How many have you been with since me?" he asked suddenly, his hand coming up to rub his forehead. "I keep trying to tell myself I don't care …"

I watched his face, watched the war of emotions dancing across his features, and I swallowed hard. "I've been in two relationships since high school, but I only slept with one of them."

Heathcliff frowned. "Was he good to you?"

"Yeah." I smiled. "He was a nice guy. The problem wasn't either of them. It was me. It's kind of hard being with someone when you keep wishing they were someone else."

Heathcliff stepped forward, but I pressed myself into the wall as if it would protect me somehow from him and from me. "You're leaving, right?" I asked.

He stopped. "I don't know."

My gaze searched his. "It's okay not to know, and I'd never expect you to stay. But, Heathcliff … I'm not sure I want to go back to that … to what we were before."

"I don't want to go back," he replied.

I knew by the look in his eyes what he meant. We'd both changed. A lot can happen in five years. We weren't the teenagers we'd once been, and yet we were. They were still there, buried deep.

"I want to show you something," Heathcliff said. Walking to the bed, he kicked open the top of his suitcase and leaned over, his hand digging in a side pocket. When he stood, he cradled a book. Even with the cover torn, repaired with tape, and marred by the elements, I knew what it was.

"*Wuthering Heights*," I breathed. "My book."

He opened the cover, revealing a folded piece of paper. I knew without looking that it was the paper I'd written in high school.

"Why?" I asked. "Why did you keep them?"

"It's funny," he laughed, "but I kept them for the same you reason you run, the same reason you walk back when you're done. When things seem to be moving too fast, I pull them out to remind me why I keep moving forward."

Dropping the book, he stalked me, his body looming over mine, his palms against the wall flanking my head. His dog tags swung between us. "You grew up good, Hawthorne."

I stared up at him, my chest heaving. "You're still growing, Heathcliff."

He laughed. "Yeah … I am."

"This is going to end," I said.

"No," Heathcliff replied. "I don't think it ever really will."

Chapter 29

My gaze remained riveted to his. "What are you doing?"

One of his hands dropped to my hip, his fingers spanning it. "There was something you said about 'dirty' and 'rode too hard' earlier."

"Heathcliff—"

His fingers ran up beneath my shirt, brushing my ribs before pausing near my bra. "It was always Max when we made love."

"Max …" I began again.

His hand found the clasp to my bra and undid it. It opened beneath my tank top, and he stared at the way the straps fell down my arms. With one swift movement, he had the tank and the bra on the floor before I even had a chance to inhale.

Leaning forward, his lips found my ear. "We've done this before, Clare. Like a mind meld, remember? The other night in the yard, I told you I wished I'd never left. You want to know why? It wasn't because of the things I've seen or the people I've lost. It's because the thing that's haunted me the most was not staying in touch with you." He nibbled on my earlobe, his breath fanning my neck. "I'm not soft anymore." His hand fell to the front of my shorts, his fingers popping open the button. "You can tell me to stop."

His head lifted, and I gazed at his face, my heart a rapid thud in my chest. "And if I'm afraid to ask you to?"

He froze. "You don't have to fear me."

"Yes, I do," I said. "I'm not afraid of Heathcliff, but I'm terrified of Max."

"That's ironic, isn't it?" he asked.

"No," I answered. "The irony isn't that I'm afraid of one and not of the other. The irony is that I want them both."

He exhaled, his fingers finishing what they'd started, my shorts pooling on the floor around my feet, my panties joining them.

As I stepped free of them, he pulled a money clip from his pocket, tugging a foil packet free before removing his jeans and boxers.

Weirdly, I was nervous, my stomach churning. Sex wasn't something new for us, but the people who were facing each other now were five years wiser, harder, and in many ways, needier than the clumsy teenagers who'd fumbled on my bed and his hooch couch.

It felt different. This wasn't sex. This wasn't even about making love. We were standing in a room full of new demons, having left the old memories and ghosts behind in our hometown. Here, we were going to be making up for the five years we'd missed.

In many ways, I wasn't prepared for the man who pushed me up against the wall, his arms lifting me into his embrace, his biceps bulging. I gripped him, letting his whisker-sharp jaw move down my neck to my chest. He suckled me, and I arched, my hands going to his hair.

He left my breasts, covering my gasping lips with his, capturing every exhaled breath as he pulled my legs around his waist, walking us to the bed.

Wrapping my hair around his hand, he pulled my head back, his troubled eyes meeting mine. "This might hurt," he said.

Laying me back, he entered me, his thrusts fast and hard and then slow and sweet. My gaze locked with his. He was right. This hurt. It wasn't physical pain. There was nothing except pleasure ripping through my body. This kind of pain was deeper than that. It was worse than the pain I'd felt when he'd taken my virginity. I'd loved the boy who'd taken my innocence, but the man who was taking me now was breaking my heart.

I'd thought my heart was broken before, but I'd been wrong. He was breaking it because, for the first time, I realized just how much I could love the complicated person he was. I'd thought I'd known him when we were teenagers, but he'd held more back than I'd ever realized. He was surrounded by family, and yet he'd always felt alone. On the other hand, all I'd really had was my uncle, and that had been enough.

How do you save a man who's still learning who he is? How do you do it so that he doesn't lose you in the process?

"We can take this slow," Heathcliff gasped.

My hands gripped him. "No," I panted. "Take me fast, and when we're cooling down we'll talk about why we should have taken our time."

He smiled, a small laugh escaping even as he thrust, his breathing growing more rapid.

He reached between us. "Come with me, Clare. I'm not doing this alone."

My hand joined his between us, our orgasms met by my small scream and his satisfied exhale.

"Clare …" he breathed. Rolling onto his back, he pulled me on top of him. "Now we can talk. We've run, so let's walk back."

Chapter 30

"Did you find what you were looking for?" I asked Heathcliff afterward.

His fingers ran lazily up and down my back. "I found a lot of places," he answered, "and a lot of people."

Lifting my head, I gazed up at his chin. "But did you find happiness?"

"No." He looked down at me. "I left that behind. You did though, didn't you? You found happiness."

I stared at him. "I found some of it. I'm waiting on the rest."

He frowned. "You shouldn't have to wait."

"Some things are worth waiting for."

Heathcliff's face transformed, a small smile blossoming. "You know, it's crazy. I think I needed the last five years. Carrying that book of yours around made me realize something." His hand slid into my hair. "Life is like a book. Some of the pages you want to rip out and others you want to keep. I've been ripping out a lot of pages lately, getting rid of the ugly stuff. The stuff that's

left behind isn't as bad as I thought it was.
You want to know what one of the things
that drew me to you was?"

"My hair?"

He chuckled. "That, too." His head
shook. "It was your house."

My eyes widened. "My house?"

"Yeah," he said. "The work I knew it
would take to bring it back to life. While
fixing it up, it started to rebuild me. For
years, I lived under this umbrella of grief
that came with being born with a stillborn
sibling." He saw my expression, and his
brows rose. "I'm not blaming my family. I
love my family. They're amazing and tight
knit. It was all me, this really stupid idea
that I must have done something in the
womb that killed my twin. He was a ghost
that haunted me. Why did I live? Logically,
I knew it had nothing to do with me, but it
plagued me anyway."

"And that made you love my house?" I
asked.

"In a weird way," he snorted. "Then it
was all about you. This girl who'd lost so
much, who was hiding behind her silence,
her wild hair, and her uncle's old clothes. It

was like when I was looking at you, I was seeing myself. Only you knew what you were hiding from. You just needed a little coaxing, a little trust, to overcome it. I was hiding in plain sight, in crowds and family and people. I've been running too long."

"Then quit," I said suddenly. "Quit running and start living."

He glanced at me. "It's a tempting offer." His fingers slid further into my hair. "I want to be inside you again," he said, "and this time, let's make it slow."

So, we did.

There's this thing love stories always forget to mention. That love isn't a constant thing. Sometimes it changes, other times it fades completely. Sometimes you have to fall in love twice to truly understand it.

People change over the years. Every so often, you have to relearn the person you're with. Heathcliff wasn't with me, but he was in my heart.

We made love two more times before he took me home that night. The plantation had never felt emptier. Even with the faint lingering odor of sweets and casseroles.

That night, the only thing I cared to smell was chicory.

Somehow, I found myself in the kitchen, the coffee pot on, the smell of my uncle's coffee floating through the air. When it was done, I hugged the warm mug I'd poured it in. I didn't drink it. I just held it and inhaled.

Heathcliff had left home to find himself and had discovered death instead. He'd taken a hard road in life, but I could only hope he was learning that sometimes it takes plunging through mud to get to the clear water.

He'd come home. That was the first step.

Chapter 31

For days, I couldn't stop thinking about Heathcliff, even with Rebecca's babbling and the night crowds at *Caffeine's*. It was like I was in high school again, lying in my bed wondering if he was thinking about me as much as I was thinking about him. Only now, he was different. He was older, broader, and—in a funny, weird kind of way—dustier. Like a vase that had sat on the hearth too long.

All I could think about was my body sprawled against his, my ear against his heart. I'd almost forgotten about his friends, about the life he had outside our town.

Until they showed up at the plantation.

I was in the kitchen working on a new recipe when Rebecca appeared in the doorway. "You expecting company?" she asked.

"No," I mumbled, half paying attention.

"Then the really pretty silver car speeding up the drive in a cloud of dirt is news to you, too?"

Her words shook me out of my reverie, and I rounded the counter, joining her at the door. Together, we peered out the window.

"A Lexus with out of state tags. Methinks you pissed off the Ginger girl," Rebecca whistled. "I'm impressed. Took an entire high school and college career before you got involved in a love triangle." She patted my back. "Don't worry. I've survived three. We've got this."

I scowled. "I'm not getting involved in anything."

"You really like to lie to yourself, girlfriend."

I snorted. "Where do you get this stuff?"

Rebecca shrugged. "I record soaps. Lots of them. If you ever just feel really bad about your life, all you have to do is watch a soap opera and," she mimicked an explosion, "boom. All better."

"I'm suddenly glad I never owned a television."

Outside, a car door slammed, and we watched as Ginger climbed out of the driver's side. She stared at the house, her hand rising to remove the expensive sunglasses on her nose. Brayden was with her, along with Chris' wife, Samantha. Samantha, who'd I'd long since started calling Sam back in high school, looked as uncomfortable as I felt.

Rebecca grunted. "By the looks of things, you're going to wish you'd seen some soaps. Trust me."

There was a knock on the door, and I stiffened, wiping flour-stained hands down a plain white apron, before marching to the foyer.

Grasping the knob, I pulled, the opening door revealing three figures on the stoop. Behind them, Heathcliff's Ford was pulling into the drive.

My lips curled into a smile, my heart fluttering. "Hi," I greeted. "This is a surprise."

Heathcliff was climbing out of his truck, his brother exiting the passenger side. Chris looked sad. Heathcliff was scowling.

Ginger was the first to speak. "Chris and Max have some business out here this afternoon, and I have to admit I was curious to see a real plantation. To see what all the fuss was about."

I stepped aside, holding the door wide, my gaze flying to Heathcliff's. Our eyes caught and then slid away. "It really isn't much," I said as they entered. "There are much bigger plantations not too far from here."

"Yes," Ginger drawled, "but *you* don't own them."

"Soap operas," Rebecca hissed in my ear as she joined us.

Ignoring her, I studied the group. "Is there something I can do for you? Would you like some coffee? Tea?"

Chris stepped forward. "Max and I need to talk to you, Hawthorne. If you don't mind, maybe Rebecca could show everyone else around the place."

My gaze flicked from Rebecca's to the group. She shrugged.

"Sure," I replied, leaning over just long enough to hiss *avoid looking at abs* in Rebecca's ear before indicating that Heathcliff and Chris should join me in the kitchen.

Rebecca's sing-song voice followed us as we walked away.

"None of you like soap operas, do you?" she was asking.

My mouth twitched as I stepped back behind the counter. Nodding at the table, I said, "Please feel free to sit. I was just working on something new."

Heathcliff's gaze wandered the room, pausing on the new stoves, the door to the walk-in freezer, and the cooling racks. "Wow, you'd think it would look smaller with all of the additions, but it doesn't."

"Odd, right?" I answered.

Chris grinned. "It smells good in here, but then again, it always does."

I shot him a look. "Not looking for handouts are we?"

He chuckled. "We should have come out sooner. It looks really nice, Hawthorne. You've done good work."

I shrugged. "Mostly thanks to Rebecca's investment." My gaze passed between the brothers. "But that's not why you're here."

"No," Chris admitted. "It's not." He shifted awkwardly. "Hawthorne, Mams passed away this morning."

The rolling pin I'd just picked up clattered to the counter. "What?"

Chris swallowed hard, his reddening eyes flicking from Heathcliff to me. Heathcliff was stoic, his face calm. There was a maelstrom of emotions in his gaze, but his face didn't reveal them.

"The thing is—" Chris began.

"She wants you to be a part of the ceremony," Heathcliff interrupted.

I stared, silence stretching. "Was it quick and painless?" I finally whispered.

Chris looked away, but Heathcliff's gaze met mine. "As peaceful as your uncle's." His hands slipped into his blue jean pockets, the gesture an old one. "She's always wanted to be cremated. Like Paps."

"She always used to say, 'I don't want to be tied down to no wooden box,'" Chris added on a chuckle. "She wanted us to spread her ashes in different places around town. There's still a lot to do, a ceremony and paperwork, but when the time comes …"

Chris paused, and Heathcliff stepped forward. "She wants you to spread a few of her ashes on your uncle Gregor's grave. She

talked to us about it yesterday before …
before her mind went. It's so she can keep
an eye on him, she said, for Hawthorne."

There are moments in life when tears
just happen, even when you have no idea
they're coming. My throat never closed up,
my face never heated, but I felt the tear that
slid down my cheek. It was a single tear, for
Mams.

"Can I do anything for any of you?" I
asked.

Chris glanced at the kitchen. "We
thought maybe you could cater a reception
after the ceremony. Something simple, and
we'd talk about pa—"

"On me, of course," I said. "I won't let
you pay me for that."

He nodded. "Thank you." His gaze
flicked to Heathcliff. "We'll let you get back
to work now. We just felt maybe this was
something we should tell you in person."

"Thank you," I murmured.

Chris inclined his head, threw one more
glance at the kitchen, and then left.
Heathcliff remained.

To fill the silence, I whispered, "I'm
sorry."

Heathcliff's gaze went to the floor. "We knew it was coming."

"That doesn't make it any easier."

He glanced up at me. "No, I guess it doesn't." He started to step toward me, and then stopped.

Where he hesitated, I didn't, my feet carrying me to him. Without a second thought, I embraced him, the hug quick but firm.

It wasn't until I stepped back that I saw Ginger standing in the doorway.

She smiled, but the gesture didn't quite make it to her eyes. "I think everyone is ready," she said.

Rebecca stepped up next her, her brows raised as she brushed past the blonde. "Well, tour went well," she said brightly, her concerned gaze swinging to Heathcliff. Mams had been a big part of our town.

"It's a quaint place," Ginger added.

Heathcliff moved toward the door, and I followed him, Rebecca behind me. I was just about to pass Ginger when her hand found my wrist, stopping me.

"He's going to leave. You know that, right?" she asked.

My gaze met hers. "I didn't ask him to stay."

Her eyes narrowed. "You wouldn't, would you?" She laughed. "You really think letting the man make his own decision is going to work in your favor?"

I frowned. "Maybe not, but at least I'll know it was his choice."

"I want him, too, you know," she said suddenly. "You aren't the only one he's shared a bed with."

"Ginger!" Heathcliff's harsh voice called.

Her head shot up, her eyes widening. I didn't hate Ginger. If anything, I pitied her. I pitied her because I knew what it was like to love Heathcliff. I also knew what it was like to lose him, and by the look in her eyes, she did, too.

That was another thing about loving Heathcliff. He'd loved people after me, and it was something I was going to have to accept.

"You should pull each other's hair," Rebecca said suddenly, watching us intently. "It's not a cat fight until someone's lost some hair."

Without acknowledging anyone, I walked into the foyer, giving Chris and his wife a final sympathetic hug before they left. Heathcliff was the last to leave. He paused at the door, his hand falling to rest next to mine, his fingers reaching for my fingers, something cold and metallic slipping into my palm.

I gripped it before it could fall, my knuckles clenched as I watched them drive away. Dust was flying in their wake when I finally opened my hand. There, in my palm, was the key to Heathcliff's building in the woods.

Chapter 32

Later that night, I stood in front of Paps' old building. The padlock dangled from the door, the window dark, but that didn't deter me.

My hand gripped the key Heathcliff had given me, my feet carrying me toward the cement block we'd always used as a step. My heart pounded as my hand rose. Opening the lock felt ritualistic, as if there should have been candles and music or a group of heralding trumpets.

Rebecca's dramatic flair was rubbing off on me.

The door swung open to reveal a dark, cavernous mouth. Reaching inside, I switched on the light and was rewarded with a yellow glow, my gaze falling over the contents within; the old couch, Heathcliff's guitar, and his stack of pieced together machinery. There was little dust, and I knew by the faint smell of disinfectant that someone had been inside recently to clean it. The thought made me think of Mams, and my face heated. She wasn't my grandmother, but she'd become a big influence in my life.

"I miss her already," Heathcliff's voice said from behind me.

Startled, I whirled to find him standing just inside the door, the darkening night framing him. He was in a dark cutoff shirt, the tattoos and muscles in his arms moving with him as he gripped the door frame. Outside, crickets sang, the frogs joining in.

"I've seen some really terrible things the past few years," Heathcliff added suddenly, his face falling. "Somehow, I've managed not to cry." He stared at me. "I should have cried when your uncle died, Hawthorne."

My hand touched my chest, just over my heart. "It was your strength that helped me through."

He shook his head. "I should have cried, and I'm sorry I didn't."

There was something strange about his voice, as if he needed my forgiveness, and I took a step toward him. "It's … okay."

He released the frame, his shoulders sagging, and I suddenly realized what he needed, suddenly realized why he'd given me the key.

Closing the distance between us, I grabbed his hand and tugged him into the room. Sitting on the couch, I brought him down next to me.

"You don't need me to tell you it's okay to cry, Heathcliff. I've done enough of that for both of us the last five years." My fingers found his chin. "Let it go."

The first tear that fell from his eyes broke me, the ones that followed rebuilt me. His head fell, his hands gripping my shoulders as he leaned into me. His height made it difficult, but I held him, his tears soaking into my shirt.

He'd needed me for this. He'd *needed* me. Sometimes that's more powerful than love. My tears joined his, leaving trails down my cheeks, my fingers sliding through his hair.

"I don't cry, Hawthorne," he choked.

My fingers tightened on his head. "Maybe you should. My uncle once told me that tears are like miniature rain storms. That they spring up when your body is so full of emotions it can't contain them anymore, your eyes the clouds. The rain falls, hard and fast, until it leaves the world, your body new again. Ready for re-growth."

His body shook, but he didn't sob, as if crying in silence was vindication enough.

I cradled him. "You can't be strong," I whispered, "if you don't allow yourself to be weak."

The tears he was shedding weren't just tears for Mams. These were more, these were years of heartache all rolled into one. Heathcliff was a dam, and his wall had been breached. Lucky for him, I was one damn good swimmer.

For a long time, we simply sat there, his body shaking, the sound of the crickets and frogs beyond a strange sort of orchestra.

When the tears finally ended, Heathcliff sat up, his face turned away. I started to reach for him, but he avoided my touch.

"Do you think I see you differently now?" I asked him. "After the tears, I mean?" He didn't say anything, and I leaned forward. "Because I do. You, in this moment when you were willing to share with me all of the pain you were feeling, just became a true hero."

Standing, I started to walk away, but his hand shot out, his fingers circling my wrist.

"Don't go," he said.

It was a déjà vu moment. I was suddenly thrown back in time to my uncle's death when I'd begged Heathcliff to stay. And in that moment, I told him the same thing he'd told me.

"I won't."

Chapter 33

For the first time in five years, I spent the night with Heathcliff in the old building in the woods. He did some work on the parts stacked against the wall, and I pulled out the couch, putting new sheets on the thin mattress. It wasn't a comfortable bed, but that didn't matter.

Grease and disinfectant. The odor wasn't necessarily a brilliant one, but it would always remind me of Heathcliff, of the dark streaks of oil on his hands, of the sound of him working.

Sitting on the edge of the bed, I watched him.

"You don't have to stay up," he said after a while.

"I like watching," I answered.

He glanced at me, dark circles marring his eyes. "You always did." He threw me a smile despite his weariness. "I don't think I ever told you how much that meant. That you came."

"You did," I replied. "You may not remember, but you told me." My gaze fell to his guitar. "Do you still play?" I asked.

His gaze followed mine. "Some. It used to pass a lot of time overseas."

"I still have the song you left me," I admitted.

"Really?" he asked. "I'm not sure if I should cringe or be impressed."

Smiling, I replied, "Impressed. Definitely impressed."

Setting a part he'd been fiddling with down on the floor, Heathcliff stood, made his way to the sink on the side of the room, and washed his hands. The citrus scent of the soap mingled with the grease, and I watched his back, my gaze roaming down his muscled arms, the way they flexed as he moved. For some reason, it moved me. It was sexy, too, but I think the reason why Heathcliff's build really affected me was because he'd earned it. Every muscle, every mark, every blemish, every callous, and every scar had been "built" over time.

A laugh escaped me, and Heathcliff turned, leaning his hip against the counter as he dried his hands on a small towel.

"What?" he asked. Even though he had no idea what had tickled me, his lips twitched at my amusement.

My head shook. "I'm sorry. It's silly, but," I smiled, "your body reminds me of a house."

He glanced down at himself, his brows arching. "A house?"

"I told you it was silly."

He stared at me, an odd look crossing his features. "No, tell me why," he said. "I never know what's going to come out of your head, Hawthorne, and it fascinates me."

My gaze passed over his face before dropping to his chest, his waist, and then his feet. "You're like the plantation. Like a foundation that's been built from the inside out. Each layer something different, unique, and beautiful, but in a way that makes you wonder if the house is haunted. Like there's too much there, too many renovations. Sometimes when I'm sitting in the kitchen, I find myself staring at the walls with this odd feeling … like the house is just going to get up one day and walk away."

Heathcliff stared, letting my words sink in, his gaze roaming over me. "I don't think people take the time to really look at each other enough," he said suddenly. "I had a buddy in the military. His grandmother was from Russia, and she'd given him this set of Matryoshka dolls. They're painted wooden dolls varying in size that fit one inside the other. We gave him such hell over those dolls." He chuckled. "They represented his family, I think. The outer doll was a woman, a different gender and person revealed as you went through them. The center doll was a baby." His gaze caught mine, boring into it. "Sometimes, I'd watch him holding that doll, and I'd find myself thinking of you. I'd picture your face on the outer doll, and on the inside there'd be the rest of us."

My breath caught, my heart beating entirely too loud. "You make me feel bigger than my skin when you talk like that," I breathed. "Like I'm not just sitting here. I'm everywhere."

"Because you are," he replied.

My lungs exhaled, emptying me, and leaving me speechless. For a long moment, we simply stared at each other, the connection finally broken when he moved to the couch bed.

Tugging his shirt over his head, he gazed down at me. "Scoot over," he ordered gently.

I moved, making room for him. He unfastened his jeans and removed them, leaving his boxers, before climbing onto the mattress with me. The bed was too small for him, and his feet hung over the end, but he didn't seem to care. Rolling onto his side, he pulled me against him, his chin resting on the top of my head.

"You remind me of Mams," Heathcliff said. "Always saying things that I feel like it would be wrong to forget."

"She was very special," I whispered.

"Yeah," he exhaled, his breath ruffling my hair, "she saw me more than anyone else in this family. Well, not really saw me. They all did I guess. She just understood me."

"She saw a lot of your Paps in you," I said suddenly.

Heathcliff's head rose. "What?"

I looked up at him. "I was visiting one summer, and she told me you reminded her of him. That you had a wanderer's soul, like he did. Like your mind and body was trapped on the earth, but your soul was somewhere else entirely." I found myself smiling, remembering her words. "She said being in love with your Paps was like being in love with a shooting star. There isn't a way you can catch one, but you can hold on to it and keep making wishes."

Heathcliff's forehead creased, his eyes on mine. "And are you?" he asked.

"Am I what?"

He blinked. "Are you holding on and making wishes?"

I froze, my pulse an erratic beat in my neck. "I don't think anyone ever quits making wishes."

He sighed, tucking me back into his side, his heart against my ear. We didn't speak. We just laid there. The crickets, the frogs, the droning sound of the window unit air conditioner, and the sound of his heartbeat had almost lulled me to sleep when Heathcliff's voice rumbled over me.

"Just don't," he insisted. "Don't quit making wishes."

There was nothing but sleep after that, his words sending me into a spiral of dreams about shooting stars. In it, I was holding onto one, tears pouring down my cheek as I struggled not to let go. *Star light, Star bright,* my dream self called out, *First star I see tonight ...*

Chapter 34

It's odd really, looking back. I felt like I was caught up in three separate love stories that had somehow coalesced into one.

The first love story was my relationship with my uncle, with the man who'd given up everything to make sure I had a healthy childhood. He'd given up his own love story to make mine come true, his relationship with the man he'd loved.

The second love story was my relationship with Heathcliff. It was a strange romance. We shared a peculiar kind of commitment, as if we couldn't escape each other, and yet it hadn't been enough to keep him with me.

The third love story was Paps and Mams, an old story I didn't really know, but that somehow felt like it mattered anyway, as if Heathcliff was a broken off piece of his grandfather, and I was a younger version of Mams.

It was three different love stories, and yet they were all the same.

The morning after our night in the building, I left Heathcliff standing in dew-covered grass, a hazy sun hanging over the trees. The air smelled like honeysuckle and dreams, as if the fog that weaved along the ground meant to keep the memory a fantasy rather than a reality.

Driving away felt wrong, like I was saying good-bye. Maybe I was. Not to what I'd shared with Heathcliff, but to adolescent expectations.

My hand gripped the steering wheel of my catering van, a tear rolling down my cheek, and I suddenly broke. My foot hit the brakes, throwing me against the seatbelt as I pulled the van into park. Unclicking my belt, I threw open the door, and jumped into the dirt road, my gaze flying to the shed.

Heathcliff was leaving, his hands in his pockets, his feet carrying him toward the trees. Dew, fog, and green foliage surrounded us. Cobwebs hung from the trees and along the ground, the kind of webs that always seemed to be there when you woke up in the morning but were gone by noon.

"I love you!" I called suddenly, my voice wavering. Heathcliff froze, his back to me, and I took a step forward. "You don't have to say anything. You don't even have to look at me. That's okay. I just needed you to know." The early morning air was heavy and wet, sitting on me like a cotton soaked blanket, and I swatted at my frizzy hair. "In my dreams, I'm standing in a kitchen cooking. Next to me is a table full of the people I love. All of them alive." Another tear rolled down my cheek. "There's meatloaf and cherry pie. No pecans anywhere. We're all barefoot because with no shoes on no one would be tempted to leave. In my dreams, I'm a buzzard, and I'm saving the world from the sun, bringing back everyone I've ever cared about."

Heathcliff turned, and I swallowed hard, words tumbling out of my mouth, so that he didn't have a chance to speak. "But this," I gestured at the woods, "isn't a dream. You say I keep people. I do. Here." I patted my chest. "I may lose them but they're kept, too, and I'll never let them go." The tears were coming fast now, and there was no way to stop them.

"Do you know why I like cooking so much?" I asked. "Because when I was growing up, I used to stare at food magazines, at the covers. The ones that featured a table full of food surrounded by family, laughter, and love. Most girls pin up pictures of celebrities. I tore out those table pictures and kept them in a drawer near my bed. They're still there." I glanced up at the sky and then back down again. "Food brings people home. It brings them together. I keep cooking because one day I keep thinking my table will be full."

My gaze went to the building we'd shared so many memories in, and I thought of Heathcliff but I thought of Mams and Uncle Gregor, too.

"I love you," I finished, "and I just thought you should know that."

Heathcliff started to step toward me, and for the first time, I turned into a true coward. For the first time since I'd known Heathcliff, I was the one to run away. Because, in that moment, I didn't need to hear him tell me he loved me. I just needed him to know that, wandering soul or no, I'd always have a plate waiting for him at my table.

So, I left, and I didn't look back.

Chapter 35

In the true scheme of things, life is love and loss. It's a never-ending cycle of the two, like a row of dominos falling over. Occasionally, when the dominos finish toppling, there's one left standing.

Mams' funeral felt like dominos. She'd always been the one left standing, even beating the odds against an illness that should have killed her much sooner. She'd been the center of her family, and she'd been yanked from it. The Vincents were a strong lot, many of them men, sons and sons of sons. Their women stood next to them, tall and proud, because to be married to a Vincent meant being strong, too. Yet, despite that strength, there wasn't a single dry-eyed Vincent that day except Heathcliff. He didn't cry because he'd shed all of his tears in the building in the woods.

Other than the service, I remained in the Vincents' kitchen with Rebecca, heating and cooking. In the kitchen, I could love better. In the kitchen, I could take all of my grief, pour it into a steaming dish, and then lay it on the table. Where I couldn't nurture their hearts, I could nurture their bodies. In a way, I'd learned that's how you survived grief. Nurture the body while the heart wore itself out.

Ginger and Brayden were still there, Brayden a comforting presence for Heathcliff. I didn't know Brayden, but I could tell just by observing the two men together that they shared a history no one would ever be able to understand. Watching them, I smiled despite the circumstances. Age, time, and loss were teaching me something. Early twenties or no, I'd learned through my experiences that it wasn't possible for one person to be everything to another person. I could love Heathcliff, but he needed people in his life who comprehended parts of him I could soothe but never fully identify with.

"Something's changed about you," Rebecca hissed in my ear.

I glanced down at her, at the empty squash casserole dish she held in her hand, and I grinned. "Not changed. Things are just coming together."

She raised her brows, her gaze flicking from me to where Heathcliff stood across the room. "With him?"

I shook my head. "No. That may never be a full reality."

She watched me. "You confound me sometimes, Hawthorne."

"Sometimes," I replied, "I confound myself."

Snorting, she left me to run water in the kitchen sink, adding the empty dish to a pile of others we'd have to clean before the end of the day.

From my corner, I watched. It was like attending a play, the mingling people swapping stories and fond memories. There was laughter, and there were tears. In the center of it all was the table, my food spread out across it.

Heathcliff's mom approached me, a smile lighting her features. "The food is good, Hawthorne," she complimented.

"Thank you."

For a moment, she stood with me, her eyes roaming the room. "They're good people, my family," she breathed, her voice full of pride.

I smiled. "They are wonderful people."

Lynn glanced at me. "You're a part of that, you know. It doesn't matter what happens with you and Max." She nodded at the room. "You are always welcome at my table."

It was the most painful and wonderful thing she could have said.

"And you," I rasped, "are always welcome at mine."

Her hand found my shoulder, and she squeezed. "You've got the same kind of gumption Mams had."

Surprised, I glanced at her. "Gumption?"

"She never expected anything from anyone. She just loved people, albeit firmly, but in a way that no matter how stern she seemed, she was never pushy. She guided people but never pushed. It's like she'd discovered that the best place to be in life was needed. She told me once that she'd felt what love felt like, so maybe she could turn the hurt she felt in losing it into love for those who may never get the chance to feel it otherwise. I see that in you, Hawthorne."

With those words, she left me. I stared after her, my heart suddenly fuller than it had ever been.

Heathcliff may never want to admit it, but the paper I'd written in high school hadn't been totally wrong. If I'd never met him, if I'd never known his family, and if I'd never loved them, then I wouldn't have learned as much about myself as I had. I wouldn't still be learning.

My gaze rose, moving across the room to where Heathcliff was standing. He was watching me, a glass of iced tea in his hand. Brayden stood next to him, his gaze flicking occasionally to Rebecca as she moved back and forth from the kitchen. There was something about the way he looked at her, a spark of interest. There was nothing unusual about it. Rebecca was a beautiful woman, after all, with a heart bigger than she'd ever admit. She was also a lost soul, her marriages proof that she was desperate for love in a way most people weren't.

She was doing another pass into the kitchen when I leaned close and whispered, "Maybe you should look at those abs."

Her gaze followed mine, and she scoffed. "Two marriages remember?"

I shrugged. "Maybe this time look at the abs and don't expect anything?"

She snorted. "I'm thinking soap operas are safer." She continued past, and I fought the urge to chuckle. Lost soul or not, she had a place at my table, too.

Maybe in a weird kind of way, losing so much in my youth had taught me that no matter how many pictures of tables I'd collected, it wouldn't matter if I didn't have the souls to put at it. The key was collecting people, to making sure there was always happiness and a steaming cup of coffee waiting for the ones I brought in.

Uncle Gregor's words suddenly made sense. He'd been right. Broken hearts weren't a bad thing. Sometimes it took a heart breaking to make it bigger. Because like anything else, a heart had to grow, and when there wasn't any more room, then it had to break to make more.

Behind me, I felt the spirits of Mams and Uncle Gregor watching me, and they were smiling.

Chapter 36

A week passed after Mams' funeral. There were no visitors, nothing except orders to fill and occasional work at *Caffeine's*. I still had the key to the building in the woods, but I didn't go back. It didn't feel right anymore, as if the spot where I'd felt so much happiness in my youth wasn't mine now. It belonged to a wandering soul who didn't need me watching him. Maybe Brayden would go with him, along with a group of his friends. Maybe there'd be poker and old stories, but either way, my story there was over.

Rebecca and I were in the kitchen laughing over chocolate dipped strawberries when the phone rang. It was a call from a lawyer. He was a sweet man who talked about my uncle and life before suddenly informing me that my presence was requested at Mams' will reading the next day.

"But I don't want anything," I protested.

The man on the other end of the line chuckled. "What she's left you is … well, I'm not quite sure anyone will …" He paused and inhaled. "It would be an honor if you joined us."

There'd been more stuttering after that, but the only thing it had gotten me was more chuckles and a promise to be there.

In the end, the call hung over my head like a cloud for the rest of the day, following me through orders, through work at *Caffeine's*, into my bed, and into the van the next morning. Outside, the sun was shining. There was no rain. I kept looking for grey clouds, but there was only blue.

The sun was hot, beating down on the van as I pulled into the small parking lot of a house that had been turned into an office. *Mellow & Mayvern*, the sign outside read. There were two other cars in the lot along with Heathcliff's black F150. With only a cursory glance at them, I entered the building. The interior had that musty smell, the kind that made you wonder what year the house had been built in, and the air was too cold, as if the air conditioner never cut off.

A young secretary, pretty with brown upswept hair, motioned me toward a small room with a long wooden table. "They're ready," she informed me.

I stepped inside, my gaze going to the family sitting around the conference room; Lynn, Dusty, Samantha, Chris, and Heathcliff. The men stood when I entered, and I took a seat at the far end of the table near a small American flag sitting in a brass holder. Rather than looking at the family, I gazed at my reflection in the shining mahogany. Being here didn't feel right.

The lawyer I'd talked to the day before was a cheery man, bald except for tufts of white hair above his ears. He wore glasses that were too small for his face, making his cheeks look like a squirrel's when it was stuffed with acorns.

"Now that everyone's here," he said. "I'm George Mayvern. I've been working with Mams for years now, mostly over her charity stuff, and I want to take a moment to express how sorry I am at your loss." He paused, but no one said anything. Laying out a stack of papers on the table in front of him, he pushed up his glasses, and said, "Mams didn't have much really. She left the family business to Dusty, and the land she and Paps owned goes to the family. She'd like her charity funds to be taken over by Lynn and Samantha."

He looked up, his gaze sweeping the table before landing on Heathcliff. "Oh, as for the land, there was one exception." He nodded at Heathcliff. "She wanted the land around the shed at the back of the property, about two acres, to go to her grandson, Max. It'll be parceled appropriately." He smiled. "And that's about it. It was pretty cut and dry ... except," he looked at me, "what she left you."

The family's gazes moved down the table toward me, and my cheeks flushed. "I'm sure whatever it is can go to the family," I stuttered. "I don't—"

A pair of old boots were suddenly slapped onto the table, a deafening silence following.

The lawyer cleared his throat, lifting a piece of paper and squinting through his glasses. "And as for my husband's old combat boots, I'd like them to go to Clare Macy," George read. "After all these years, they aren't much to look at it. They've seen a lot of rough roads." The lawyer looked up at me. "Give them to Clare, and tell her I know she'll understand why."

I stared, my gaze locked on the boots, my hands trembling where they rested in my lap under the table.

Mams had given me Paps' shoes.

Around me, the family started speaking, their voices rising as they asked the lawyer about other parts of the will, but the only thing I saw were the boots.

She'd given me her husband's shoes.

I thought of Heathcliff's sneakers resting in my bedroom closet, and I had to clench my fists to control the shaking in my body.

At some point someone spoke to me, a small container slid in front of my face.

"A little bit of Mams' ashes," Lynn said near my ear. "We figured you might want to spread them on your uncle's grave alone."

Vaguely, I remembered thanking her, remembered asking if I could sit a little longer as everyone left. But as for everything else, I couldn't recall it. As much as I hated to admit it, I didn't even remember Heathcliff.

There was only me, a long table, and a pair of old boots.

Chapter 37

For an hour, I sat in the conference room staring at the boots. I knew why Mams had given them to me. I understood it more than I'd like to admit, my heart filling with fondness for the old woman as I finally stood.

Reaching for the shoes, I picked them up, cradling them against my chest, my eyes welling with tears. To most people, they were shoes. For Mams, I had no doubt they'd been filled with memories. Shoes are often overlooked by people. They were worn on the feet, after all. How many stop to look down at their feet?

However, it was the feet that did the walking, the feet that did the running, and the feet that did the resting.

There was no going home now.

Climbing into the catering van, I set Paps' boots and the small container of ashes reverently in the passenger's seat, my fingers lingering over them before starting the vehicle.

As I backed out of the lot, I rolled the windows down, the wind rushing in around me, the gravel crunching under my tires.

The wind freed me. It tugged at my hair, pulling and pushing it around my face, the sun pouring in through the windshield. The smell of honeysuckle, azaleas, magnolias, and even the occasional rank chicken house flooded my nostrils through the window, hugging me. The wind smelled like home. The wind *was* home. Like shoes, the wind saw everything, and then carried what it saw to the four corners of the earth. If the wind could talk, it could tell an infinite amount of stories.

I was almost out of town when I turned onto a long dirt road. On one side was a large grass-covered hill, trees in the distance. Wild yellow flowers bloomed like a blanket of melted sunshine over the expanse. On the opposite side was a cemetery, an arched wrought iron gate marking the entrance.

Parking on the side of the road, I climbed free of the van, stopping only long enough to get the small container of ashes out of the passenger side. The boots I brought with me, too, even though I had no intention of leaving them behind.

My uncle's grave was just inside the gate on top of a rise, his tombstone overlooking the sea of yellow across the road. In the sky, buzzards circled, probably eyeing a dead carcass, but it seemed fitting somehow.

Pausing before the simple arched stone that marked Gregor's resting place, I nodded at the yellow hill. "You have a nice view. That's good." Setting Pap's boots just at the foot of Gregor's grave, I held up the container of ashes. "I brought you a visitor." Lifting the lid, I felt a tear roll down my cheek as I poured the ashes into my palm. "She's going to keep you company, Uncle, when I can't be here."

Maybe there should have been more words than that, but nothing came, my throat closing up as I sprinkled Mams' ashes over the ground at my feet. The wind carried some of them away, twirling them up toward the sky and down into the sunny field, and I watched them.

"I'm going to keep you both," I whispered, patting my chest, "here." My hand came down to rest on the tombstone, the etched words, *Here rests a kind soul and a doting father,* staring back at me. "You'll always have a place at my table."

Across from us the yellow field shone. Above us, the buzzards flew. Clouds sent shadows over the area, but it never rained. The sun beat down, lighting the grave, the old pair of boots, and a wild-haired woman holding an empty silver container.

The wind blew, carrying away my story.

Epilogue

Paps' boots got a place of honor just inside the front door, forever a symbol that he was a part of the plantation. Things returned to normal around the house. The catering business bloomed, and Rebecca set up an online service that let us ship all over the States, with the hopes that we could eventually make it international. *Caffeine's* also flourished, and we built on an extra building that offered baked goods from the plantation. Against all odds, we were becoming a success. It would take a long time to pay off the debts I owed because of school and the upkeep the plantation required, but I was making it.

Once again, Heathcliff left. There'd been no good-bye. I think, in retrospect, we were past good-byes. He had a job out-of-state, a life away from our small town, and it was enough for me knowing he was still wandering, trying to find that piece of his soul that was missing. No matter the distance, no matter what he needed to find out about himself, I wasn't going anywhere.

My table was full, with ghosts, family, and friends. Even so, I left one space open … waiting.

Two years passed.

In those two years, Rebecca and I had developed a name for ourselves, the business continuing to expand. Rebecca had attempted two more serious relationships but bailed out before it could result in marriage. In the end, she'd started spending more time with the men in her soaps than she did in real life. I would have been worried if her constant soap opera babbling didn't keep *Caffeine's* customers so enthralled. Rebecca was a natural storyteller.

The plantation was rarely empty now. When we weren't working, there were always visitors; Heathcliff's family, Mams' lawyer, women from town, and even Rebecca's mother, who was trying to repair her relationship with Rebecca despite the distance between her and her daughter.

I'd just finished a long, exhausting morning catering an event, and was parking the van at the plantation when I noticed something unusual on the porch.

Climbing free of the vehicle, I walked cautiously toward the house, my eyes widening. There, hanging from the brass fitting on the light next to the front door was a pair of tennis shoes. I knew these shoes. They were the sneakers Heathcliff had worn when we'd graduated high school, a replica of the *keep me* ones he'd left behind.

The ones dangling in front of my face now were even more worn than the ones I had upstairs. Scratches, dirt, and oil streaked them, the bottom of one of them starting to come undone at the seams. There was permanent marker etched into the sides. On one shoe was written, *Hawthorne*. On the other was scrawled, *Heathcliff*.

"It seemed fitting," a voice, *his* voice, called from behind me, "that when I decided to hang up my shoes, that it should be here."

Slowly, I turned.

"That is," he continued, "if you have room for me."

Heathcliff looked no different, other than a tan and a few extra scars, than he'd looked two years before. He leaned against the porch column, his hands tucked into his blue jean pockets. He wore a black T-shirt across his chest, the word *Vincent's* etched across the front. I knew by the way it was scripted that this *Vincent's* wasn't related to the hardware store.

His gaze followed mine, and he smiled. "It's a new business, not quite a year old, but it's already doing well. I get to do what I love, and I can go to where the jobs are if needed. But," he pushed himself away from the column, "this weary traveler is ready to come home."

My gaze fell to his feet. They were bare.

Tears threatening, I breathed, "There's always room at my table for you." My eyes traveled back up his body to his face, our eyes catching.

"It's been a long, rough road, Hawthorne," he said, his arms opening.

Without a second thought, I rushed into his embrace. "It's better to travel it with someone who knows the road. Welcome home."

His arms closed around me, tight and desperate, his relieved sigh fanning my hair. "Home. God, Hawthorne, why did it take me so long?"

I glanced up at him. "You had to do it. For your sake."

Smiling softly, his face lowered, his whispered, "I love you," barely escaping his mouth before our lips met.

Behind us, his shoes dangled, moving with the strong afternoon breeze, two words flashing.

Hawthorne and Heathcliff.

About the Author

R.K. Ryals is the author of emotional and gripping young adult and new adult paranormal romance, contemporary romance, and fantasy. With a strong passion for charity and literacy, she works as a full time writer encouraging people to "share the love of reading one book at a time." An avid animal lover and self-proclaimed coffee-holic, R.K. Ryals was born in Jackson, Mississippi and makes her home in the Southern U.S. with her husband, her three daughters, a rescue dog named Oscar the Grouch, A Shitzsu named Tinkerbell, an OCD cat, and a coffee pot she honestly couldn't live without. Should she ever become the owner of a fire-breathing dragon (tame of course), her life would be complete. Visit her at www.authorrkryals.com.

Other works available:

<u>The Redemption Series</u>
Redemption
Ransom

Retribution
Revelation

The Acropolis Series
The Acropolis
The Labyrinth
Deliverance

The Thorne Trilogy
Cursed
Possessed
Dancing with the Devil

The Scribes of Medeisia Series
Mark of the Mage
Fist of the Furor
City in Ruins

The Singing River

The Story of Awkward

In the Land of Tea and Ravens

CPSIA information can be obtained at www.ICGtesting.com
Printed in the USA
LVOW07s2344190916

505345LV00001B/110/P

9 781515 003830